AND THEN THERE'S MARGARET...

CAROLYN CLARKE

Black Rose Writing | Texas

The author grants the final approval for this literary material.

Third printing

This is a work of fiction. Names, characters, businesses, places, events, and incidents are either the products of the author's imagination or used in a fictitious manner. Any resemblance to actual persons, living or dead, or actual events is purely coincidental.

ISBN: 978-1-68433-993-8 (Paperback); 978-1-68513-214-9 (Hardcover)
PUBLISHED BY BLACK ROSE WRITING
www.blackrosewriting.com

Printed in the United States of America
Suggested Retail Price (SRP) $20.95 (Paperback); $25.95 (Hardcover)

And Then There's Margaret is printed in Sabon

*As a planet-friendly publisher, Black Rose Writing does its best to eliminate unnecessary waste to reduce paper usage and energy costs, while never compromising the reading experience. As a result, the final word count vs. page count may not meet common expectations.

To Tony and the girls, with love and gratitude.
And to my mother-in-law. Although I never got to meet
you, I know we would've been good friends.

PRAISE FOR

AND THEN THERE'S MARGARET...

"*And Then There's Margaret* is a lively, satirical, contemporary debut by Carolyn Clarke, a talented writer (and also a heralded book blogger)."

–Marilyn Simon Rothstein, author of
Crazy to Leave You and *Separate & Lift*

"*And Then There's Margaret...* is a wonderful, fun confection of a tale, written with verve and humor. Clarke has illuminated every married woman's nightmare - the mother-in-law who majors in criticism - and written it in such a way that had me blurting out my coffee."

–Melodie Campbell, Award-winning author of
The Goddaughter series

"Carolyn Clarke's skillful and subtle storytelling in *And Then There's Margaret*, a playful coming-of (middle)-age novel, navigates a path that is funny without being absurd while creating a relatable narrator who encounters a magnificent little-old-lady menace."

–*Indie Reader*

"The emotions of the characters are expressed with whip-smart commentaries and readers will enjoy watching these characters as they deal with issues that Allie's children are facing, including a dubious boyfriend. Throughout, Clarke mesmerizes with her dazzling prose and her ability to write details into the inner worlds of the characters — they are complex and emotionally rich. This is a remarkable debut you won't want to miss."

–The Book Commentary

"It's a well-written story with crisp, clear dialog that engages you from the start and characters that you can't help but relate to...With plenty of action and no small amount of humor, this is a great story to while away a few hours on a rainy day or on the beach."

–Readers' Favorite

"In this hilarious, down-to-Earth read, debut author Carolyn Clarke has created charming and fascinating characters that could come from any home on any block and because they feel so human, you'll want to stay with them until the very last page."

–Chicklit Café

"Loved it! Carolyn Clarke weaves the plot with skill, and her characters are all convincing, with their flaws and quirks. Moreover, the wittiness of the writing enlightened the story. Here, day-to-day life is never boring."

–Reedsy Discovery

ACKNOWLEDGEMENTS

A special thanks to all those who have been a part of my getting there; my first, second, and third draft beta readers and my dearest family, friends and colleagues who encouraged me to write this book and cheered me on to finish it.

I also owe an enormous debt of gratitude to those who gave me constructive comments and suggestions on one or more chapters including, Anthony Teekasingh, Karen Samson and Marcella Corroeli Jager.

AND THEN THERE'S MARGARET...

1 - Goodbye George, Hello Margaret

It takes effort to hate the things that make you unhappy. Like cold winters, rude people and when it comes to world problems that'll never end, government corruption. I spend more time hating and being angry than I do smiling. I could go on, but what I really mean is, I strongly dislike these things just as much as being called the M-word by some young, toned, *Gwyneth Paltrow* look-alike with perfect breasts and a soft voice that adds a touch of sweetness to obvious condescension. *Now* there are those who might see this word as a courtesy, a sign of deference or respect, but in my world, *ma'am* is what you call someone you think is simple and safe. Old *and* inconsequential. Unless I become the *Queen of England*, don't ever call me *ma'am*. It's dismissive and ego bruising.

"Everything okay, *ma'am?*" asked the pretty girl, *Gwyneth*, again, who was waiting for me to finish filling out the fitness membership form.

I nodded mutely with a clenched jaw, trying to get my pen to work.

Tap. Tap.

Scribble. Scribble.

I shook it in the air and then scribbled more vertical lines on the top of the form before banging it on the desk. Frustration mounting, I shut my eyes and took a deep, calming breath. When I opened them, *Gwyneth* was staring at me while simultaneously tucking a loose strand of unnatural blond lustrous hair behind her delicate little ear.

"Meditative breathing," she said, smiling approvingly. "It's a great technique. I use it too." She reached across the end of the glossy white counter and rolled forward a *New Body Fitness* pen with the pen she had in her hand. "Here, why don't you try this one?"

Oh, she was good. Trying to disarm me with feigned empathy.

I dropped my useless ballpoint into my oversized purse, tucking a loose strand of my own, graying and somewhat less lustrous hair behind my ear too, as I reached out for the pen. I knew I was being petty. In the real world, not including my paranoia, she was just trying to be polite in her own way.

"Okay.... so you just need to fill out this part here and we'll be done," she said, clapping her hands as if toasting the moment.

Her overbearing enthusiasm failed to change my mood. I took another deep breath, squinting back at the membership application. You'd think I was here for a job interview. Needless to say, beyond the usual contact stuff, they wanted information I *really* didn't care to share.

Age:

Current weight:

My numbers are no one's business.

Do you consider yourself obese?

Oh, c'mon! No, I don't, I wrote.

Do you exercise daily?

If a slow walk around the block with a really distracted dog counts, then yes!

What are your goals?

My goals? *My first goal would be to murder whoever created the form.*

I guess I still had enough self-restraint to stop my hands from writing my exact thoughts, though. Instead, I contemplated writing a more typical response. Get back in shape. I was once a runner. *Oh, wait... and to enjoy life again.* Enjoy and smile—like how I felt as a kid from the moment I'd wake up to the moment I'd go to bed, because my day, in its entirety, revolved around twiddling my thumbs as I made life-changing decisions to watch either *Scooby-Doo* or *Legend Zelda*, with a bowl of *Froot Loops* or *Frosted Flakes* on my lap.

When I lifted my eyes, *Gwyneth* was busy on her cell, undoubtedly making up for lost time on social media. *Stop.* No one probably ever told the poor child it was impolite to be texting or *sexting*, or who knows what else while you were supposed to be taking care of a potential new gym member. And it wasn't her fault I had to write *yes* to the overweight question. Somewhere between my second childbirth and forty-fifth birthday, my weight has edged closer to the higher end of the overweight category on the *Body Mass Index* calculator—causing strained back muscles that make me sometimes walk with an octogenarian stride. I've let myself go, living on autopilot for the past twenty years, and there's no one to blame except myself. Maybe the founders of *Netflix* and *Tony's Pepperoni.* They haven't helped either.

When Gwyneth finally saw me looking, she quickly put down her phone, smiled broadly and said as though sharing a confidence, "Sorry, I've been waiting for an important message."

Before I could respond, Carrie Underwood's *Blown Away* ringtone bellowed from the depths of my purse. It was Hank, my husband. And since he was visiting his father at the hospital, he was probably requesting a quiet night and a little comfort food.

I dug my phone out, signaling *Gwyneth* to give me a minute. "Hey baby, should I call Tony's Pepperoni?" I said, anticipating his request as I stepped away from the counter.

Hank didn't answer. Perhaps our twenty-one-year-old daughter, Samantha, had flunked her college exams, *or* her younger brother, Cameron, once again, was the cause of a fender bender as he practiced driving with his father. Pausing for a moment, I recited my *Be Here* mantra three times, as if it would give me extraordinary powers or something to stay present and not get lost in creeping dreaded thoughts.

"He's gone, Allie..." Hank finally said.

"Gone? We ordered from him last week, didn't we?"

"No, Allie, not him," he said flatly. And then I thought he was referring to Baily, our monster labradoodle, who'd discovered an exciting world beyond the backyard gate. But Hank's shaky voice made it clear it was far more tragic. "Mom was feeding him her tapioca pudding and he... he shook his head for her to stop and then... he closed his eyes and ..."

It took me a moment. "Oh, Hank..." I said, as the weight of what he was saying finally hit me. *He's gone. My beloved father-in-law, George.* I raised my head and stared blankly at the thin layer of dust collecting on the leaves of a dying poinsettia plant and then at my ragged looking fingernails. *George is gone.*

Hank let out a little cry and then a tremendous wave of awkwardness of not knowing what to say next overwhelmed me. I stood in disbelief as he struggled to get words out. "He looked fine... he was... and then—wait, hold on."

I took another deep breath, feeling a stinging sensation in my eyes so bad I closed them. *He's gone.* After all the time mentally preparing for the day, I felt I'd been punched hard in the gut. We didn't expect him to survive into the new year, but to our surprise, he did—making us mistakenly believe he was getting stronger and ready to go home in a few days.

A moment later, Hank returned. "Allie, you there?"

I stood up taller, reaching into my purse for car keys. "Yep. I'm here, sweetie." My voice reverberated with sadness. "I'm on my way now. I love you—"

"Okay, but hurry. I'm not sure what to do or even what to say to her." *Her,* meaning his mother Margaret. Suddenly, a picture flashed before my eyes—a disturbing image of Margaret yelling at the nurses and blaming them for her husband's death. I blinked away the scene and focused on Hank.

"Most people need to be comforted at a time like this," I said. In Margaret's case, held and restrained was more like it because I could hear her in the background, crying and telling Hank what to say to me. "I'll be there as soon as I get Cam—he'll want to come too."

After a quick goodbye, I looked over at *Gwyneth*, who was now leaning against a high black stool and talking on her phone. "... *absolutely and thank you for the opportunity*," I overheard her say.

I flapped the registration form at her with a pounding heart, all while trying to maintain my composure. "Excuse me," I said after I got her attention. "I'm gonna have to come back. My father-in-law just passed." My lips quivered as the words reached my heart.

She obviously didn't understand my word choice for *died* because she hid her phone under some papers and then bounced over with a bright smile.

Keeping my eyes on her, she quickly scanned the form before glancing at me with her wrinkle-free skin. Her smile faded. I could see she wasn't pleased, given we'd spent the past twenty minutes going through the gym's elaborate registration process. "When should we expect you back—uhhh... Mrs... uh—"

"Allison—Allison Montgomery," I said, pointing impatiently at my name in big bold letters on the top of the form. *Idiot.*

"Allison, sorry. Did you want to reschedule, Allison, or come back later?" I could hardly think as she flipped through the schedule mechanically, inhaling deeply, and clicking and unclicking her pen. Moments later, "We can book you in on Tuesday at three o'clock, and if you need to cancel, just let us know. Does that work?"

"Sure," I said stiffly. "That's fine. I'll call if it doesn't."

As I shouldered open the heavy gym door and hurried out into the bitter cold, my cell rang with a vulgar rap song Cameron had recently set on it for his ring tone.

He didn't waste any time when I answered. "Did you hear?" he said, choking back tears.

"I did, honey, and I'm on my way to get you. I'll need to come in and change first though."

"I'm at Kyle's..." he said faintly.

Kyle, Cameron's best friend, lives ten minutes in the opposite direction. Showing up at the hospital in yoga pants *and* a sweatshirt would not go over well with Margaret, but there was no choice, I reasoned. It would be a lot worse if I didn't get there before the staff took George's body away.

"Okay," I said, sounding surprisingly calm. "I'll be there in ten minutes."

I fiddled with the radio as I drove. I was hoping to find some calming music to keep me from slipping into a downward emotional spiral. But with rush hour in full swing, all I could find was news or commercials. Numb and dazed, I turned the radio off and drove in silence along the snow-lined streets amidst the fading light. Suddenly, another wave of emotions crashed over me. A tear escaped again. *How was I going to cope without George?* I swallowed, trying to catch my breath as warm tears rolled down my cheeks. And then, unexpectedly, feelings hidden deep inside surfaced. I gripped the steering wheel a little more tightly with a racing heart. And that's when it hit me. I realized what it might mean. It wasn't just the darkness of George's death I was afraid of. It was *what*, or *who*, was lurking behind it... Hank's mother... my mother-in-law, a master manipulator, and the source of much of my anxiety, insecurity and frustration since the day we'd met.

Maybe I should be blaming *her* for my weight gain and what might become a tense marriage for Hank and me.

Hate is a strong word. *Sometimes.*

2 - GUESS WHO'S COMING TO DINNER

I navigated through traffic, barely. I couldn't stop thinking about how much I was going to miss him. George had been like a second father to me. He accepted me for who I was. I loved him for that. Sadly, it was the exact opposite of the relationship I had with Margaret. After every visit *to* her and every visit *from* her, I'd always feel so angry—angry, trapped and frustrated. George knew and had *always* tried to act as a buffer between Margaret and me.

Twenty-five minutes later, in Kyle's driveway, I sent another text to Samantha. It was strange I hadn't heard back from her. Very strange. Unless she was driving, she'd usually respond within milliseconds. I took a deep breath, feeling my throat constricting at the end of it.

When I looked up, Cameron was coming out of Kyle's house. Weighed down by his heavy backpack and his two-pound winter coat, he walked over to the driver's side and opened the door. "Aren't I driving?"

I gave him an apologetic but bright smile. "Oh, sweetie, I don't think now's the time. We're already late and traffic's ugly." I could see the disappointment register on his face, but something else was there. Something deeper. The news of his grandfather's passing was probably starting to hit him. "How 'bout you drive home after the hospital."

"*Fine*. Whatever. I'll just fail my road test on Monday," he mumbled reflexively.

"Well, maybe Dad can take you—" Cameron shut the car door before I could finish.

Flustered, I blew the hair out of my eyes and watched as he marched slightly around the front of the car to the passenger side. The fact that he was now dragging his expensive coat like an *old dirty blanket* confirmed what I'd seen in his eyes. He got in, fastened his seat belt, and slumped down in the seat. I gave him a moment before pulling out of the driveway.

Cameron looks like his father. Tall, lean and handsome. But his personality he got from his grandfather. Like George, Cameron is warm and compassionate but also light-hearted—when he's feeling good. Despite Cameron's sullen and teenage self-absorption, he's still my baby and even though he's growing up, we're still connected—far more than Samantha and I are, or have ever been, really. She's fiercely independent and has been since the day she learned to use her potty.

When Cameron finally looked my way, I gave him my warmest, most loving smile. He reciprocated half-heartedly, then turned and pulled his hood over his head.

We drove another five minutes in silence before I tried again. I reached over and squeezed his knee. He moved it away. It hardly surprised me, still, I tried not to take that, or his fake smile, personally.

I took a deep breath before attempting a conversation. "You okay?" I asked, feeling a bit frustrated by the line of other frustrated drivers behind a slow poke in an old minivan.

"Yeah," he replied, the warmth back in his voice.

"Wanna talk about Grandpa?" I asked tentatively, aware it was Cameron's first real experience with death, *not* counting our cat, Ruby, two golden hamsters, four Beta fish, and, most recently, the sad *slow* death of Izzy—his beloved and good-natured bearded dragon.

"No," Cameron said, a little too quickly. "I'm *okay*, Mom," he added.

"Cam, it's okay to cry, you know."

"I know—I mean, it's not like any of this is surprising," he mused. After a moment, he pulled his hood down and then looked right at me.

"I'm actually kinda relieved, if you wanna know the truth," he said. "I didn't like seeing him suffer. He wasn't happy."

I pondered this for a bit and then smiled. "Yeah—I don't think so either," I said, letting out a deep breath I didn't know I was holding. "Grandpa put up a good, long fight, but I think there comes a point when your body is ready to shut down and your spirit is ready to move on."

"Yeah... and as Grandpa used to say about his friends who were dead or dying—*they left the building a long time ago.*"

We burst out laughing, which seemed to release the built-up nervous energy in the core of my stomach I had about saying goodbye to George.

Despite tight shoulders, I leaned toward Cameron when we stopped at a red light. "George," I said, nudging him to jump in, "if you're up there already and can hear us, we miss you."

"And if you see Izzy—tell him I say *hi*," Cameron said. "I love you, Grampa," he added with a shaky voice.

I nodded. He nodded. And when I saw a little tear roll down the side of his nose, I gave his hand a tight squeeze. He gave me a quick but sad smile, and then, weaving his fingers through mine, turned and stared out the window. Grieving together, we drove the rest of the way in silence.

It took nearly ten minutes to find a parking spot close to the hospital's entrance. Cameron stayed in the car while I hurried to get a parking ticket from the machine. I wasn't sure how long we'd be, considering George had already *left the building,* so I paid the maximum in case there was paperwork.

Back at the car, Cameron was on his phone. "*When?*" I heard him say to the person on the other end. "Well, tell her to wait. We'll be there in five." He hung up and looked at me. "That was Sam. Grandma's getting impatient and she's calling someone to take Grandpa's body away—"

"Sam's there? She never called *or* texted me back," I said, trying to keep the frustration out of my voice. "Did she seem upset—oh, never mind." Out of respect for George, I let it go. I threw the parking ticket on the dashboard and grabbed my purse. "*C'mon*. Let's get up there *before* Grandma has the funeral."

Not surprisingly, Cameron didn't respond. He doesn't like getting involved in our mother-daughter drama, and my comments about Margaret tend to make him uncomfortable—for the most part, he did always agree with them.

"And put on your coat," I snapped a bit. "It's winter out here."

He grabbed it, flipped it over his shoulders and followed me through the poorly lit parking lot and then through the big glass doors. As we walked through the spacious foyer with its distinctive hospital smell, I focused on pleasant thoughts. It was a brand-new facility, complete with electric fireplaces, expensive but impressive gift shops and a Starbucks coffee station. Everywhere you looked, there were trained and energetic volunteers helping to make things run more smoothly. But it still felt eerie. And depressing. Seeing patients and visitors milling around added to the general uneasiness I felt about hospitals. It's heart-breaking to watch people in distress as they cope with their injuries, illnesses, or surgeries— or those of their loved ones. Unless you're in the maternity ward or the outpatient wing, you can't mask the sense of gloom that fills the air—no matter how many colorful balloons or flowers you add.

When we neared the elevator, I turned to Cameron. "You must be hungry," I said, reaching to straighten his thick wavy hair. "We'll grab something on the way home, *okay?*" We followed the crowd like penguins into the elevator. "And pull up your pants," I whispered, winking at him as he wiggled them up with one hand and fixed his hair with the other.

Cameron reached through the people in front of us and pressed the button, then we both stared awkwardly at the indicator as we approached the eighth floor. When we stepped off the elevator, I took a deep, *deep* breath. With my germ phobia on high alert, I put both hands under the hands-free sanitizer on the wall, twice, and continued taking small, shallow breaths as we walked down the brightly lit hall. We passed some rather chatty staff hanging around the nurses' desk—like a scene out of *Grey's Anatomy.*

"*Allison!*"

Surprised to hear my name, I stopped and turned to see George's favorite nurse, Helen, a compassionate and seasoned nurse with a robust frame. In stylish pink scrubs and a fashionable mask covered in unicorns hanging from one ear, she walked toward us with her arms wide open, breaking the rules of any recent *Hugger's Guide.*

"He went without much pain," she said, pulling me close and patting my back.

After a few seconds, she reached out her arms to Cameron before giving him a tight squeeze. "He's at peace now," she said.

Cameron nodded, smiling shyly.

Helen's expression changed when she looked back at me. "Margaret's not, though—" She shook her head. "We had to get your daughter to take her out of the room after she gave one of our nurses a bloody nose."

"*Oh....*" I unzipped my coat and stuffed my hat into my coat pocket, without taking my eyes off her. "What happened?" I asked, certain I didn't want to know.

She paused before she replied, her head falling. "It was an accident, of course—she was trying her version of resuscitation on George. We couldn't get her off him." Helen managed to keep a straight face. "She's a feisty old girl. Anyway, don't be alarmed if you see blood on the sheets."

"Sorry, Helen," I said. "I hope she hasn't caused *too* much trouble around here."

She let out a little sigh. "It's okay. I know it hasn't been easy for her."

"Yeah, I know... but I'm sure it hasn't been for the staff either—so thank you." I gave her a quick but heartfelt hug before motioning Cameron to follow me down the hall.

"YOU MAY NEED TO CONSIDER HAVING HER STAY WITH YOU FOR A WHILE," Helen called out.

I froze in my tracks, squeezing my eyes tight. *What?*

"Mom, you *okay?*"

No.

"Yep," I said, not moving as I switched my heavy purse to the other shoulder.

"*Mom?*"

I drew in my breath, holding it as long as I could. "I'm *fine!*" I said at last. I continued walking, forcing a smile as I changed up my mantra from *I'm thankful for what I have, even if it's not perfect* to *my curses become my blessings.*

When we got to George's room, I slowly peeked inside. Samantha was sitting on the end of the bed reading some hospital pamphlet with her headphones on, and Hank, in his wrinkled cotton dress shirt, was pacing back and forth in front of the window while talking on his phone. And... then there was Margaret. She was the first to spot us as she stood by the bed, holding George's hand. "*Finally,*" she muttered. She looked at her wristwatch and then back at me, frowning because of my yoga pants, I was sure.

My curses become my blessings.

My curses become my blessings.

My curses become my blessin—

"Sorry we're so late," I said, and before I knew it, I found myself walking toward her with my arms outstretched. Sure, I was still angry and upset for her giving Samantha money *and* a car so she could move out and go away to school—without our permission. And a thousand other things over the years related to her *one-woman campaign* against me. But right now, with George now gone, I couldn't help but feel overwhelming sympathy for her. Besides, I love her son. We have that in common. And I had loved George with all my heart. We shared that too.

I took a deep breath, catching sight of George's pale and waxy face over Margaret's shoulder as she accepted my hug. It was hard to comprehend it was him. He appeared strangely different with his jaw slightly opened but looked remarkably at peace. The unreality of it all made me shiver.

When Margaret let go of me, she reached out and gave Cameron a hug before turning back to George. Stunned and slightly queasy, I watched as she took George's black comb off the rectangular overbed table and start detangling the snarls out of his thin gray hair.

I was about to remark on the strange scene in front of me when Samantha pulled her headphones down and jumped off the bed. "*Hey*, Mom." She crossed the room for a hug, seeming surprisingly composed. She gave Cameron a quick squeeze before flopping in one of the tanned sleeper chairs beside George's bed. "What took you guys so long?" she asked, struggling with the lever on her chair.

Before I could answer, Hank was there, wrapping his arms securely around me, reminding me how well my shoulders fit under his arms. It had been a long time since we'd hugged so tightly. Hugged period. I had almost forgotten how warm and fuzzy it felt. Without letting go as we rocked from side to side, he turned toward Samantha. "It doesn't matter— we're all here now. So, let's say our *goodbyes* and let them get in here and take Grandpa's body downstairs."

Hank and I held each other for a while longer until he suddenly pushed me back and gasped, "MOM!" He sprinted to the other side of the bed. "*What are you doing?*"

I looked behind me and saw Margaret cutting George's hair with a tiny pair of nail scissors. Just in time, I swallowed the tiny bubble of laughter surfacing from the pit of my stomach.

Margaret cocked her head to one side. "He needs a trim," she replied defensively. There was a pause, and then she stood up. "I *was* going to do it today anyway."

Hank carefully peeled the scissors out of her frail looking fingers. "Don't worry about it now—they'll take care of everything at the funeral home."

"*What?*" She looked annoyed and perplexed at the same time. "Well, they'd better—it's a bloody mess," she said, sitting back on the bed, sulking with narrow-set eyes.

Cameron plopped down in the other chair, looking as startled as his sister. Surely it felt disturbing and surreal being in the room with their grandpa's *dead* body. It felt surreal to me. And weird. As much as I wanted to give George a goodbye kiss, I couldn't bring myself to do it. His body was stiffening, turning a purplish-blue tinge, and I didn't want his cold skin against my lips to be one of my last memories of him.

I could tell everyone was struggling, trying to keep it together, except for Margaret. She was busy cleaning George's ears with a cotton swab. Hank was about to say something when, as if by magic, Helen appeared in the doorway. "The gurney's here," she said tenderly. Behind her stood two young men in full surgical garb, ready to take on the task of removing George's body from the room. It was all part of the awkward process that follows the death of a loved one in a hospital.

We huddled around the bed one last time as George lay there, without a flicker of life in his body. I said my silent goodbye through a wild wave of sadness and hopelessness, half expecting him to open one of his eyes, like he would after taking one of his naps.

A heavy silence permeated the room until Hank cleared his throat. He was overwhelmed, I could tell. And when he's overwhelmed, he gets antsy. "Okay everybody... time to go." He tucked in his shirt before grabbing his phone off the table.

When the two sweet looking men entered after Helen, we all headed for the door, except Margaret. "Make sure to keep him covered. He doesn't like to be cold," she instructed the orderlies, looking quite perturbed.

My eyes widened. For a split second, I thought she was making a joke about cold, dead bodies. But then I saw the look on her face and realized she was just being Margaret.

I watched as Hank gave her a gentle squeeze on the shoulder. "Don't worry, Mom. They'll take care of him. Let's go," he whispered, guiding her to the door.

Helen smiled with kind and compassionate eyes. "We'll be done in about twenty minutes—" she said to us. "You can come back and get his belongings then."

Hank tried to get Margaret to go with him and the kids to the cafeteria. She refused to follow. I invited her to come with me, in search of a bathroom and a card for the eighth-floor staff, but she shook her head.

"I'm not going anywhere," she said firmly, sounding a bit belligerent. "*Someone* needs to make sure these two men do right by your father."

I exchanged a look with Hank. *Was I surprised she was already causing another scene?* Neither of us insisted on her coming, so we left her standing in the doorway, like a sentry with arms folded and eyes fixed on Helen and the transport team.

Sure enough, when we got back, Margaret was in the room, carefully wrapping up the wilted flowers sent by George's well-wishers. I sat on the edge of the bed, exhausted, while taking in the quiet stillness of the room. In a sense, we were free. No longer would we be held captive by the hospital, and it felt oddly liberating. I stretched my back, experiencing a warm loving light filling up my senses. *George, is that you?*

Seconds later, Margaret interrupted, declaring in her default tone, "This stuff isn't going to pack up itself."

Snapped back to reality, I took a calming breath. "You're *right*, Margaret. Let's get to it," I said smiling, smiling as I tenderly rotated my shoulders.

I could see a mix of gratitude and relief spread across Hank's face when my eyes found his. If it had been any other time or place, my response to her might've been different. *I assure you.*

We re-read the *get-well* cards lined up along the window sill, threw out the half-emptied juice bottles and gathered up all the wrinkled tubes of ointments. Margaret picked up George's knit socks and flannel pajamas scattered throughout the room. She smelled them first, of course, before stuffing them into an overflowing garbage bin next to the bed.

Not long after, we all had our coats on and were ready to leave when Margaret flopped on the bed. She let out a lengthy, audible sigh for everyone to hear before moaning, "*God... I'm hungry.*"

When I turned around, she quickly looked up at the ceiling. She let out another long sigh, rolling halfway over toward the window in her heavy wool coat.

"*Mom, why don't you just come over and have dinner with us?*" I heard Hank say.

I whipped my head around, giving him a wide-eyed, blank stare.

"Well..." She paused, as if trying to manage a response. "If you *think* it's best—I suppose I *could*," she mumbled into the mattress.

I almost exhaled a long audible sigh too, eyeing the eight-storey window and thinking about a good-old fashioned Bohemian style solution. *Just. One. Push.* I smiled and nodded instead. *Of course Margaret was coming home to have dinner with us. Her husband just died. What else were we going to do? Drop her off at a McDonalds?*

3 – In the Beginning

If Margaret and I *had* gotten along over the years, and I really wish we had, I would've treated her like I treat my own mother. I would've made duo hair appointments and surprised her with lunch at trendy restaurants downtown. I would've gone out of my way to pick up the milk she'd forgotten and gladly have swung by to drop it off. I would've inquired about her health, taken notes on her cooking tips, and happily listened to her weekly stories about her neighbors and frustrations.

I would've been the perfect daughter-in-law.

Positive.

Loving.

And attentive.

But, somehow, out of *all* the protective mothers out there who would've embraced a relationship with their new daughter-in-law, I'd ended up with a mother-in-law more reminiscent of *Cruella De Vil*.

When I first met Margaret, I knew immediately the two of us would never be friends. Before greeting me in her front hallway, she looked me over—from my freshly styled hair down to the pretty silver sandals I'd worn for the occasion—and asked pointedly, "Did you bring a pair of socks with you?"

The second thing that came out of his mother's mouth was even snootier. She looked right past me to her son. "Henry, please. Could you show your girlfriend to the bathroom so she can wash her feet?"

"Mom, *relax!*" Hank snapped, looking mortified as he stepped out of his runners and into his *house shoes*, which were already lined up for him next to a basket of slippers.

Even though I felt humiliated by Margaret's comments about my "dirty feet", I made myself smile before tiptoeing behind Hank as we moved across the perfectly vacuumed carpets to the bathroom which, by the way, smelled like rose petals and was even covered in rose petal wallpaper.

The truth was, Margaret had been angry even before I got there. She didn't like the idea of her son, and only child, getting serious with anyone other than Sandra, the daughter of a long-time family friend and someone whom Margaret adored. The golden girl represented everything Margaret wanted in a daughter-in-law—she was a soon-to-be lawyer from a well-known, respected family with beautiful genes to pass on to Margaret's future grandchildren.

The problem was, Hank didn't love Sandra. While he'd known her since childhood and they'd seen each other at many family functions and get-togethers over the years, Hank saw Sandra as more of a "cousin"—and a pretentious, stuck-up one at that. Of course, he'd always tried to be respectful and polite to her whenever their paths crossed—as you might with a prickly member of your extended family.

Hank has always said he loved me from the moment we met, but it took time before my reciprocity surfaced. Albeit good-looking, he was *too* nice with his incessant compliments and adoration. But soon after processing my attraction to him, he'd won my heart, and I realized we had more things in common than not—besides not having any siblings, we both liked bloody horror movies, hated country music, and loved anything spicy. But more importantly, we made each other laugh. He'd always tell me how I was like wearing his favorite pajama bottoms.

Hank's upbringing beat mine hands down, but he never made me feel inadequate or inferior—that was Margaret's mission. Sadly, his mother's disapproval of me was hard on him. She *was* his mother, after all, and he loved her, and she was devoted to him. But when I came into his life and it became clear I was there to stay, he began to feel her wrath. Thankfully, he stood up for me when Margaret said I wasn't as *smart* or as *ambitious* as he was.

I have to admit, she was probably right about the *ambition* part. At twenty-two, I wasn't ready to take on the world, even with my shiny new bachelor's degree. I wasn't ready for a grown-up job that required me to wear grown-up clothes. I was happy and content waiting tables at the *Wild West Sports Bar*, making generous tips and drinking free vodka cocktails, while most of my friends were swiveling awkwardly in their office chairs, trying to make their fancy degrees seem worthwhile. So, there I was, back in my twenties, feeling proud for doing my own laundry, paying my own rent and cooking something more complex than spaghetti and meatballs for my roommates while Margaret was applauding Hank—and herself— for snagging a high-paying financial analyst position with a big downtown firm weeks *before* graduation.

A year after we'd started dating, Hank invited me to his friend's wedding. It involved a one-night stay in a four-star hotel and back then, you didn't invite your girlfriend to a wedding that included a continental breakfast if you weren't serious. After a few drinks at the open bar, Hank had come back to our table and proposed to me while the other guests were off dancing to the third *Madonna* song of the evening.

As my feet tapped to the beat under the white linen tablecloth, Hank took my hand, leaned in, and half-shouted in my ear because of the music, "So, when are you and I getting married?"

My feet stopped tapping. I wasn't sure if he was joking or if he was serious. It was all so confusing. We loved each other and people do impulsive things at a wedding, but his mother didn't like me. And I wasn't sure if there really was a next step for us.

He must've sensed my confusion because he took a swig of his beer and restated the question, looking deep into my eyes. "Allie, I love you.

We belong together. And I don't care what anyone says. Will you marry me?"

I remembered pulling away and giving him a shy, half-amused smile. Looking deep into his eyes, I accepted with a brief nod. And then I looked away and focused on the sea of people in their stocking feet, loosening up on the dance floor and yelling into each other's faces the words of the song. *What was wrong with me?* I thought hard. Most girls would've been jumping up for joy, barely able to contain their excitement at the thought of getting engaged and being the center of attention at an extravagant wedding, but all I remember was the way my joy was undercut by an overpowering sense of dread—Margaret was going to be my mother-in-law.

Hank had later confessed he wasn't heartbroken by my unenthusiastic response to his proposal. Despite his best efforts, he blamed his imprudent marriage question on the free drinks and excitement of being at his first major wedding.

My lukewarm reaction was because of my non-existent relationship with his mother. And because of this, it had been causing the protective wall I'd built for myself to get higher. Whenever Hank called his parents on Sunday night after his roommates had gone off to their hangouts, I'd notice how calm and relaxed he was when speaking to his dad, but how tense and defensive he'd become when he talked to his mother—probably because they were arguing about me. He'd always looked so frustrated and exhausted after he hung up.

Of course, Hank was a natural shoo-in with my parents, especially when compared to all the *not so charming* boys I had brought home. When I told them our first date had been at an art gallery instead of a drive-in, they were hooked. From then on, even after my father died, my mother would always ask how Hank was doing before inquiring about me. She loved him. And he loved her, too.

Two months after Hank's impulsive, alcohol inspired proposal and my unenthusiastic, anxiety-laden acceptance, we told his parents. We were having dinner—right in the middle of dessert—and as soon as the words left Hank's lips, Margaret stood up abruptly, looked at me and then glared at Hank declaring, "You know we're *not* too happy about this." Without another word, she took her plate of cherry cheesecake and stormed off into the kitchen.

When Margaret started banging dishes and slamming cupboard doors, Hank put his hand on mine, sighed deeply, and then went to calm her down. Meanwhile, George walked me to the front door and thanked me for coming.

He gave me a warm, comforting hug. "Don't take it personally. There's no girl in the world she'd actually approve of." He helped me with my sweater. "I'll talk some sense into her. You're a lovely girl, Allie, and you make Hank happy... that's all that matters." He looked at my feet. "Love the sandals, by the way," he said with a giant smile before giving me another tight squeeze.

George was that kind of person. Kind-hearted, gentle, and generous. *He married Margaret and spent the rest of his life with her, so what did that say?*

In the spring of the following year, Hank and I got married. We'd both wanted a small and intimate wedding, surrounded by those closest to us and at the city's stunning botanical gardens. But, of course, after Margaret had left two angry phone messages and dropped a major guilt trip on Hank, the plug was pulled on those plans. *She* decided we were getting married at the country club *she* and George belonged to and made all the arrangements. Our original sixty-person guest list grew to a grandiose party of over two hundred. Of course, it had all made sense to me. George came from old money and had had a successful career, which allowed Margaret to play the part of a high society lady, complete with her ladies' luncheons and golf club fundraisers. And let's be honest. After feeling the shame of her son marrying a lowly sports bar waitress, she certainly didn't want to expose herself to the shame of us having our reception in a glass atrium that she said resembled a cheap goldfish bowl.

But having thought giving in to her demands about the wedding would have appeased her, I was brought back to reality the very day we got back from our honeymoon. That's when Margaret started leaving daily voicemail messages reminding me of the importance of separating the whites from the darks, ironing Hank's cotton shirts on low, and having hot and hearty meals ready and on the table when he walked through the front door at the end of his long, hard day. And because she had a key to the lovely new house George had generously helped us buy, she could come over whether we were home or not. And she did. Frequently. Afterward, she'd call to criticize me for having left cereal bowls and coffee cups in the sink or strands of hair on the bathroom floor. She would even put Hank's favorite meals in our fridge—after cleaning it out, of course. Infuriating? You bet.

All of it continued well into our sixth month of marriage until I *finally* snapped. I called Margaret to give her a piece of my mind. Later that evening, Hank sat speechless on the sofa with his hands around his head, listening to me recount the phone conversation I had had with his mother. He'd had enough too, especially when she called to leave another message right in the middle of our first real fight as a married couple. She blabbered on and on about me and then about the ugly tea stains in the mugs she'd bought for us. Hank finally picked up the phone in the middle of her sentence. "Mom, I can't see this working out..."

Apparently, she started crying and yelling before telling Hank, "If I'm ruining your life, I just won't speak to you anymore. EVER!" Then she hung up on him.

While that could've been my greatest victory—I'll admit, a small smile had formed on my lips when I thought I'd never have to see her again—but it didn't last. I felt bad. Logic? Because I loved Hank too much to see him in such pain. After a few weeks of watching my poor husband suffer, I did what I had to do. I called Margaret. I swallowed my pride and apologized for getting upset and told her I appreciated her suggestions and help around the house.

I'd taken the high road and felt refreshed that Hank was feeling better. But that didn't mean everything was free of big waves. Three days later, Margaret left a letter for me on the kitchen counter saying that maybe I wasn't so evil but that I did need to find a worthy job so I could look and feel better about myself and because serving drinks to dirty old men at a sport bar was neither *proper* nor *lady-like*, especially since Hank was establishing himself in his career. She ended it all by wishing me a good weekend and that she liked the new bamboo blinds on the kitchen window—but she also said she could see out of the window better if it wasn't so filthy. *Filthy*... spelled out in capital letters.

One thing was perfectly clear. If I wanted to stay married *and* if I wanted Hank to be happy, Margaret had to be in the picture. So, I took a deep breath and after careful consideration, I tore up the letter. I never told Hank about it and resolved to avoid Margaret whenever possible. But life had other plans. When the grown-up job I'd been avoiding, and the kids that were never planned came along, I caved under the pressure. We needed an extra pair of hands around the house to help keep our children safe in a happy and healthy environment. Unfortunately, it was the opening she was waiting for to sink her claws into us for good.

As a child, it was not how I imagined my marriage to be.

4 – One Too Many Cooks

It was eight thirty when Cameron and I got back to the car. I fished out my keys with chattering teeth and shivering legs and offered them to him.

"You sure?"

I nodded even though I had many qualms about teenage drivers. "Just need to make a stop at the store," I said, giving him a quick smile before hurrying around to the passenger side and jumping in.

While we waited for the car to warm up, Cameron turned to me, suddenly sounding about six years old. "So... am I going to have to cancel my driving test?"

I gazed at him through the darkness. "Let's see how the weekend unfolds, Cam."

He didn't respond right away. "Okay," he said at last, his face falling with disappointment.

I put my hand on his leg. "Don't worry. I'll make sure you get to take it." And I meant it. Getting his license might keep him from focusing on the loss of his grandpa. The only problem is Margaret. She was likely to see it as disrespectful. At least she would blame me, not Cameron.

With the car warmed up, we drove to the grocery store. Under normal circumstances, I would've balked at putting together a full-on meal late in the evening, but I decided it would be better for everyone if I kept my mouth shut because nothing charming would've come out of it anyway.

Cameron seemed to have read my mind. "Why don't we just order pizza? I'm sure—"

"Really?" I adjusted my seat forward. "Can you imagine the look on your grandma's face if we walked in with a large pepperoni pizza?"

"Right," he said without looking at me, "store it is."

Generally speaking, I *hate* to cook. It takes too much time and although I try to make healthy and tasty meals, it feels mostly like a wasted effort. None of us are picky eaters and no matter what you make, there are always dirty dishes to deal with—partly why I avoid any recipe requiring three or more pans. Interestingly enough, there *always* seems to be another edition of a carefully wrapped and unmarked *Healthy Meals in Thirty Minutes* cookbook under our Christmas tree every year.

Cameron found a parking spot close to *Urban Fresh Market's* entrance. "Do I have to come in?" he asked, turning off the car.

"Nah, it's okay," I said quickly, too quickly. But truth was, I needed the alone time, the physical and mental space to process my emotions— even if only for a few minutes and in a grocery store full of hungry, cranky shoppers. I put my hand on his arm. "Great job getting us here. I'm proud of you."

He settled into the car seat, giving me a lively smile before I clutched my purse close and ran for the doors. When they opened, I felt the familiar flood of strangely comforting warm air from the overhead vents. As much as I find grocery shopping to be a chore, for some reason, the store itself feels like a sanctuary. It's a place where I can "be", while roaming through aisles and humming along to the store's soft rock music in the background.

After adjusting my bulky winter coat and wrestling a grocery cart from the corral, Billy Joel's *Uptown Girl* rang out in my purse. Mindful that my brief break to sort through feelings would be over, I dug out my phone anyway because it was Val, a dear friend I'd found and kept out of the thousands of people at university. Val, who could make a late-night shop for milk or eggs feel like a spontaneous and wild adventure, lives around the corner from us, and is one of the few people in my life who didn't consume my energy. Whenever one of us needs to talk or complain about a bunch of things, we'd be there for each other at a moment's notice—and depending on the time of day, with a bottle of wine and chocolate covered almonds. Whether I needed cheering up because of a recently discovered chin hair or a sounding board for my waning libido, she is my go-to girl— and vice versa. She's also the one I'd express a multitude of emotions to about my incredibly challenging and thorny relationship with Margaret. Val understands. She had a difficult mother-in-law once.

Val has also had to deal with *Peter the Cheater*, her womanizing ex-husband. For whatever reason, she can't seem to get him out of her system. So the good thing is, apart from learning how to lead a decent sex life at our age, after listening to her issues, I'd often feel better about mine.

Bracing for her reaction to the jumbled text I'd sent her from the hospital bathroom earlier, I answered.

"Got your text...how *are* you?" she said right away.

"Exhausted—I'm at the store now getting something for dinner."

"*Jesus*, Allie. Just order a *frickin'* pizza or something," she blurted out. "The last thing you need is to spend two hours in a kitchen trying to impress her." She paused and I could hear her bracelets jingling over the phone—likely from lifting her wine up to her mouth. She continued after swallowing rather loudly. "And you know *exactly* how that's gonna end up."

I let out a sigh, pushing the most annoying cart I could've possibly grabbed around the produce section.

"All I'm saying is, you need to accept her for who she is—right now— for your own peace of mind. She's not going to change—" Her bling-bling jingled away. "*She's* a bitter old woman," she declared.

My mouth watered. I could almost smell the familiar nutty scent of our favorite white. "Should I get salmon or chicken?" I asked, throwing an English cucumber and a bag of baby carrots into the shopping cart.

"Salmon," she responded.

"Potatoes or rice—wait—never mind," I said, "I'm going with rice." It's the one thing I like when I'm feeling hungry and out of sorts and wanting a thousand of something on my plate.

I chose a thick slab of Atlantic salmon from the seafood counter and then because I didn't have a grocery list, I grabbed a few more bottles of wine and various other things we probably didn't need going back and forth across the store. While Val continued complaining about mother-in-laws in general, I waited in the one and only checkout line the store had open.

"Okay, I'm heading to the car now," I announced not long after getting through the line. "I'll call if I need an escape."

Back at the car, Cameron was deeply engaged in his phone.

"What did ya get?" he said, not looking up from the bright screen.

"Salmon," I replied, grabbing his phone and putting it in the cup holder. "Concentrate."

He shook his head, turning on the engine. "No one likes it except for you and Dad—"

"Your grandma *loves* salmon—"

"No, she doesn't," he corrected. "Don't you remember it gave her food poisoning on that cruise she took with Grandpa two years ago?"

I flinched at the realization as I threw two of the three bags of groceries in the back seat behind me.

He gave me a quick look. "She said she feels sick when she thinks of salmon."

I gave a humorless laugh before pulling a face and swallowing the lump in my throat. It didn't matter. In Margaret's eyes, my dinner was going to be a complete failure regardless of what we had. "Well... leftovers it is then," I said, decisively.

I pulled out my phone and looked at the time. Hank was probably with Margaret at her condo still. She wanted to change out of her *hospital clothes*, as she put it, before coming to dinner. Nonetheless, my fingers raced over the keys.

[Dinner might be a disaster. Got salmon... will have to be leftovers]

Hank responded immediately.

[Yikes! Home soon. XOXO]

Cameron didn't say anything as we drove home. He was focused on the road which was good because it was giving me time to regain control of my emotions and to prepare for more when his grandmother soon discovered tonight's dinner was going to be last night's spicy meatloaf and a string bean casserole.

In the driveway, I smiled proudly after he turned off the car. "Just gotta nail your parking and you're good."

We hurried into the house and were greeted wholeheartedly by Baily, with one of my wooly socks in his mouth. "Thank you, *baby*," I said, tugging it out from between his teeth. He wagged his tail insanely, as if to say, *there's a million things I wanna do with you guys now that you're home.* I cannot comprehend when people tell me they don't love dogs.

While we were putting our things away in the stuffed closet full of hangers and winter coats, I heard Samantha on her phone seemingly giving an inventory of what we had in the fridge. That was ominous.

Moments later, she popped her head around the corner of the kitchen. "That was Grandma—" she said, sounding relieved, "and she's bringing dinner."

"Well..." I said, keeping the sarcasm out of my voice, "... isn't that a blessing." I kicked off my runners, shuffled to the kitchen and went straight to the fridge after planting a kiss on the back of her head. I missed her living in the house. Sadly, we haven't been talking much since she dropped out of her theater and drama program last year and enrolled in an interior design program at a distant college—*distant* being the operative word that hurt us the most. Besides her being away, Hank and I couldn't support her vision of *now* wanting to become the next designer queen after wanting to give some of Hollywood's best actresses a run for their money. If Margaret hadn't swooped in, giving Samantha a big fat check, we'd be talking more than we do now. *And what sane grown-up hands over that kind of money to a kid whose brain isn't even fully developed yet?* All we could do was watch our overly impulsive and somewhat naive firstborn happily pack her bags and move three hours away to a strange city. Hank cried when Samantha drove off. If I hadn't been so mad, I might've cried too. I'd put up with Margaret's numerous affronts over the years, but helping my child leave home without my permission was a lot to bear.

I left the kids talking in the kitchen and collapsed on the living room sofa with a full, to the rim, glass of Chardonnay. I knew when I'd been beaten by something as simple as dinner, but I was too tired to care. Right now, there was me, my wine, and a handful of chocolate covered almonds. I raised my glass, preparing for *Hurricane Margaret*. "Here's to you, George. May you rest in peace..." I took a big sip, letting the wine come in contact with all my taste buds before swallowing and then raised my glass up in the air again, "... and here's to me. May I live in peace."

5 – A Suitcase Full of...

Hank's car headlights lit up the living room when I was only halfway through my glass of wine. *Damn.* I was hoping for a surge of warmth throughout my body before Margaret got here. I gulped down the rest of it before peeling myself off the comfortable leather sofa. *Showtime.* I'd already given Margaret enough satisfaction by screwing up on the food. I wasn't about to give her the satisfaction of not having the table properly set and waiting. Two minutes at most was all I had, so I hurried to the kitchen.

Like a pro, I whizzed around, dropping dinner plates and matching flatware onto the kitchen table. I lit a cranberry candle, got out Margaret's Christmas present—a fancy *Pottery Barn* placemat and napkin set—and topped up last night's salad with cucumbers and carrots all before the front door opened. *Boom! There's no way Gwyneth, that flawless beauty from the fitness club, could've pulled that off.*

I could hear Margaret explaining to Hank why she, and only she, should take care of George's funeral arrangements when they walked through the front door. Moments later, Hank walked into the kitchen carrying a foil-covered tray that smelled of Italian goodness and then came Margaret, with her maroon slippers and matching velour outfit, right behind him—who was still talking *at* Hank as she rolled in a suitcase.

My eyes followed the suitcase, a *large Caribbean blue* suitcase which screamed *more* than one night. And when she threw it up on the kitchen chair, opened it, and then rummaged through it like a homeless person looking for food in a trash bin, my legs got all jellylike and rubbery.

Hank took out the Scotch bottle from the kitchen cabinet. "I sent you a text," he mouthed sheepishly. He took his time unscrewing the cap and then poured himself a generous double.

I wiped off the horror-stricken look I was sure had spread across my face as Margaret spun around in our direction. She held up two cans in the air. "I brought tomato soup—" she announced, "and the lasagna Edith made for me last night." She pointed to the tray on the stove with a long-crooked finger that was capped off by intense crimson nail polish.

I was really at a loss for words so quickly forced a bright smile. I surprised myself. "Wow! Thank *God* for Campbell's and helpful neighbors—"

"Well, we should be eating *something* healthy tonight," she stated.

Artificial soup?

I gave her another bright smile, taking the cans from her hands and putting them on the counter. My smile vanished. "Thanks for bringing dinner, Margaret—"

"How about some wine tonight, Mom?" Hank asked, reaching into the cupboard for a glass.

She eyed the glassful I'd poured myself and said indignantly, but proudly, "*Wine*—I haven't drunk it in *years*—and besides, the wine you have gives me headaches." She looked at Hank as he sipped his scotch. "One of us should stay sober over the next few days—don't you think?" She repositioned the forks and knives and then straightened the napkins on the table. "*Someone* had taste buying this placemat set for you, Allison," she mumbled in my direction, playing to the gallery again.

Hank gave me a *don't-pay-attention-to-her* shake of his head before joining Margaret at the table. I let it pass and after an exaggerated grunt of exhaustion, and frustration, I turned on the oven and then busied myself with converting a stale French baguette into garlic bread. It felt like another world. Flat and gray. If George would've been in the kitchen, he would've given me the most fetching smile. He had my back whenever I felt I was being attacked. I shuddered, closing my eyes briefly.

Margaret got up from the table and strode purposefully to the stove. Moments later, "I'd like to create a list of errands and chores we're going to need to do before the funeral." She opened one of the soup cans and then spooned globs of its content into a sauce pot. Before Hank and I could answer, she waved the spoon in front of her and told us, like a pair of two-year-olds, "You should both clean up before dinner." She licked the spoon before putting it back into the pot, adding smugly, "And change your clothes. They're contaminated with germs from that dirty hospital." I heard her ramble on about other matters, but I was already halfway up the stairs, leaving Hank in the kitchen to deal with his mother.

Cameron and Samantha were sitting on Cameron's bed, disagreeing about something when I popped my head in. The pair of them stopped talking when they saw me. Taking note, I made my way to the bed, trying not to stumble over Baily or the heap of clothes in the middle of the floor. "Dinner should be ready soon," I said, eyeing them closely.

Neither of them answered. Instead, Samantha shuffled over on the bed to make space for me, then sprang up and crossed the room while admiring her own pretty face in the mirror. She pulled her black knit leggings further up her tiny waist and flipped her long dark hair away from her shoulders as she continued making the *duck face* she normally does whenever there's a mirror around.

Curiosity set in. I cleared my throat, looking pointedly at Samantha when she turned around. "So, how come you were at the hospital so quickly?"

Silence.

She went back to fiddling with the various objects on Cameron's tall dresser. "Mom, family was really important to Grandpa, wasn't it?" she said, somewhat tentatively.

Puzzled, I turned to Cameron.

"Don't look at me—" he said firmly with a small grin. "I just live here." He pulled his hoodie off and then threw it in the basket full of clean clothes—missing altogether.

I was about to press the issue with Samantha and now, the entire laundry process with Cameron, when the floorboards outside Cameron's room creaked. It was Hank and his body filled the doorway as he leaned against the door jamb, with ankles crossed and arms folded—even after twenty-two years of marriage, he's still very attractive—a swimmer's body and face now distinguished with fine lines, wrinkles, and gray-lined temples. It's unfair he still has his gorgeous looks. However, the hormonal rollercoaster I've been on means Hank hasn't been getting much from me in the bedroom these days. I don't doubt that's Mother Nature's wicked sense of humor as she tries to keep things fair in the midlife marriage stage.

"You guys ready for dinner?" Hank said in a mellow voice.

"I am," Samantha answered first before kissing her dad on the cheek.

Hank rubbed her slender shoulder before turning to Cameron. "Why don't you two go down and keep Grandma company while we get changed."

Without waiting for a response, he gave them a long, genuine smile. But I didn't. I gave them a sidelong glance before I followed Hank down the hall and into our partially re-painted bedroom. Long story short, Margaret had decided for some reason or another our bedroom needed a makeover when Hank and I were away in November. She must've thought it was a good idea—a good enough idea to have had Cameron take a picture of her handyman in front of a stepladder, in our bedroom, and send it to us. I swore at the *f-ing* phone as soon as I saw it, while Hank hit the speed dial button to call the project off. I never had the chance to tell her how I felt about it, nor about the ridiculous peach color she'd chosen, because after we got back, George was rushed to the hospital the next morning.

Hank slipped into the bathroom while I changed into my favorite jeans and green knitted sweater. A few minutes later, Hank emerged, looking refreshed and ready to eat.

"Something's up with Sam because she..." I heard my voice trail off as I watched him change into his grungy sweatpants and hole-filled sweatshirt from his university days—both *very* unsuitable for public viewing.

"Okay, well... is it good or bad—actually... I don't want to know—not right now anyway," he replied dryly, sitting on the end of the bed with sad tired eyes.

Darkness was descending on him. Not giving it any thought, I went over and cradled his head in my arms, tenderly kissing his smooth, shiny bald spot. I stayed like that for a bit thinking how our new reality would be void of all the mental space taken up by George's doctor appointments and chemotherapy treatments, and the hope and gloom that came with every prognosis. Over the years, we'd felt optimistic on his good days and then sank into hopelessness during his bad ones, feeling emotionally and mentally drained. I think we were all, except Margaret, ready to see George relieved of his suffering. Every trip to the hospital, he cried. We cried. It was agonizing.

Sensing Hank was contemplating something as he lightly tapped his feet against the hardwood floor, I involuntary let go of his head and stepped back. He gave off a loud, gaping yawn. What came out of his mouth next, in the form of a statement rather than a question, made my stomach drop and my breathing difficult. "My mom can stay in Sam's room."

What?

My throat tightened simultaneously when my shoulders slumped. *Here goes.* "Sure—" I said, trying hard to sound warm and receptive. I swallowed hard again, already feeling resentful. "But for how long?" I asked, also trying hard to sound like a caring and responsive wife.

"For as long as she wants. She'll need the support while she grieves."

I smiled at him. "Oh," was all I could say, while picking imaginary lint off his red sweatshirt.

He stood up, laying his hands lovingly on my tight shoulders.

"Okay," I said after what might've seemed like a long pause.

"When she's ready," he said, "and maybe she'll surprise us, we can help her re-settle back at her place." He squeezed my shoulders. "Promise."

I didn't mean to, but I nodded glumly. There was no choice in the matter. Deep down, I knew it was the right thing to do. We did the same thing with my mother. However, when we invited her to stay after my dad died, it turned out she had only needed a few days. Relieved from the pressures of caring for him and running a house, she made the necessary arrangements with her sister and was on a plane to the Sunshine State of Florida before we knew it. Since then, she'd been living in a retirement community and enjoying the perks of year-round golf, afternoon cocktails by the pool, and... *the attention of wealthy widowed men who could still get it up, but were morons*—her words, not mine.

Hank was about to say something, when his cell phone rang with a shrillness that startled us both. "Are you teaching tomorrow?" he asked before reaching into his pocket to answer it.

"Substitute teacher," I mouthed, feeling that sense of overall doom in my belly about my job. It'd been almost twenty years of teaching and until only recently, I'd been asking myself why—besides helping to pay those bills that keep showing up each month—it no longer brings me joy except for the expensive perfumes, candles, and gift cards from parents twice a year.

He blew me a kiss, which lately was uncharacteristic of him, before switching to business mode with the caller. I blew one back and then felt irrationally panicked again and a little sick to my stomach thinking about Margaret's suitcase sitting on the kitchen chair.

The doorbell rang the moment I got to the bottom of the stairs. Margaret appeared from the kitchen and lumbered toward the door, wiping her hands on the decorative checkered tea towel I had hanging on the oven door. "How could you invite someone over tonight, of *all* nights?" she said, shaking her head side to side and sending her short curls flying in every direction.

Of course I ignored her accusation as I held Baily back and pulled open the door. And when I did, my eyes sprang open. *It was definitely not Avon.*

Margaret drew a sharp breath. "Keith!" she called out, nearly pushing me over to get to him. "What are *you* doing here?"

"I heard about George—" he said. "I just wanted to make sure you were okay."

She lowered her gaze. "Oh, that's so kind of you," she gushed. "Honestly, I don't know how I feel, but I'm glad you're here."

She pulled the gorgeous looking guy with hazel eyes and perfect hair into the house by his bright blue parka before turning to me. "Allison, this is Keith—Keith, this is my daughter-in-law, Allison." She smiled adoringly, caressing my back before saying, "You know, the one whose bedroom we *were* re-doing before Henry stopped the project."

And this is my mother-in-law. Sweet and courteous one second, cold and snooty the next.

My smile turned to a feral grin when realizing he'd been the one on the stepladder in the photo Cameron sent us in November. Although reeking of cologne, he looked like a gentle giant with his wide smile and friendly eyes.

He bowed his head slightly. "Nice to *finally* meet you, Allison," he said.

Finally? A tight-lipped smile took over my mouth again. "You, too," I said. Cautiously.

Keith grinned again and then turned his attention back to Margaret, giving her a big, long hug.

As I leaned against the wall, wondering *how* Keith had heard about George, not to mention *why* he was here, Samantha came bouncing into the foyer. No wonder a torturous shiver ran down my spine as I watched her swinging her hips toward Keith with a radiant smile. Well. They had my attention now.

Was Margaret as shocked as I was? Either she was oblivious to the steamy looks between the two of them or was intentionally playing dumb. She might be many things, but oblivious isn't one of them. Whatever was going on, in the middle of the foyer, she knew.

We all turned as Hank descended the stairs with Cameron in tow, dressed now in a pair of jeans and a flannel shirt.

Samantha grabbed Keith's arm, pulling him toward Hank. "This is Keith, Dad," she said, still holding onto his arm.

Margaret tapped Hank's shoulder. "He's the one who installed the bathroom railing for your father," she said, tugging Keith away from Samantha's tight hold.

"*Ah*. Right," Hank nodded, giving him a half, but honest smile.

Almost losing his footing, Keith bowed his head for the second time this evening. "It's good to *finally* put a face to the name."

Again with the *finally*.

Keith looked at Cameron and nodded. Cameron nodded back, completely unmoved. Not even a smile.

Samantha exhaled deeply. "Since we're all here," she said before clearing her throat and standing a bit taller, "there's something I want to tell—"

"Keith, how 'bout you stay for some lasagna," Margaret piped up before Samantha could finish. And before Hank had a chance to fully clue into his daughter's proud introduction of his mother's handyman, Margaret was herding us into the kitchen like cattle, yammering to Keith about George's last moments at the hospital.

6 – Love and Other Four-Letter Words

Margaret had us move with our dinner plates in hand from the kitchen table to the dining room table—a dark cappuccino table used when Cameron has a big school project, when I feel compelled to prep at home the *not-so-simple* crafts for my senior kindergarten class at Hillmount Academy, or for Sunday night dinners and holiday feasts. Tonight would mark the first time the table would serve as the gathering place to eat, following a family death. With growling stomachs and heavy hearts, we positioned ourselves around it and sat down. I immediately felt George's absence and sensed Margaret did too, when she laid her hand on top of Keith's calloused hand, squeezing it. "Let's pray," she commanded, then stood up.

Yes, pray. When Margaret is here, we'd say a prayer before meals. We'd say the *Bless Us O Lord* prayer, holding hands like steadfast worshippers in big circles.

Margaret led the prayer, and as we always did, we stood up. She resents the no-church rule in our home. But I'm not riddled with guilt or shame. I do believe, and I say this with the utmost respect, that I get the same satisfaction and enlightenment with a good book or my Friday night wine that Margaret gets from sitting in a hard-wooden pew for an hour, with the same church rituals, readings, and songs.

We all joined in the prayer—except for our newfound guest, Keith. I studied him as he shifted uncomfortably from one foot to the other, looking at us as if we were mocking him in a foreign language. I wasn't sure if he was uneasy because he wasn't the praying kind or because Samantha, who continued sneaking glances his way, was trying to make whatever they had going on "official" in front of her family on the night of her grandfather's death.

It was Hank who broke the silence after we said *amen* and sat down again. "So, Sam, what did you want to tell us? Did you change your program at school again?" he said, his voice sounding shaky before putting a forkful of lasagna in his mouth.

Seriously? Had he not been paying attention to the body language going on under our noses between his daughter and Margaret's contractor? "Well, not exactly," she said quietly. She shifted uncomfortably in her chair. "I—"

Annoyingly, Margaret tapped her glass with her fork, like they do at weddings, to get everyone's attention. "First, let's all say something to my beloved husband." She looked over at Hank. "And to your father... *and* to your grandfather we lost today." She glanced at Cameron, who was picking away at the lasagna on his plate, and then at Samantha, who seemed utterly deflated by the interruption.

I caught Margaret's eye as she took a slow sip of water, feeling a bit like odd man out. "And father-in-law," I said, flashing pride from my voice as I sat back in my chair.

"Of course, Allison," she quickly replied in her condescending tone. "Your father-in-law too."

Hank shook his head in dismay without looking at her before smiling kindly at me. "I'll go first, if I may."

Margaret nodded, breathing deeply, readying herself. "Go ahead, Henry."

He cleared his throat, concentrating. "Dad, you were always someone I could count on. You were a friend... and your strength showed us how to put up a good fight to the end." I watched as tears welled in his eyes. "I love you—and I'll miss you," he said, lifting his glass toward us.

We reached across the table with our raised glasses, trying to clink ours with his.

"Who wants to go next?" Margaret said, blowing her nose into a man-sized tissue.

"I'll go," Cameron said, straightening up in his chair. "Ready?" We all nodded and then I gave him a reassuring smile, which he seemed to find calming. "You were an *amazing* Grandpa—the best," he said. "I'm going to... I'm going to miss talking to you..." There was a pause. And then he added brightly, "And I hope you can now be in peace without pain."

"*Hear, hear!*" Keith shouted before taking a drink of the Scotch Hank had poured him. Margaret squeezed Keith's free hand, nodding in agreement before blowing her nose in the balled-up tissue again.

"My turn," Samantha said, with one hand firmly clasped in the other. "I never got to say goodbye to you today, so I'm sorry about that. But I think..." she said, closing her eyes after flashing a smile at Keith, "I felt your blessing."

Blessing?

I was about to take Samantha into the kitchen for a little one-on-one when Keith jumped up to save Margaret from toppling over on her chair as she stood up. Back on her feet again, Margaret raised her glass, taking the floor. She wiped her damp eyes and started with, "You're in God's hands now, George. My long service in taking care of you has come to an honorable end..."

Alas, her short tribute to George turned into a long tribute to herself as she recited all the wonderful things she'd done for him over the years. When she finished speaking—and Keith finished clapping like a trained circus seal—she turned her attention toward me and just like that, she said, "Did you want to get dessert going, Allison?"

"I think we're still eating here, Margaret," I boldly asserted, swallowing the food in my mouth, nearly choking. I washed the rest of it down with more wine while everyone looked my way.

"Mom, sit down and let us finish," Hank scolded her, reaching for the salt in front of him after soothing me with his eyes.

"Don't you want to say something, Mom?" Cameron asked meaningfully.

Relieved I'd been passed over, I shook my head, blasting around a smile—it seemed like the appropriate thing to do. I wasn't comfortable expressing my feelings about George in front of everyone. Besides, I was afraid of slurring my words.

I took the last bite of my garlic bread and excused myself, taking empty plates and Samantha with me to the kitchen.

"What's going on in there?" I growled after dumping the plates into the sink.

"What do ya mean?" she said.

"Oh, *c'mon* Sam," I retorted. "What's with all the looks between you and Keith?"

She stood there with confidence. "We're in love," she stated.

In love? I stared at her, speechless as the room spun.

"Mom... you okay?"

I pulled myself back to the present. "I'm not sure what to say. You've had a lot of boyfriends in the past... but Keith? He's *way* too old for you—he's what—thirty?"

"He's *only* twenty-nine."

"Oh... well... then twenty-nine," I scoffed, folding my arms. I leaned against the counter. "When—and how did you meet him?"

She squirmed a bit. "We met at Grandma's in September when he was installing something. Sorry, but everyone was so busy and stressed with everything, and I didn't want to cause any problems... so... I didn't say anything—but she's okay with it."

"What?" I said, throwing my hands in the air. "How could she have kept this from us?"

"Maybe 'cause she didn't want Grandpa—"

"Your grandpa wouldn't have been too pleased about this, Sam." Her shoulders and head dropped toward the floor. I continued, breathing deeply to stay the course. "She didn't say anything because it would've meant losing Keith as her handyman or whatever else he does for her." Okay, I wasn't really being fair. But the one thing guaranteed to make me crazy was someone messing with my kids. I shook my head at no one in particular, pulling out dessert spoons from the kitchen drawer. "Wait—" I slammed the drawer shut, turning back to her. "What was that little speech you gave in there?" My stomach twisted. "*Please* tell me you're not pregnant."

She didn't respond.

My jaw dropped.

"Mom, I really love him," she said, with *way* too much enthusiasm.

"This is *not* good, Samantha." I looked at her closely, wishing I was sitting under a palm tree on a white sandy beach somewhere—back to my single carefree days. There'd been less to worry about. "Does your grandma know?" I said, feeling incredibly dizzy.

"No..." She checked to see if anyone was coming from the dining room. "I realized when—"

"Realized? Did you go to the doctor's or something?" I said, disturbed I was having this conversation with her. "And what about your birth control pills?"

"I stopped because my face was breaking out in pimples." She stared at the floor again, twisting the ends of her hair with her fingers. "I thought this would've been good news with Grandpa dying and everything—"

"*Good news?* You can't be serious." I sighed deeply, sad she'd left me out of her decision to ditch the pill. Even though she's considered an adult, she's still one of my babies. And babies are *definitely* not ready to take care of their own babies. "You have your *whole* life ahead of you—what about school?"

The conversation paused for a moment and she kicked some crumbs on the floor with her neon pink sock. "Well, that was the *other* thing I wanted to tell you guys—"

"*What?*" I snapped, leaning toward her and staring right into her eyes.

She backed away from me, shrugging. "Well... it's just that I'm learning more about interior design from Keith than I was at school—"

"Let me guess—you're running off with him to host your own design show on *HGTV?*"

She clicked her tongue, slightly too hard. "Not now... but maybe *one* day."

I raised my eyebrows as far as they could go. *Not the response I wanted to hear.* This was sheer madness.

She cleared her throat. "I've been helping Keith with some projects—and like you, I'm *really* good at picking out colors and coordinating things. He's been teaching me—plus his dad one day might give him some business or something."

Okay, if Samantha had anything to do with the peach fizz color on our bedroom walls, then she might need to rethink her design calling.

"I didn't go back to school because Grandma said she desperately needed the help," she blurted out with some defensiveness in her voice.

"Oh, so your grandma knew about school too?" I said. *Damn her. And desperately needed the help? Damn her again.* Margaret has had an entire crew at her beck and call—Hank and me—not to mention, her neighbors, the home support staff from the hospital, and now it seemed, Keith.

"Everything's going to be okay, Mom. Don't worry," she finally said with twitching lips.

"*Don't worry?*" I said, stepping back to look at her fully. "This is *a lot* to take in right now." I gave her a penetrating stare. "When was your period due?"

"About ten days ago—and I'm *never* late."

My heart rate doubled as I turned away and stared at the wall. Shocked and hurt, I took a deep cleansing breath and turned around to her. "I need you to go back in there and act normal," I ordered, finding myself texting Val to bring over a home pregnancy test. Discreetly I warned. "And stop playing footsies with Keith under the table—your dad just lost his father and doesn't need to know about *any* of this right now."

As though awakening to her own reality, she lowered her head. "Fine," she said, trying hard to keep her chin from trembling.

Seconds later, Margaret floated in with the half-eaten lasagna tray. I didn't speak as I loaded cups and plates into the dishwasher and tried to ebb tears flowing in my eyes. I was hurt. Deeply hurt. And I was angry, and not because she was pouring my unfinished wine down the kitchen drain.

"How come you didn't tell us about the unwise choices Sam's been making?" I finally said, blinking back tears.

"What are you talking about?" she asked, foraging inside the fridge.

I tried to exercise some patience but couldn't. "Keith as her boyfriend—her quitting school," I fired back.

Margaret took her head out of the fridge and turned to me, wagging her finger. "There was just a death in the family, so don't you go gettin' all yelly at me."

"I *know* that, Margaret. But right now, we have a crisis on our hands." I grabbed out of her hand the piece of lemon pie I had hidden behind the milk carton in the fridge. "And just so you know—she thinks she's pregnant!" I hissed in her ear.

"Samantha's *pregnant?*" she cried out.

And as if on cue, Hank and Keith walked into the kitchen with the rest of the dirty dishes. I watched Margaret cower in the corner as she realized she'd spoken a little *too* loudly.

"Samantha's *pregnant?*" Hank echoed. Maybe he had been paying attention because he seemed to be foaming at the mouth when he looked back at Keith.

•   •   •

After the evening came to an abrupt halt, Hank told Keith to leave and then Margaret to settle herself in Samantha's room. It'd been an exhausting and emotional day, and Samantha's two bombshells had only fueled it. But it relieved us to know the biggest one she dropped, never hit the ground. Turned out the two pregnancy tests Val had helped her with, were negative. However, Samantha quitting school and falling in love with Keith would call for some much-needed parental intervention, regardless of whether she wanted it.

"Thanks for coming to the rescue," I said to Val while we waited for Baily to relieve himself in the neighbor's frozen garden.

I watched her blow smoke into the damp air. "I wasn't going to leave you with all that." She shook her head. "*God*, that Margaret is something else. She actually seemed heartbroken she wasn't going to be a great grandmother."

"I know," I said, "and when you were upstairs with Sam, I heard her telling Keith he was going to make a wonderful father." I took a deep drag from Val's cigarette, a terrible and nasty habit whenever I'm with her. "*Un*believable."

"Yeah, and all I could think about when we were waiting for the results was the possibility of hearing a child referring to you as *Grandma*," Val said, poking me in the arm.

I winced, allowing myself a deep breath.

She laughed, stomping out her cigarette with her stylish boot. "But I would've had your back with some cool granny names like *Gigi*... or *Bibi*... or *I* know—what about *Alibaba*—"

"Don't even go there," I said, bumping her affectionately as we continued walking. My stomach dropped at the very thought of being a grandmother at my age.

Five minutes later, we gave each other a big, long squeeze before she headed into her empty house. I couldn't help but feel jealous of her having all that quiet, private space when I watched her close the door behind her. There's something *awfully* liberating about being home and not having to worry about the needs of anyone but yourself. Call me selfish. I wouldn't be *too* paralyzed with guilt.

7 – To Do or Not to Do

Are you there, George? It's me, Allie.

I miss you but feel your love all around as I sit here in front of the living room window basking in the warm, soothing sun. Please don't misunderstand me if you can feel my happy relief now that the emotional burden has been lifted. I'll grieve this tremendous loss in my life, but with comfort, knowing you're in a much better place. How could you not be? You're at peace, free from all your pain and suffering.

Outside, I see those tall green cedars you convinced us to plant years ago. Like sturdy courageous soldiers, side by side as the harsh winds ruffle them, they remind me of the determination and strength you had. Oh, and there's Cameron. I can see him behind the wheel in Hank's car, slowly and cautiously backing out onto the freshly plowed street.

Thank you for nudging your son and grandchildren to take Margaret to church today and for putting the thought of a nice lunch afterwards, and perhaps even a movie, in their heads.

I'll thoroughly enjoy the peace and quiet.

Cough. Cough.

Sniffle. Sniffle.

Wink. Wink.

I miss you dearly,

Allie xoxo

(and sorry for not going to church, but if I recall, you were never really fond of going either)

Of course that didn't mean Margaret was going to let me get away with not going to church, being that it was the first Sunday since George's death. Even though I was seemingly under the weather, she thought, quite frankly, I could show my respect and make it up to the *Holy One* by doing a few things around the house while they were gone.

One was to clean Samantha's bedroom, which I haven't stepped in since Christmas. It's Margaret's room now, leaving Samantha sleeping in a small, damp and windowless room in the basement. I do get it. Samantha isn't the tidiest person—she makes Cameron's bedroom look immaculate. Whenever she's home, I have to pry open her door, with the books and clothes behind it. A hodgepodge of damp towels, papers and half-eaten bags of potato chips and skittles would be strewn across her bed and dusty night table. It's been a mystery to me—her small regard in keeping one room clean. Yet she keeps her entire apartment near school, which is now under discussion, spotless. When she's home and maybe because I spent most of my thirties nagging her about it, I don't say a word so she'll come back more often. Hank never says a word either when he sees me going in there with Lysol and a garbage bag after she leaves. His basement office is much like her bedroom. Underneath the chaos, I'm sure there's a system only evident to them.

The second task Margaret had assigned me to do was to keep an eye on her beef stew in the slow cooker. She scribbled out step-by-step instructions as if I'd never made it before:

Please stir the stew in one hour and then add water (if needed)

Stir the stew again after one hour and add more water (if needed)

Turn the slow cooker down to low. Make sure the stew is not too watery... and so on.

But what she hadn't put in her simple instructions was to taste it, then sprinkle in some salt—hell, sprinkle in some pepper, too, even if it didn't need it. *Stamp that baby and make it your own!*

Finally, she wanted me to contact George's friends about the funeral arrangements. I was honored to do this for his final tribute, but when I saw the phone numbers she'd written in her loopy and unreadable handwriting, a small bead of sweat trickled down my back and I began to panic.

I should've gone to church. It would've been less stressful than fretting over my mother-in-law's *to-do* list. Could she not see I was coming down with a cold? And even if I really did have a terrible, debilitating virus, to her it still meant bucking up and toughing it out—not lying down for hours watching mindless TV, eating chocolate bonbons, and drinking warm cups of green tea. Now if it were Hank or the kids, it'd be a different story. They'd get the royal treatment, with some homemade chicken soup and *Schweppes Ginger Ale.*

In the kitchen, I reached for my readers and called the first person on Margaret's list. Several attempts later, when I got the numbers right, I found out that Ted, one of George's teammates from the bowling club, was no longer with us. He'd *left the building* years ago. But as luck would have it, when the next person I called (George's good friend named Ray) eagerly took over my task, telling me he'd contact everyone else on the list and then some, I jumped for joy. *Thank God* for *Facebook* enthusiasts. And from what I'd learned, George had been one of them too—a *regular user* Ray said, stating that George's photos and informative posts and re-posts of someone else's repost, which were often hilarious he said, would be dearly missed.

Call me old and boring, but I don't understand the obsession with social media. I'm not particularly interested in sharing my life and thoughts with the rest of the world. It can bring out the assholes too. And while on the topic, why does sharing highly edited images of humdrum moments in one's life and envying the trappings of success in another's provide an incredible source of entertainment for some? I'd been purposely avoiding social media and face-to-face apps, bound by a phone all day and compulsively checking clicks and likes. Even though, as many people remind me, social media platforms have become a primary source of official information and don't forget, many like to say, a great way for parents and grandparents to battle boredom or get caught up with family and friends though live chatting or entertain or embarrass them through photos and stupid videos. Maybe that's why I still have a basic phone with a basic plan. It's less work. I'm not really expected to do much from it.

After ending the phone call with Ray, it'd suddenly occurred to me that if I didn't hop on the social community train to instantly connect or reconnect with those who'd played a part in my growing-up years, I might not have a whole lot of people coming to my funeral. Not that I would know or anything, but still.

When nudging a resistant Baily to go to the bathroom outside in the backyard, my cell phone pinged with a text.

Val.
[MF?]
Me.
[YES!!!!!!]

And in exactly twelve minutes, Val was standing at the front door holding my mocha Frappuccino in one hand and her shiny metallic purse in the other. She was a vision, like a *James Bond* girl who'd just walked off the set with her purple beret and tanned suede boots. Imagine wearing all that stuff and pulling it off at our age. And that perfectly blonde coiffed hair only reminded me of the lifeless mass of hair I had going on.

"You're my hero," I said, drooling over the sight of my coffee as she handed it to me.

She laughed, but then stopped abruptly. She took off her oversized sunglasses, examining me. When she leaned in closer, I could smell her minty gum. "What the *hell* is on your face?" she said.

I took a few steps back. "What?"

She cocked her head, pushing me toward the hallway mirror. "Look for yourself."

I peered in the mirror, exhaling. I tried to remain in good-humor with the gravy spots splattered on my forehead from stirring Margaret's beef stew. *Note to self—Never let pretty friends visit when a) You haven't been keeping up with your grays, b) Your face direly needs a good scrub and an expensive night cream, and c) You've eaten salty snacks far too late in the evening, you've ended up looking like a bloated goat.*

Val kept mum, giving me one of her tender smiles as I rubbed the dried-up spots with the sleeve of my scarlet robe. Looking happy and bright, she peeled out of her knee-high boots while telling me about her most recent house showing, and then, of course, telling me about the date she had last night.

"Is this the same guy you saw on Friday?" I asked, cautiously taking the first sip of my hot coffee.

She batted her eyelids, grinning. "Yep, and get this. I—"

"Wow, he must be pretty special."

She ignored my sarcasm and continued. "I found out he has a grown son that recently moved back in with him."

"And?" I said, not sure why that seemed relevant or surprising. In this tough economy, the check-out time has been pushed up in some parent hotels to age thirty.

"He's twenty-nine... lives here in the city..." she said slowly.

Maybe it was the angle, but her eyes looked huge. I tilted my head, staring at her as intently as she was staring at me. "I still don't get—"

"*Keith!*" she wailed, shaking her head.

"*Keith?*" I repeated, trying to grasp what she'd said. "How do you know it's him?" I asked. "That'd be a small world if it was…"

"Because—" She paused for a moment. "When he told me about his recently *divorced* son, who was broke and how he was helping him with renovation jobs to pay off some serious debt, I asked for a description, hoping for a name," she said in one big breath.

I shook my head. "*And?*"

"When he said *Keith*, I nearly fell off the chair," she said. I stood there, mouth agape, naturally.

Stunned at the chances Val had been on a date—make that two dates—with Keith's father, I obviously had to inquire further. "Did you tell him you met Keith on Thursday—*and* your friend's daughter thought she was pregnant with his child?" I said, shuddering at the image of Samantha with a pregnant belly.

"No… of course not," she said, following me into the kitchen. "But when Robert said his son has too many girlfriends to count, I nearly fell off my chair again."

"What!" I said, thinking about my poor child.

"Yep, that's what he said," Val confirmed. "We need to warn Sam she's not the only one he's seeing."

"Yes. Yes, we do." I stared through her, nodding absently, recalling having seen Margaret handing over cash to Keith before he'd left the house Thursday night. A thick rush of anger went through me, wondering if she was paying him for a job he did, or if she'd been hit up for money. I decided to keep that sighting to myself. It was the safest course of action right now, plus I didn't have the energy to delve into it. Making a conscious choice of changing the subject to keep my adrenaline and cortisol levels from rising further, I got Val to tell me about the hair products she's been using and then, since I had the next three days off work, I had her set me up with her manicurist and her overly expensive hair stylist. Before I knew it, our time had come to a sudden end after reading a text from Cameron.

[Gran's tired. Home in 20]

Fuckety Fuck.

Val's face was a mix of disappointment and sympathy as she picked up her purse and stood up. "You okay?"

"Uh-huh." I tightened the belt on my robe in a meaningful way, cursing again for feeling immensely cheated on my *me* time—and for feeling so agitated that Margaret would soon be walking through the front door.

I watched Val walk to her fancy black Sedan parked in the driveway. Not only does she have a great sense of style with a fun and rewarding real estate career, but she has the freedom to make her own decisions. She can be whoever she wants, whenever. I can't. It feels like I'm walking in waist deep water against the pressures of being the "perfect" mom, wife, and kindergarten teacher. And now that Margaret is with us, what will become of me? My marriage? My sanity? I already struggle to find the time and energy for the things that make me feel happy and alive, like listening to music in places other than my car, antiquing furniture *and* training for 50K marathons—okay, 5K marathons. But still.

I drank the last few drops of my cold coffee and climbed the stairs with a tight chest. The fact I had gravy caked on my face and hadn't washed my hair in three days was probably not helping my heavy mood. At the top of the stairs, I heard car doors slamming shut, one by one, in the driveway. My back suddenly tightened too, picturing Margaret looking at her beef stew that hadn't been tended to in two hours and at the uncleaned spectacle of Samantha's room.

Screw it. I headed to the bathroom for a long hot shower.

8 - A Cold Day in July

Besides the grocery store, the shower is a sanctuary for me too. Maybe because I grew up with a shitty hot water tank that standing under steamy water and spacing out as I watch my worries go down the drain is blissful. And when I'm done, I feel like a new person, a shiny clean person. Hank would complain about the water I'd waste and would ask me what I was doing in there. I'd always give him a blank stare. *I dunno*, I'd say, feeling guilty every time. But what I did know was that some of my best thinking got done in the shower. Apart from planning out meals or work outfits, it's a chance to reflect—reflect alone and to the sounds of a rushing waterfall.

I'll never forget the shower I had years ago, when my toes and the bottom of my feet shriveled up so badly, I could hardly walk. I was in pain, fitting to what had happened that afternoon. And let me start off by saying I don't always allow myself to get mad. I mean really mad. Either I'm tough to crack unless pushed off the edge, or I avoid my temperature rising because of the cognitive distortion it can have on rational thinking. But anger really besieged me that day. Not only did I release emotions I had about Margaret and her coveting control over the kitchen again, but I felt like my marriage was crumbling.

It all happened on the day George had confided in me about his failing health. Earlier, Margaret had been rearranging the entire contents of our kitchen, while making snide comments about my housekeeping abilities.

The annoyance manifested into my mood. I could feel the heat within and then an uncomfortable tension in my throat. Enough that I wanted to suffocate her with the tea towels she had in her hands. But I didn't. Instead, I yanked them away and then threw them in the top cupboard. And since I was already feeling quite moody and tense because Hank and I were in a difficult season in our marriage, I slammed the cupboard door, hitting her head with the edge of it. It did straddle the line of being an accident, of course. However, she screamed in pain and then stomped to the basement to summon Hank. Shortly after, he came up from the basement. He then had the nerve to tell me I was being ungrateful. Her twisted and fabricated story had me screaming and reminding him that when she came over and did her *white glove inspection*, he needed to *step in* or be the one to *step out*.

Hank looked at me coldly. "She's just trying to help, Allie."

"Help—my ass," I hissed loud enough for Margaret's sake because I knew she was at the bottom of the basement stairs with a cupped hand around her ear. "She's disrespectful. And she's only cleaning so she can snoop." I took a deep breath to cut through the fog before continuing. "And another thing—why the hell does she feel the need to be here all the time making dinner—"

"Why don't you just let her cook, and you enjoy it. It's less work for you and besides, you don't even like to make..."

I didn't stick around to hear him defending her, so I ran upstairs, locking the bedroom door behind me. I jumped in the shower, held my breath, and then screamed like a child because I couldn't find a reason to be happy anymore. My attention suddenly narrowed. I wanted to leave Hank, letting his mother have him all to herself. Childish? Yes. But Margaret brought out the worst in me.

After the water had turned cold and I had no tears left, I got out of the shower. I hated myself for struggling knowingly with my irrational fear of Margaret which was obviously leading me to the dark angry side, so I mentally prepared myself to call an end to the latest kitchen battle. I had to focus on my breathing when I saw George's size eleven shoes at the front door and Hank's leather sandals, the kids' foam crocs, and Margaret's orthopedic shoes gone from it.

George was sitting at the kitchen island seemingly lost in thought as his big strong hands held a tea mug in them. "George?" I said, half startling him as I walked on the sides of my sore pruney feet. "What are you doing here all alone?"

He glanced up at me. "Oh... there you are," he said, smiling. "Thought I'd stay and say hello."

"Well, that was nice of you." I squeezed his shoulders tight and sat next to him, tense and agitated, but delighted he was there. I hesitated a moment. "Guess you heard Margaret's version of what happened."

He grinned. "I didn't let her finish and had Hank and the kids take her home."

"Oh." I let out a long sigh, peering over at his mug. "More tea?"

Without waiting for a reply, I jumped off the stool. I did my best not to think about Hank or Margaret but couldn't. I filled the kettle with water, turning to him. "Were they upset you stayed?"

He shook his head. "I told them I had a few errands to do."

I smiled fondly at him. "Oh, so you lied."

He'd laughed a genuine laugh before standing and handing me his mug. "Your eyes are all puffy. Were you crying?"

I nodded solemnly. "She really threw me off more than usual today."

"I get it, Allie," he said. "She's not an easy person."

She's a force of nature. I nodded again, recalling a similar conversation we'd had about Margaret and her lack of boundaries. George had summed it up to her needing to feel important in Hank's life. I took a deep breath, happy I felt comfortable enough to talk to him about my marital life. "I'm almost used to her behavior, but your son taking her side is probably what *really* upset me." I paused, watching him struggle uncomfortably getting back on the stool. "It's only added to the disconnect I've been feeling between us lately too," I said. I leaned against the counter, wiping my wet eye. I remember questioning our marriage four and a half years ago, wondering if Hank and I had outgrown one another. We'd go days without talking when his mother and I were in a grudge match. And with the demands of work and family, our time and enjoyment of doing things together had fizzled out too. Watching horror movies were a thing of the past and grabbing breakfast after a Saturday morning run was becoming a chore too. We were both exhausted at the end of the work week to put the effort into making our relationship a smooth one over the weekend.

George listened intently and when I finally stopped, he took an uneasy breath. "You obviously care about Hank, or you wouldn't be so upset," he said.

I bobbed my head up and down in agreement. "He's my best friend, but maybe we just have different ideas of what we want now."

"Right. Well, as long as neither of you have to give anything up important to you, then wanting different things is okay," he'd said.

"That's true," I agreed.

Without asking for details, he continued. "No one fits a hundred percent, so couples have to avoid looking for perfections—look at Margaret and me. I've had to accept that from her the same way she's had to accept that from me. Over the years, we've offered a lot of strengths to the marriage—I've been a stable man for her, nothing flashy," he said with a little laugh. "It's all about the three Ss—"

"The *three* Ss?" I echoed softly. He nodded. I nodded. "Does one of them have to do with *sex?*" I said, feeling the familiar blush whenever I said the word.

His eyes widened as he shook his head, smiling. "*Safety, security* and *stability*," he said, pronouncing each word slowly and carefully. "Like a safe harbor to come home to."

He was the wisest man I knew. I smiled back, filling his mug with hot water and a fresh tea bag, surprised *sex* wasn't one of them. "Well, Hank definitely represents *all* three Ss to me...and I know he's content with the way things are."

"Uh-huh," he said. "Like me, he doesn't need a whole lot to have his needs met. I'm happy and content just with the cooking Margaret has done over all these years. She takes good care of me." He grinned and then patted his large and somewhat bloated looking stomach.

I resisted the urge to complain further. Even though I'd been feeling resentful because life hadn't gone back to being easy and playful since the kids were born, I didn't want George to have to worry about Hank and me.

Seconds later, he'd winced in pain when he shifted his weight on the stool. I gave him a slight smile before noticing dark circles and heavy bags under his eyes. "You okay?" He didn't reply at first until I gave him a serious but thoughtful look. "George, is something wrong?" For an instance, I was puzzled.

He looked up at long last, saddened. "I don't want anyone to worry, yet," he said.

"*Yet?*" My stomach dropped, feeling as though it'd been punched. "Worry about what?"

And that's when George had made me promise not to say a word, especially to Margaret, about being diagnosed with stage II colon cancer. He'd wanted to get another opinion before having to decide what he would say, and how he would say it, to her.

My stomach turned cold. "Oh, God, George," I cried, shocked with disbelief as he told me about his symptoms and the details revealed with a specialist. With watery eyes, I put on a brave face as he stood there, his broad shoulders drooping. It was strange because I'd only ever known him as a big jolly man. I cupped my hand to my forehead. "I'm going with you to get this second opinion," I said and then reached out to hug him.

We moved into the living room and for the next hour, I let him do the talking. After, we sat in a comfortable silence until he stood up and stretched out his back. "I better be on my way, love," he said, handing me his mug full of cold tea.

"Well, thank you for sharing this with me, George," I said—although part of me worried about keeping it a secret. *How could you act normal with news like that, especially around those who don't know, without imploding?* I gave him another good long hug.

Not a second after he left, I realized my mood had shifted. George's news had put things in perspective. So I called Margaret. I called to apologize for hitting her in the head with the cupboard door *and* to tell her how grateful I was for all her help around the house. I didn't know if I had called out of compassion. Or guilt. But what I did know was, I was going to have to put some effort into our relationship once she found out George had been diagnosed with cancer.

Unfortunately, George's second opinion had shown the same result as the first, so I put on that brave face again, all while falling apart inside when he told Hank and Margaret the heart-breaking news in our living room. They were devastated, but like George and I had been, optimistic if he agreed to surgery. Margaret, however, was furious with me. Limited in her readiness to deal with his diagnosis, she'd called the next day, blaming me for letting George's cancer fester for two weeks. After I'd hung up with her and wiped the tears from my swollen eyes, I made a pot roast dinner. And all I remember thinking when I was making that dinner four and a half years ago was what Hank would need most from me—a supportive, non-complaining wife when it came to his mother. *I tried. I really tried.*

•   •   •

I lathered myself in orange blossom body wash, half smiling as I pictured Margaret in the kitchen inspecting her dried-out beef stew in the cooker. For some reason, it felt good. However, not long after taking a deep breath of the sweet, floral fragrance, the water turned scalding hot. "Oh, *c'mon!*" I yelled, jumping out of the lava-like water with stinging skin. We all knew the *no flushing any of the toilets when someone is taking a shower* rule in the house. After waiting patiently for the stupid toilet tank to fill with water,

I waved my hand under the shower head and then got back in only to burn myself with another pressure drop. "What the *hell*!" I squealed, leaping over the side of the tub, nearly falling. Cold and dripping water on the tiny bathroom mat, it'd occurred to me Margaret was playing with the toilet, mad no doubt that her stew hadn't been given a good stir, and Samantha's room was still a mess. *Well, damn you, Margaret!*

9 - PISTOLS AT DAWN

Are you there, George? It's me, Allie.

Do you sleep where you are? If not, I really don't want to go there. But if it's paradise like everyone says, maybe sleep isn't necessary. Then again... who wouldn't want to take a long, cozy nap under the canopy of a great big willow tree in the warm breeze?

I haven't been getting much sleep lately. Sleeping next to what sounds like a wounded warthog keeps me up at night and makes me anxious. My howls fall on Hank's deaf ears. The only thing that seems to stop him is if I kick his runner's knee. And if that doesn't work, I usually have to find another bed in the house. Unfortunately, those two beds are occupied by Margaret and Sam, so I've had no choice but to sleep on the living room sofa... only to be awakened early by the sounds of banging, clattering, and clinking going on in the kitchen.

Was Margaret always this much of an early bird? Six thirty a.m.? Doable. But five o'clock? If I don't get my seven hours of uninterrupted sleep, things are soon going to get ugly around here. I know she's the woman you married, but even with you up there, I don't think I can ever stop asking, "Why, George? Why?"

Wish you were here,

Allie xoxo

Exhausted and with sore muscles, I grabbed my pillow and heavy duvet and tried to sneak back upstairs before Margaret saw me. But it was too late, Baily had come running out of the kitchen with a wagging tail, whimpering for some rubs and breakfast as he stretched out his hind legs.

I felt a pulse in my neck when Margaret came out and flicked on the hallway light. "What are you doing with all your bedding?" She glanced at her wristwatch with a cocked eyebrow. "It's a little early to start laundry, don't you think... Samantha's still sleeping down there."

Refusing to be taken down by her this early in the morning, I tried to keep the irritation out of my voice as she followed me in her old floral robe. "I'm going back up to bed, if that's okay," I said halfway up the stairs.

"Okay, but when you get up, I'm going to help you do a deep clean... especially on all the floors and the bathtub upstairs."

First, it was nice she wanted to help with the post-funeral reception she'd talked Hank into having here instead of at the funeral home, but how dirty did she think the house was? Second, what did she think the guests were going to do? Inspect the floors? Take a shower? A quick surface clean was all this house was going to get from me. You do a deep clean *after* all the guests—including some high-energy kids and real power drinkers—had finished traipsing throughout the house, spilling their drinks, and dropping pastry crumbs everywhere.

"You probably don't notice because you're used to it, but there are a lot of odors in the house too," she added, flapping her big chest.

It might be you, Margaret. I clenched my jaw, wisely holding my tongue. I can't say my facial expression mirrored the same depth of wisdom. "Uh, I didn't notice. We should open the windows then," I mumbled back from the top of the stairs. I turned the hall light off, leaving her standing in the dark with Baily.

"Oh, and one more thing—" she said, her voice bouncing off the walls and echoing up the stairs, sounding deceptively charming and caring. "We should probably cover the living room sofa if sleeping on it is going to become a habit."

Habit? I wouldn't make sleeping on a sofa a habit. Hank and I had spent too much on a luxury mattress, hoping to solve the myriad of sleeping issues we've been having. Besides midlife aches and pains, we've been despairing over Hank's supersonic snoring, my night sweats, our frequent trips to the bathroom, his restless leg syndrome, our disparate bedtimes, and depending on the temperature outside, the right room temperature inside, which determines if it's a fan-on or fan-off kind of night. I feel bad. He feels bad. Next stop? Separate beds. I love my husband, but at times, I need my own bed. And sleeping in Samantha's bed before it'd been taken over had been a slice of heaven.

I could barely make out Margaret's silhouette in the dawn light. "Absolutely. You go right ahead and cover it," I slurred, turning inward and giving her a villainous smile and then outward giving her my middle finger.

• • •

Hours later, I woke up in an otherwise empty bed and to the loud, shrieking sound of the vacuum cleaner. Dazed and confused, I rolled over toward Hank's bedside table and forced my eyes to focus on the red-lit numbers of our old clunky digital clock. 11:10 a.m. *Crap.* I rolled back over, ignoring the pangs of guilt slicing through my gut.

I stared at the outdated popcorn ceiling and focused on my Kegel exercises—a tall order from my doctor I try to do every morning, even though I'm convinced they accomplish nothing.

Squeeze. Count to eight.

Relax. Count to eight.

Squeeze. Count to eight—Unfortunately, I didn't get much past the second round. Right there in the middle of it all, the deep rumble of the vacuum cleaner Margaret had no doubt commandeered, roared closer to the second floor, warning me to get moving. I inhaled and closed my eyes, adamant about not feeling lazy about all the cleaning she'd be sure to tell me she did while I'd been sleeping the morning away.

At eleven thirty, the vacuum cleaner fell silent. *Get up.* I twisted my body around and put my feet on the cold floor, bribing myself with morning coffee. When I reached into the wicker basket under the night table, my stomach tightened. I gasped actually because I'd taken my phone down with me last night and forgotten about it when I came back up in the morning. I moaned back into the bed. I was stuck—trapped and alone in my bedroom without my *personal assistant* who handles all my incoming calls and texts, and with the ability on its little black screen to find instant answers to all the random questions that pop up in my mind like *Glenn Close's* latest movie or the health benefits of using organic coconut oil.

I looked at the clock again. 11:45 a.m. *Get up.* For a few moments, I couldn't move. I simply didn't want to get out of the warm comfortable bed. But then I bribed myself with a *big* mug of steaming coffee and now with the possibility of having important and exciting messages waiting for me on my phone.

I dragged my sleepy body toward the bathroom. Before going in, I shuffled over to the window and pulled back the curtains, blinking as the bright sun blinded me. I blinked again to get rid of the blur of seeing only one car in the driveway. The empty driveway, with the exception of my Honda, meant Hank was somewhere in his, Samantha was somewhere in hers, and Cameron, who'd soon be joining the ranks of inexperienced teen drivers, was somewhere in school. I was alone in the house. Alone with Margaret and the damn vacuum cleaner shrieking again as it made its way toward this end of the hallway.

Finally, it was quiet which made me feel better in contemplating my next move. I got dressed and then sat on the end of the bed, brushing my tangled hair out. I couldn't decide whether to make a beeline for the front door or head to the kitchen and get the coffee I'd promised myself before taking control of the cleaning around here.

My head jerked up when a sharp rap hit our bedroom door. Before I could reply, the door flung wide open. With my *Painted Ladies of San*

Francisco tea towel slung over her shoulder, Margaret stood there as I sat with my knitted beige sweater draped across my thighs and my paddle hairbrush in my hand.

"Oh, *there* you are," she said. She folded her arms across her chest. "I was beginning to get worried with you alone in this gloomy room." The smug expression on her face grated on my nerves. *Sorry, Margaret. I'm not the depressed mess you think I am.*

After a silence, the first sign of caffeine withdrawal reared its ugly head in my right temple and down the back of my neck. Inhaling deeply, I gave her a bright smile. "I'm fine, Margaret," I said through several little forced coughs. "I've been resting and fighting this cold." I sniffed slightly.

She moved closer to the dresser. Antsy, it seemed. "Sometimes the best way to get rid of a cold is to get moving," she said, poking her finger deep into the soil of one of the Boston fern plant "projects" she'd given us to help keep our household air clean and pure. She shook her head, obviously disappointed her finger had come out bone dry.

Without warning, I felt that familiar creeping sensation in my toes. The intense heat rushed to my chest and then up to my brow, causing my face to turn sweaty, and no doubt, glowing red. I took a deep breath and let it go, while Margaret stood there watching me.

I desperately needed water, but before I could get to the bathroom, Margaret emerged from it holding our toothbrush holder cup filled with some. Honestly, I thought she was reaching out, you know, woman to woman, when she stopped and looked at me intently. But then she resumed walking and walked right past me to dump the water onto the fern.

I released another in-held breath, shaking my head for her to see. "Sorry Margaret, but I've got to go. Even though I'm not feeling great—" I gave another cough and wiped my forehead with the back of my hand. "I have a few appointments I need to get to."

When she spun around, our eyes met. "Well, you don't look good at all." She gave me a piercing look. "And do you think it's wise to be out spreading all your germs? If you ask me, it might be better to sweat it out cleaning," she mumbled, carrying the makeshift watering can back to the bathroom.

"It's a cold, and I'll be *very* careful not to sneeze on anyone." Exasperated, I left the bedroom.

"Well, what time will you be home?" she said, following me down the hallway. "Henry would like it if you took me to the mall this afternoon... I need to find a dress and some shoes."

I stepped over the abandoned vacuum cleaner lying in the middle of the floor and turned back at the stairs. "Well," I said, suddenly feeling sorry for her, "I don't think it can be me, Margaret. Maybe Hank can take you later. Or Sam?" I suggested hopefully before making my way down the stairs with her following close behind.

"I'd like to get there before the school kids do. Henry's busy with meetings, and Samantha drove back to her apartment to get more clothes," she said. "And *you* might want to go shopping too and find something that fits."

Fits? Okay now she's really making me feel like an Orc.

I thought about Hank and if he had told Margaret I could take her. He would've known better, no? But I knew he had a busy day filled with meetings and after, was taking Cameron to his driving test. And Samantha probably just left, which meant she wasn't coming back anytime soon.

"I'm sure I have something in my closet," I told her, knowing for a fact I didn't. I hadn't given funeral dressing, especially for a family member who'd died in the middle of winter, enough attention when it came to my bright color wardrobe. I would need to devote some time into finding something somber and respectful.

Margaret followed me into the living room as I searched for my phone. It wasn't on the coffee table, so I tore apart the sofa with her hovering close by.

"Did you lose something?" she said almost in a gripe.

"Yeah, my phone," I replied quickly, whipping my head to her.

"You could've just told me before tearing the sofa apart," she said, slowly reaching into her apron pocket and then struggling to get it out. "I *was* bringing it to you because it was making all kinds of sounds."

I snatched it from her hand. "Thank you," I said, trying to get a grip on myself.

"By the way, Henry was calling you and had to call me on the home phone. Good thing I was here. He was getting worried." She put the sofa pillows back in place. "Don't worry, though. I told him you were still sleeping when he last called."

I didn't respond because I was too busy staring at my poor... disabled... phone. Someone, and I won't name any names here, had attempted to enter my four-digit password one too many times. And that someone, again not naming *any* names, had managed to lock me out of my device for the next one hundred and forty minutes. I looked at her, taking a quick breath in and exhaling loudly.

Margaret stood there seemingly unaware she had killed my device. "So?" she said as though looking for an answer.

I blinked, suddenly weary. "So... so *what*?"

She clasped her hands together. "Are we going to the mall or shall I just wear an old worn-out dress to my husband's funeral?"

I unclenched my fists, resenting having to be the one to take her to the bloody mall, but decided right then and there, and going forward, for my sake—and in case George was watching over—to keep things calm as best as I could. Giving her a quick smile, I made my way to the front hall closet. I raised my chin after putting on my coat and grabbing my purse. *I'm trying here, George.* "I'll be waiting in the car for you," I said as pleasantly as I could before stepping into my clunky boots and marching out the door.

10 - Runaway Dress

My head was splitting, demanding coffee, by the time Margaret made it out of the house and into the car. I adjusted the rear-view mirror and watched her climb into the back seat, then waited until our eyes met.

"We're only going down the street, so why don't you sit up in the front?" I said, tapping the head rest of the seat. Tapping and smiling.

She took her eyes off me and pulled the seat belt strap across her shoulders, locking herself in. "You know I'm not too crazy about your driving, Allison," she responded after a short silence.

No wonder the furrow forming between my eyebrows had been getting deeper.

Her eyes met mine again when I readjusted the mirror. "Don't worry. I'm fine back here," she said stiffly. She then nervously checked behind her on the left and then again on the right as I reversed out of the driveway. It's like *Driving Miss Daisy*. Not only does she make me feel like the hired help by chauffeuring her around, but she also fits the definition of a backseat driver. All her instructing and criticizing is comical actually, especially for someone who'd never learned to drive.

"Suit yourself," I whispered underneath my breath, because for some reason, she has no problem sitting up front whenever Hank's driving. Although an incredibly competent driver, he's also terrifyingly aggressive. As cars slow down, he speeds up, zipping in and out of traffic and then slamming on his brakes, inches from rear bumpers. It's like taking my life into my hands every time I get into the passenger seat. Road trips with him send me into anxiety tailspins.

We drove for the six minutes to the shopping mall. Thankfully, Margaret kept her unwanted driving advice to herself. She did, however, keep her wary eyes on traffic and the intersection pedestrians in front of us. I would've driven an extra twenty miles to the three hundred plus store outlet mall in the next city, but because she was with me, this mall would have to suffice for funeral clothes shopping.

After what seemed like a tense drive, my body relaxed when we entered the distinctly warmer air of Bellsville Square—sometimes referred to as *Hells-ville* Square because of its lack of character and branded shops. Like cooking, I don't enjoy shopping for the sake of it. And when with someone who is, I'm usually the one finding all the benches to sit on, making a whole lot of impatient huffing sounds so we can go home. Not to sound like a killjoy for those who can't live without trying on cute clothes and accessories, but everything I see in stores and the obnoxious music blaring through speakers makes me irrationally irritable. I'm fine when I shop for something specific, like a birthday present or a new pair of pajamas but wandering aimlessly in and out of shops sucks the life right out of me.

We walked toward the bright center courtyard filled with young moms and their happy toddlers. "Let's go get you your coffee first," Margaret said.

I immediately pepped up. "Oh, yes," I said, suddenly feeling grateful, but a bit taken aback by her considerate gesture. *Heck, she could poison your coffee.* I chuckled as the thought penetrated my mind. Although I consider Margaret capable of several unsavory deeds, I really don't think she has the heart to maim or kill.

When we turned the corner, we both instinctively stopped and quietly gawked at the Valentine necklace and earring sets showcased in one of the five jewelry stores this mall offered for its semi-reckless shoppers.

Margaret broke the silence as I was imagining Hank clasping a necklace around my neck, like you'd see in a sappy romance movie. "Oh, that reminds me. I found this when I was cleaning this morning..." She dug into her coat pocket and then handed me a tiny golden hoop earring that looked like the set she'd given me for my fortieth birthday. "Just in case you wanted to buy another pair today," she said. She touched my arm. "I know they were your favorite."

I feigned surprise when I plucked it out of her hand. *No. No, they were not my favorite.* They were a cheap pair of gold-plated earrings she'd given me for my birthday that made the holes in my ears itch and swell up.

I smiled as best I could. "Oh... I must've dropped it," I lied. Oddly enough, I'd found the earring in the groove of Hank's car floor mat around Christmas time. I'd put this earring, made of actual gold, in one of my coat pockets, not wanting to think about it. Though of course, I did. What was a woman's earring doing in Hank's car? It wasn't mine. If the inside of his car were a crime scene, the earring I was holding would've been held as evidence. If part of an infidelity investigation, then it'd be held as potential evidence.

I shook my head, quickly putting the made-up silly idea of a hot and steamy encounter in Hank's car out of mind. I'd gone down that road with him last year when I accused him of having a *thing* with Robyn, a beautiful redhead who works at an investment company Hank does business with. Robyn had swaggered down the hotel's wide carpeted corridor to say hello at one of his summer conferences we attended. If he hadn't stumbled on his words and looked at her the way he did, I wouldn't have become so insecure and suspicious. After being introduced to her, the two of them rambled on about the latest interest rates—with Robyn occasionally touching Hank's arm or shoulder, agreeing and disagreeing with him. Strangely jealous and feeling a bit territorial, I moved in closer to him. I nodded confidently, as if I knew what they were talking about with all their investment jargon, trying to ignore the fact that my bladder desperately needed relief. Robyn had stopped talking as I'd turned to look down the corridor, scoping out a bathroom. "So... what do you do, Allison?" she asked, giving me a rather bothersome up and down glance.

Since then, whenever I'd hear him utter her name over the phone with partners or clients, intense waves of low self-esteem would kick in as my confidence sunk considerably. However, Hank had made it clear nothing has happened, nor ever would with her. He'd once said she was merely a confidence booster, but he had no interest in an affair with her, or anyone else for that matter. His tender words that I was the only one he had eyes for, soothed me. But the reality is... well, there's *some* reality in two people being married for over twenty years, isn't there?

It hasn't been easy warding off the notion of Robyn pursuing my midlife husband. My mind conjures up images of him riding off into the sunset in a red convertible, with her and her long white silky scarf flapping to one side in the wind.

I squinted at the earring again. "Thanks for finding it," I said, lightly prodding Margaret away from the dazzling jewelry window display, toward the escalator.

Apart from this tiny golden culprit in the palm of my hand, this had been the second time where Margaret claimed she found something that was in someone else's pocket. The first time I'd actually caught her digging around in my front hall closet going through the coats. When I asked her what she was doing, she said she noticed we had change in them. The real kicker to this incident was that later, she had the gall to ask if I wanted the cherry lip balm she'd found in one of *my* pockets.

I'd never fully understood why she was hunting in our coats for spare change and had never brought this odd behavior up to Hank but was now considering it—and the lone star earring I'd just dropped into my purse.

After ordering, we sat in the food court overlooking the cascading fountain on the first floor. As I drank my coffee in large mouthfuls and nibbled on a sesame bagel, Margaret complained about the price of clothes, about her sugary coffee, and about the number of raisins in her bran muffin. I nodded silently, trying to pacify her worries. But truth was,

I had bigger fish to fry—getting us out of the mall, each with a dress and a pair of shoes.

"Okay, Margaret—" I stood up quickly, squishing my bagel wrapper, "let's head to *Jaspers* and see if we can find some dresses," I said, suddenly feeling back in control. She nodded primly and then followed me through the maze of blue fiberglass tables and chairs.

I turned to make sure she was behind me when we reached the main area of the mall. If I must say, I appreciated her more like this, when she wasn't saying anything. I found myself humming as Margaret continued following me.

Upon entering *Jaspers*, I stopped when I heard her behind me. "I don't like this place," she complained.

My eyes narrowed. "Is there something wrong with this store, Margaret?" I asked, gritting my teeth.

She stood there, pulling her old white purse up to her shoulder. "It looks like a place where waitresses and bartenders would shop, not where I could get an outfit for my husband's funeral," she replied, turning her nose up as if a bad smell was in the air.

The only bad smell I could perceive was her attitude. She had successfully taken a jab at my waitressing days, while making it seem like she was only stating a rather obvious point.

"Alright then, let's go. You pick the store," I said as pleasantly as I could manage.

The glee that spread across her face was smacked of victory. I should've known when she followed me without a fuss, she already had something planned.

After twenty minutes of walking past shops and tiny kiosks with aggressive salespeople trying to spread moisturizer on our palms, and then going up and down the escalator twice, she finally led us to an expensive, high-end ladies fashion store that had recently opened in the far end of the mall.

I entered the store behind her with an aching back, trying not to roll my eyes when I saw a tall, un-busy and dressed-to-the-nines sales associate glance up over her glasses from behind the counter. She gave a curt smile. I was quite sure she was deciding if we were worth the effort to walk out from behind the counter to properly greet and help us—me in my bulky winter coat and salt-stained boots and Margaret with her prim hairdo and dated makeup.

Minutes later, after presumably making a flattering assessment of us, she approached with a warm and genuine smile when we stopped to take in the overall layout of the store. She asked how she could help us on this *fine* day—her words exactly. It certainly was no fine day for me, and I was tempted to tell her this, but kept that piece of information to myself. It wasn't her fault I was saddled with the responsibility of taking Margaret shopping.

"Could you please show us your collection of black dresses?" Margaret said. "I assume your store is color coded?"

I said nothing.

"Of course," the associate said, giving us a radiant smile. "This way."

She led us past rows and rows of stylish pant suits, as well as evening dresses, which were indeed color coded. *How did Margaret know that? Right, she'd been here before.* The realization irritated me further. When we got to the section of black outfits, the sales associate with a name tag that read Donna left us with the invitation to call her if we needed help. Moments later, I could see her silently watching us take off our coats and setting our purses on the nearby cushy stools as she tidied nearby clothing racks.

Their dress collection was indeed impressive, but I wanted nothing more than to sit on one of the funky red sofas and see if my phone had come back to life. And that's exactly what I did after grabbing my purse.

"Would you not rather look at a dress for yourself?" Margaret said.

"Er, sure. But I need to reply to some messages, so you go ahead," I said.

She stalked off toward the other racks, muttering something about priorities.

Ignoring her, I fetched my phone out of my purse once I settled on the sofa. To my relief, it had turned on. There were several missed calls from Hank and a message he was going to be late getting Cameron to his road test. I replied, sparing him my current reality about his mother being a giant pain in the ass. There was a voicemail message from Cameron frantically looking for me because he had the time wrong for his test, and oddly enough, a text from Samantha that Keith had saved the day and was going to take Cameron because she was still at her apartment. Lastly, there were a string of texts from Val reminding me about the hair and nail appointments she'd set up in the afternoon.

Two beauty appointments scheduled back to back? I raised my head to tell Margaret we'd have to cut our time short, but she was nowhere to be seen. Seconds later, I lowered my head to text Val. When I was about to hit *send*, I saw a pair of nude stocking feet in front of me. I slowly raised my head.

"Are you going to keep your head buried in that thing all day?" she said, dressed in a lacy black dress and a cashmere cardigan.

I jumped to my feet. "That's a nice dress. You should get it." It was probably the first time I would give her a compliment I meant. Plus, I needed her to like it so we could go.

She smiled self-consciously, patting the dress on her body. "I know, right?" She turned, twisting her head so she could see the back of herself in the mirror.

"Go ahead and try some outfits on." She took the cardigan off, admiring herself even more. "I'll wait."

"You don't have to do that. Why don't you get changed and go pay—"

Her head tilted to one side. "I insist. Besides, I can't have you showing up at George's funeral looking like this."

The most important thing here was to keep my cool. I stood taller with composure—we simply had to move this along because we still had shoes to find. So, with the intention of trying on the first thing I saw in my size, I moved toward the rack of dresses. Fortunately for me, the first dress I grabbed was an adorable pencil style dress in my size, with long sleeves. It was simple, but it'd been a while since I'd worn anything mature and classic like this—not to mention, expensive. I eagerly went to try it on.

Convinced the dress was made for me, I hesitated a moment before walking out of the change room to admire myself in the floor-length mirror. The last shopping trip with Margaret had been a harrowing experience. I'd been filled with high hopes of form fitting stretchy jeans hiding my broad hips, and when I'd come out of the change room under the unflattering fluorescent lights, there she was—her reflection in the distorted mirror telling me I needed to stop dressing like a teenage hooker. When I turned back to see the real her, who was *supposed to be* in the bookstore next door, and the herd of teenage girls standing there giggling and whispering to their alpha leader, my self-esteem plummeted. Duped into believing a woman my age shouldn't be wearing tight, skimpy clothes, I'd gone home that day feeling embarrassed. And old.

Sucking in my tummy, I walked out of the dressing room with confidence. I liked what I saw. However, my moment of self-love was cut short when Margaret snorted from the bench.

"You look pregnant," she said, getting up to look at herself again, this time with her shoes on. "You might want to get something to hide your belly."

Breathe, Allie. Breathe. But I couldn't. I'd had enough of her condescension for one day. I was already feeling bad for letting my body go, and I certainly didn't need her shoving it down my throat. "Margaret, I know you're going through a difficult time right now, but we all are." I took a deep breath in, moving up to her face with a tight grin. "I'm your son's wife. Like it or not, you have no right to be *such* a bitch," I said firmly, with some regret.

Donna poked her head around the corner. "Everything okay in here?"

"No. No, it's not!" Margaret fired back. "My husband just died." And in a flash, she was on her feet and running with her purse and my car keys.

When did she take my keys?

"Come back!" I shouted, flying after her before realizing I was wearing the store's dress too. Of course, Margaret had set off the alarms as she ran *out* of the store.

With my credit card in hand, I was able to talk to the security guard that showed up within seconds. She didn't wait to see what happened after because she ran out of the store again, sobbing openly.

I changed back into my clothes and grabbed our coats. Out of breath when I spotted her running toward the entrance we'd come in, I stopped and called out to her. But it was too late. Margaret was already out of the doors.

When I got to the car, huffing and puffing, she was inside the car crying in the driver's seat. I tried to open the door, but she'd locked it. She wouldn't even look my way when I held up her coat. About to pull my hair out? Yes.

Allowing her a moment, I hurried back to the entrance, positioning myself inside where I could watch her. I took a calming breath, checking a text from Cameron. He'd passed his test. *Finally, some good news.* Looking at the time, I realized I had less than an hour to get to my hair appointment. I shook my head sourly, willing her to get out of the car and return to the mall to find shoes for her and a cheaper dress for me. I shifted my weight to the other foot, reading my horoscope for the day, which said I'd find comfort in words and communication. An unexpected burst of laughter came out of me.

Although I felt somewhat bad for upsetting her, my mother-in-law's party had lasted long enough. This was more about her personality and our relationship than it could ever be about George's death. I marched back to the car and rapped on the window. She looked up and seconds later, slowly opened the door before slamming it shut. She grabbed her coat and bag of clothes out of my hands before walking around to the passenger's side. Of course I wasn't expecting any kind of *thank you* for having bought the four-hundred-dollar dress and the hundred dollar cardigan she was wearing.

I stretched out my hand. "Car keys, please," I said good-naturedly.

Her red, puffy eyes widened when she looked at the car.

NOOOO, I silently shouted as I double checked the door. Yup. Locked. With the keys on the seat.

Margaret shook her head. "Sorry," she said in a small voice.

At that moment, I couldn't find the strength or heart to chide her. *Who's the adult now?* Instead of taking the easy route and calling my roadside service membership, I sent a message to Cameron, first congratulating him on his test and then asking if he was still with Keith— of all people. His reply came immediately. And after a few more exchanges with him, my eyes met with hers. "Cam and Keith are coming with the spare key," I informed her.

Seeming a bit confused, she nodded and then followed me into the mall without a word. We stood at opposite ends of the entrance doors. I gave her a big smile as she stood tall, clutching her purse and scowling. Seconds later, a bigger smile came from within after checking the time. Even though I'd be leaving this mall without a dress or shoes, I was happier knowing I was going to make it to my appointments after all—once I palmed Margaret off on Cameron and Keith.

11 - Driving Miss Margaret

Are you there, George? It's me, Allie.

I miss you. But Margaret misses you more. She had a meltdown at the mall yesterday, and let me point out, she started it. One minute, she was admiring the dress she had on while telling me how terrible I looked in mine, and the next minute—after a few words from me—she was running out the mall in full crisis mode. And guess who had to pay for the most expensive dress from that store, let alone mall?

But you'd be happy to know I soldiered on, giving myself permission to spend a little on me—something you were always telling me to do. I got a chic bold hairstyle and pink nails. I like the hair, but the nails? A bit out of my comfort zone. But a much better choice than the bright orange color Maribel, the beautician, tried to talk me into trying—and this was just before she'd pointed out rather loudly, I might add, that I should get my mustache done too. And then after my nails, instead of going home, I treated myself to a fish and chip dinner and a late-night movie.

I'll see you at your funeral on Wednesday. Don't be disappointed if you see most of us crying. I know you wouldn't want that, so I'll do my best to keep everyone smiling, celebrating your life. But beware... that kind of farewell isn't for everyone, George. Margaret is going to expect the sober dignity of a solemn event.

I miss you.

Allie xoxo

For the first time in a long time, I got out of bed feeling rested. Could it be because I felt strangely motivated to get to my gym orientation so I could start shedding some of this unwanted fat affecting my body mechanics? Or was it because I slept soundly through the night? If the latter, that could only mean one thing. Hank hadn't come to bed. Could I blame him for not coming up last night? He had to listen to my complaining when I got home, which I promised myself I wouldn't do, about his mother's behavior at the mall, and then of course, about my latest insecurities—including Robyn.

Hank was the first to see me when I eventually made my way down into the kitchen. "Hey sleepy head," he said, opening the squeaky dishwasher door.

Cameron spoke up next, staring at me as he drowned his pancakes in thick syrup. "Cool hair, Mom."

"Thank you," I said, tugging at the back of his shirt affectionately.

I was surprised they didn't crack a joke about it. I put my hands to my head. After trying to style it like they did in the salon, I felt like a honey blonde version of *Peter Pan*.

Hank must've read my mind when I seized the coffee mug he was offering. "Sorry I didn't make it to bed last night. I was making notes for Dad's eulogy," he said.

"Oh, right," I said, suddenly feeling less insecure about having slept alone. "Need any help?"

He gave a gaping yawn. "No, think I'm done." He squeezed my hand. "Thought it might've been nice for you to get some sleep without my snoring, so I slept on the sofa."

"Thanks, I did," I said softly, piling Hank's famous fluffy pancakes onto a plate. *And we need to talk about Margaret.*

Margaret, who was perched like a bird on one of the kitchen stools, rolled her eyes.

Trying to stay positive and assertive, I placed a kiss on Hank's lips and then dropped one on the back of Cameron's head. My eyes caught Margaret's. "Good morning," I said, parading over to the table with my coffee and pancakes.

"Morning," she mumbled against her favorite porcelain teacup she'd brought from her condo.

"Don't you have something to say to Allie?" Hank said, giving her a meaningful stare.

She practically slammed her cup down on the counter. "Do I?"

"Mom..." Hank said, shaking his head vigorously.

"*Fine*," she responded as she got down from her stool to wash and then dry her cup with a paper towel. Finally, she breathed in heavily with her back to me. "I'm sorry for what I said yesterday and for all the troubles I've put you through. It wasn't my intention to hurt you." And then begrudgingly, she added, "Forgive me."

I took a big gulp of coffee, rolling my eyes hard. I didn't want a confrontation, and I certainly didn't want to humiliate her with all that could've come out of my mouth in response to her contrived apology. Instead, I accepted it with a simple nod when she turned around. She didn't deserve anything else from me when her childlike mind believed every wrong could be righted with a string of empty words.

She gave me a blank expression before she carefully put her teacup back into the cupboard, behind all the others.

Hank wagged his head slowly, struggling to get Baily's leash on for his morning walk. When he looked back at me, he put on a cheerful smile. "I'm going to take Cam shopping for a suit today."

I whipped my head toward Cameron. "When's Sam coming back?" I said with desperate, frantic eyes.

"Oh, yeah. She called and said her car's still with the mechanic. So maybe dinnertime. Not sure," he responded, *completely* unaware of my predicament. I didn't want to have to cancel my gym orientation, on top of all the other things I'd planned to do.

I refused to meet Margaret's eyes when I sagged into the kitchen chair, utterly disappointed. "Well, I hope she gets it fixed today," was all I could say because it was Samantha who was supposed to take Margaret to her condo to collect more things for George's funeral. And knowing Margaret, most of the things she'd collect would be her belongings. She'd brought everything but the kitchen sink to our house.

•　　•　　•

I prided myself on not making a scene after getting stuck with Margaret. I wanted to keep the peace for tomorrow—and give Hank and Cameron some Father Son time.

The drive to Margaret's condo was surprisingly quiet. It seemed for once she didn't plan to launch her usual collection of remarks. A small part of me felt sorry for her again—maybe going to the condo would dredge up memories.

I was deep in thought at an intersection when Margaret finally spoke.

"Sorry, what?" I said with a raised eyebrow.

I caught her through the rear-view mirror shaking her head sourly. "I was talking about the funeral," she huffed impatiently. "I think George would be okay with an open casket. He doesn't look too bad."

Yes. Yes, he does. Anyone who's dead looks bad. I gripped the steering wheel, mentally scolding myself for wanting to give my real opinion if she were asking for one—which if she was, it'd be too late anyway. I knew she was being her usual self, acting like she needed a different opinion when she had indeed, already made up her mind.

"It's fine. It'll all be fine," I lied, hoping George wouldn't hurl lightning bolts down at me. George had loved attention, but I highly doubted he would want to be on public display at his funeral with an open casket. It was quite disturbing to see someone's mouth and all the surrounding skin contorted and pulled in an unnatural manner when morticians had to glue the orifices of eyes and mouth shut. Need I say more? I've had to repeatedly look at photos of my father to remember how he looked in life instead of seeing the image of his face burned in my memory at his funeral years ago. I've been to two of those types of funerals, and I was hoping not to *ever* have to attend a third one. They were morbid, quite frankly. I inhaled deeply. Not the time to argue, so I nodded agreeably while she continued talking in the back seat.

Shortly after we kicked off our boots, Margaret walked straight to her bedroom down the narrow hall, leaving me standing alone in their spacious and spotless living room. An acrid smell of lemons, with a touch of burning engine oil, permeated the thick warm air. Maybe it was in response to the aroma of Margaret's furniture polish she used on every piece of wood this place had that intense feelings began to surface. I could almost see George's large frame in his favorite blue reclining chair.

It didn't take me long before I was sitting and melting into it. The smell of him suddenly filled my nostrils as I heard his deep chuckle when he'd joke during the rare times we had dinner here. God, I'm going to miss his positive and light energy. It had helped to keep me sane and out of the dark, negative energy Margaret spewed around her all the time. *Ying, yang.* It's a dynamic force when balanced.

I basked in the euphoria of being close to George again. In hopes of finding more traces of him, I rubbed my hands along the worn-out armrests and sniffed the tightly woven fabric where his head would rest. On impulse, I pulled the lever to recline but nothing happened, so I kicked back hard with some force, ending up in zero-gravity position.

Moments later, I jumped a bit when I saw Margaret's eyes pointing down at me. "I'm all set," she said softly and then strangely, smiled. The chair made a terrible clunking sound when I flipped it back into an upright position. I fully expected her to say something about me sniffing out George's recliner, but she didn't. She just stood there, a bit unsteady on her feet with a framed photo of George and his favorite ball cap, looking like a lost child.

For the first time, I *wanted* to hug her. But I couldn't. I couldn't open my heart—because surely, she'd reject my sympathy embrace. She didn't resist when I took everything from her, including what was in her other hand—undoubtedly more of her belongings. We locked the door behind us and headed to the car, saying nothing.

"Where to next?" I asked, successfully keeping the frustration of knowing there was a "next" out of my voice. I had less than two hours to get to the gym, but I'd rather lose an arm than mention that to her. I didn't want to give Margaret an opening into any conversation revolving around my body. *Obviously.*

"*Oh,* we could go to the bakery to be sure our order is right for tomorrow," she said.

"Okay," I mumbled slowly, watching her open the car's *front* passenger door.

"After, let's stop by the florist and double check the bouquets," she said, climbing into the seat and then reaching behind her for the shoulder strap.

I found myself smiling. "*Okay,*" I mumbled again, pretending not to notice her decision to sit up front. A breakthrough? Doubt it. But it did make me feel better.

Margaret wiped her eyes with a tissue before blowing her nose. "We should probably see if they have everything ready at the funeral home too."

Or we could call all these places and save some time, was what I wanted to say. And where was her other chauffeur Keith? My heart constricted at the thought of Samantha having any involvement with him.

Margaret's quality control mission to the bakery, florist, and funeral home took up the next hour and a half. Weirdly, and maybe because I was driving and seemingly in charge of operations, there was some harmony. She was different. Nice as pie. Yes, I was treading carefully, but it didn't feel like we were walking through a minefield like it usually does when we're together. And when it's just the two of us.

Unfortunately, I didn't have time to take her home, so much to my chagrin, I had to explain first where we were going, and secondly, what a gym orientation was. "You should be mourning George—not your twenty-four-year-old body," she drawled, as if I were some kind of idiot.

After parking the car, Margaret was following me through the gym doors, back to her *on-stage* personality, uptight and slightly manic. "You know, Allison, you could save your money by spending more time cleaning the house if you wanted to trim down." She took a bite of the ham and cheese sandwich I bought her at the bakery. "I once read that a good spring cleaning can burn more calories than running in those marathons you and Henry used to do," she said between chews.

Good news for those who like to work up a sweat vacuuming carpets and mopping floors.

I tuned Margaret out after spotting *Gwyneth* at the reception desk. When we got there, I knocked a couple of times on the counter to get her attention because her nose was buried in her phone. She raised her eyes. Clearly I'd interrupted her mid-sentence with whatever she was typing. I wanted to smack her over the head with my gym bag but managed a smile instead. I didn't succeed at motherhood by acting on impulse, though I was tempted. And recently *more* tempted. *Gwyneth* smiled back at me when I threw my bag on the counter with some force. "Here for the orientation, *ma'am?*" she said.

And then there was Margaret. "I don't know why you're bothering with this gym thing. You're never going to look like *them*." She made a sweeping gesture of her hand toward the row of treadmill enthusiasts. "Or *her*," she said under her breath as she turned back to *Gwyneth*.

I hadn't expected *Gwyneth* to raise her eyebrows at Margaret, but she did.

Margaret put both hands on the counter. "Enjoy that pretty face and body while you can. It's not going to last..." My jaw dropped. The shift of attention, away from me, felt good... for a quick second, because Margaret then pointed to me with her eyes to sum up her entire case in point. "I can guarantee you that," she added.

I had no words, and neither did *Gwyneth*.

Gwyneth recovered quickly, standing taller and giving me a quick smile before pulling out a big red binder from the drawer. "Allison, right?"

"Yes, Allison Montgomery," I confirmed, forcing a smile.

Moments later, I told Margaret to sit in the reception area after I was successfully registered by what seemed like a more attentive *Gwyneth*. She'd probably gotten a little flash of what her world might look like if she had a mother-in-law like Margaret.

It appeared Margaret was exhausted from the day's activities when I stepped out of the change room. There she was, sitting quietly on the sofa. It wasn't surprising. Being a constant pain in the ass took a lot of work. Whatever reason was fine for me as long as she wasn't breathing down my neck and muttering about what a waste of money this whole *getting back into shape* process was.

Forty minutes later, the small orientation group finished getting the *do's* and *don'ts* of the fitness center by a perky instructor in her mid-thirties who felt more like a salesperson than a personal trainer. It was feeling like a giant conspiracy as she tried to push expensive training sessions, workout apparel and nutritional supplements on us. Some of the bright-eyed and bushy-tailed group members stayed to start their first workout, but I simply wasn't able to. Not with Margaret at the reception desk. I could read her lips and body language from across the gym. I might have known she'd be there, fussing about the noise level and the uncomfortable dirty sofa. I grabbed my bag and hurried to the front, gently yanking Margaret past the desk, as you would a toddler who was about to have a tantrum. *Maybe I did need a personal trainer. A certified one who could help me build the strength needed for my mother-in-law.*

As I struggled to push open the gym doors with Margaret behind, I could feel *Gwyneth's* eyes bore through me. At that moment, besides feeling a wave of hot air flash up the front of my body, my pulse was throbbing. I was surrounded by these ridiculous people at this phase in my life. I thought about this for a moment, and wouldn't you know it, I envied Val for the third time this week.

· · ·

Samantha and Keith were getting out of her car when we turned onto our street. And there was Margaret, sitting in the back, beaming, and unclasping her seat belt before we got to the driveway. I gripped the steering wheel, cursing myself for not having told Samantha yet about Keith's alleged behavior with women and his money troubles.

Once parked, I opened the car door slowly, nodding stiffly at Keith's greetings. I was sure he could tell by the expression on my face I wasn't up for any small talk, so his attention shifted to a kinder audience—Margaret. They hugged while I went and opened the front door, questioning Samantha about her past two-day whereabouts. Her car repair story wasn't adding up, but I was too frazzled to probe further.

Mindful I was operating at a lower vibe than the three chatting behind me, I went straight to the kitchen—and that's when it hit me. I still didn't have a dress or shoes. I wanted to scream. No, cry. I mentally assessed the limited outfits in my closet and then in Val's as I opened the fridge door. I didn't care if Margaret was going to throw a fit about me drinking wine well before dinner time because a) I'd definitely earned it, b) she was part of the reason I needed it, and c) Keith was in *my* house. *If she was going to go that route of condemnation, I was ready to kick up a storm.*

12 - The Funeral Crasher

The last goodbye was today. A tough one.

I could see the emotional toll of Hank's father's death on his face when I found him deep in thought, staring at the floor while he brushed his teeth.

"You okay?" I said, looking across the bathroom at him.

A moment passed before he twisted around and spat the toothpaste in the sink. After rinsing his mouth, I handed him a towel before wrapping my arms around his waist.

"I didn't think it'd be so hard," he said, burying his head into my neck. "Things have been so crazy with work that I haven't really thought about all that's happened. But it's sinking in now."

I gave him another good hug, kissing his cheek.

"My own mortality seems more real." He sighed deeply. "I feel so lost."

My eyes teared over. "Oh, Hank... I understand." And I did. A dead or dying parent at any age can transform your life and thoughts—it's that complete loss of childhood and innocence. And it doesn't matter whether that parent was loved or resented, or whether the relationship was warm or cold. From what I'd learned, losing a parent is life-altering. Suddenly, it can make you feel all grown up. There should be some recognition of parental death as a profound milestone in adulthood, don't you think? When I became fatherless, it felt as though my lifelong identity died along with him.

Hank cleared his throat. "I'm going to sneak out of here and get a bite to eat. I need to lighten up my speech—it's too somber."

"Good idea—he'd want that," I said on behalf of George. "Focus on the happy full life he had."

He kissed my forehead. "I'll meet you guys at the funeral hall."

"Okay," I agreed, giving him a gentle smile.

As soon as he was out of the bathroom, I picked up my hairbrush and frowned in the mirror again. *If only a bad hair day was a hairstyle.* Still unhappy after spending twenty minutes re-doing my hair, I went down to the kitchen anyway.

I could hear Samantha and my mother talking online when I reached the bottom of the stairs. Unfortunately, or fortunately, depending on how you look at it, my mother couldn't come to the funeral. When she'd told me about her sinus infection, we both agreed she not take any chances flying on an airplane with a painful, stuffed-up nose.

Truth be told, it's a relief for her not to be here at the same time as Margaret. The last time she was, the sight of them in the same room was enough headache and when they chose to engage, it was simply exhausting to watch and moderate their communication. My mother's fun and flamboyant nature would often overshadow Margaret's energy—it's like pairing an unusual oil and bitter vinegar for a salad dressing. The two just can't balance out, no matter how much you tweak it.

"Is that you, dear?" my mother said, presumably spotting me at the coffee machine.

"Hey, Mom," I said quickly, waving at the screen. "How are your sinuses?"

Samantha, obviously bored and disgusted listening to her detailed response about her symptoms, slid out of the kitchen chair and retreated downstairs. I slid in right behind her on the warm seat, adjusting the computer screen.

"What did you do to your *hair?*" my mother shrieked.

"That *bad?*" I moaned.

"Well, it makes you look..." I waited patiently while she blew her nose. "Well, it's hard to say without really seeing it, but you look tired to me."

Tired? It's a compliment to say such a thing in some African countries. But here, in the Western world, it's considered a shit move because it usually means one of two things; you look like crap, explain yourself or you look bad—worse than usual. I settled back into the chair with a heavy sigh. I invariably set myself up with the next question that came off my lips. "So—what's the weather like today?" I asked, and thought *Oh God, here we go with her five-minute comparison between our cold and drab winters to the warm ones she was now used to.*

Margaret, meanwhile, was busy setting out the fine china she'd rented from a full-service tabletop rental company along with an assortment of fancy shaped bowls she'd brought from her condo. When she neared, I could sense she was getting annoyed with my mother and me as we talked about the latest gossip happening in the sunny tropics. She deliberately started banging dishes and cupboard doors needlessly.

My mother stopped mid-sentence after Margaret banged the dishwasher door shut rather loudly. "Okay, I better let you go so you can get organized." And then, "Margaret, are you there?" She gave me a little wink as Margaret walked over to the computer with a stack of white linen napkins in her hand.

With a bit of irritation in her voice, Margaret peered at the computer screen. "What is it, Rosemary?"

My mother got right to it. "I wanted to tell you again how sorry I am for your loss. It'll get easier with time." She coughed into her sleeve. "And don't you worry. I'll come for a visit as soon as my doctor gives me the go-ahead."

I was quite sure Margaret hadn't been worrying, but she thanked my mother anyway. And then, "Okay, Rosemary. We've got lots to do around here." Her finger hovered over the power button. "Allison will talk to you later." And just like that, as if I were a lazy teenager talking to a reckless friend, Margaret pressed the button and closed the computer before I had a chance to say good-bye.

When I turned my head up at Margaret, she rolled her eyes back. I was about to roll mine far back too, but given the day, I decided to stay pleasant, getting up to rinse my coffee cup before giving her a quick smile. "I'm going to go wake up Cam."

"No need to. He's been up since eight," she said, "helping me."

I turned toward the basement stairs. "Oh, is he cleaning down there?"

"No." She paused. "I sent him to pick up more things at the grocery store."

"*What?*" And there it was—that sinking feeling in the pit of my stomach.

"He'll be fine, Allison," she reassured me.

I took a deep breath before explaining, like you would to a young child, the challenges of rush hour traffic for a new driver. A very new driver.

She stared at me blankly. "Nobody around here wanted to take me to the store last night so—"

"That was last night. You should've asked this morning." I grabbed my cup out of the sink for more coffee. "Cameron is barely functional at school, let alone driving this early in the day." My limbs went weak, and palpitations started as I envisioned Cameron in the chaos of mid-morning traffic and making left turns at busy intersections.

Margaret opened the freezer door. "You're going to add more wrinkles to your face if you keep worrying about him. He's not a baby, you know."

With her hand still wrapped around the freezer handle, I closed the door with a bit of force. "Don't talk to me like that," I snapped.

She gave me a bitter stare. I gave her a bitter stare back. "I know you're trying to have this lavish reception to impress your friends, but you don't need to stress out others. No one coming today will expect all this, and they sure as heck won't be inspecting the cleanliness of this house either,"

I said, surprised she hadn't requested a live orchestra or at least an ensemble.

Her reply? *I didn't care enough of what people thought about the way I lived.*

My reply to her absurdity? Nothing, because that's when I heard Cameron cry out for help at the front door.

Margaret sung out behind me as I hurried to it. "*See*, Allison. He did it! You gotta trust him." I ignored her need for recognition and gave Cameron a congratulatory hug as he kicked off his boots.

"I was awesome!" he said, looking quite pleased as he stood there with his arms weighed down by grocery bags.

"Course you were," I said. Amused, I shook my head as I glared at Margaret who stood there shrugging. I took the heaviest bag from his hands, giving him a proud smile. "Baby steps, okay?"

•   •   •

Three hours later, we spotted Hank getting out of his car after we pulled into the funeral home parking lot. By now, my neck was itchy and inflamed—a small reminder as to why this old black dress of mine had been cast away in the depths of my closet for so many years.

Once parked, we all walked toward the doors together. I tried not to look spitefully at Margaret's regal black dress popping out from under her coat as she walked in front of Hank and me, with the kids on either side of her.

As soon as we got through the heavy wooden doors, we were greeted by the friendly and professional staff. Of course, they had better be friendly and professional. Death is a booming industry, and the sales practices and markups they'd used on us when we came to help Margaret with the arrangements were shocking. When we walked out of there, we were all feeling guilt-ridden for not having chosen their luxury package, which included handmade casket carvings and some real 'out of the box' features such as jazz music playing in the background and butterflies being released to lighten the mood and make George's eternal sleep a nice one— gone were the days of solemn church funerals and receptions with crust-free sandwiches and coffee or tea served in Styrofoam cups.

After our coats were hung up, the staff led us into a small oak-paneled room across from the chapel. Settled on their tiny sofa, my throat started closing when the funeral officiant instructed and reminded us on the order of events and what we and our guests could and couldn't do. The experience felt peculiar and overwhelming, especially when one of the staff members stepped aside. I couldn't resist looking at George's casket at the front of the chapel.

I squeezed Hank's hand as we were led to the chapel to be with George before people arrived. We paused when we got to the entrance of it. None of us seemed to have the courage to approach the casket, except for Margaret. Impressively, she walked up and adjusted the arrangement of flowers and framed photos of George. She then bent over the casket as if she were saying something to him. And like that, she walked back to join us again. Moments later, Hank and the kids went up and said their goodbyes. I stayed behind, taking deep breaths, and trying to swallow the lump nestled deep in my throat. *George is gone... like gone gone.*

The minutes flew by and before we knew it, we were receiving guests—one, sometimes two or three at a time. Hank remained at Margaret's side, squeezing her hand, steadying her. I suspected everyone, including Margaret, hadn't expected the strange emotions surfacing. It all happened quickly as we stood listening to friends and family all saying contradictory things such as *stay strong* and *it's okay to cry.* How can you do both?

Keith was the last in line. I politely accepted his condolences and then watched him move on to the others. Samantha, of course, had already grabbed her purse before he got to her, ready to walk up the bluey green carpet with him by her side.

I took Hank's other hand, motioning him into the chapel. It was time for the funeral to begin. As we filed in, somberly walking up the aisle to the emotional piano music playing, something caught my eye. I did a double-take and noticed... *beautiful, long flowing red* hair. I spun my head around, with my arm still looped around Hank's. When we reached our front row seats and sat down, the salty tingling sensation formed in my eyes. I took a deep, calming breath, focusing straight ahead. I wasn't sure if my tears were because of seeing George's lifeless body in front of me, the energy it took and was going to take to manage Margaret, or because of seeing Robyn and that gorgeous mane of hers.

13 – Reception, Deception

Are you there, George? It's me, Allie.

You never told me you busked your way across Europe with your friend, Ray, and that you walked the Great Wall of China. I learned more about you from the wonderful tributes given by your friends and family than I did while you were alive. That's sad actually... how we don't really know someone until they're gone.

Sorry to have been a bit distracted when Revered Paul spoke. Hank's comment this morning about feeling his own mortality got me wondering if that's why Peter cheated on Val when his mother died. Is this what I might be in for with Hank? If you're capable of warning your loved ones down here of anything significant in the pipeline, please do give me a sign. It doesn't have to be anything spectacular—a simple cool breeze on my arm or a bird dropping just missing me will do.

Thinking of you always,

Allie xoxo

Back at the house, Margaret, the *star* of the day, saw to everyone's needs as I stood, lost and drained in the corner of my own living room, chatting with some of Margaret's curious condo neighbors, including Edith—the chef of Thursday night's lasagna dinner. I felt trapped as they huddled around me with their raised eyebrows, questioning George's last moments at the hospital. I could tell they hadn't wanted to upset Margaret about all the dreadful details like the time of his death or his last words, so I filled them in. Edith was about to open her mouth and ask another question when I spotted Val at the front door with Robert. My sad and pensive mood immediately lifted.

Val knew just what to do. After removing her various wool layers, she hurried over and then she leaned forward, tugging on my elbow and smiling brightly at the group in front of me. "You're needed in the kitchen, Allison," she said slowly and loudly like you would with the hard of hearing.

"You, okay?" she asked when we made it to the other side of the room.

"I don't know," I said, peering around, looking for Hank in the crowd of people.

She introduced Robert and me quickly. After we said our hellos, Val whispered something in his ear before turning to me. "*C'mon*," she said quietly, "let's get out of here for a bit."

I gave Robert a gracious smile as Val pulled me away. If I had it right, date number three for them, or was it four, had been a funeral, then an after-funeral reception. This *must* be serious. She turned her head back as I trailed behind her through the crowd near the kitchen. "Garage?" she said. I nodded eagerly as we headed through the kitchen and into the adjoining mud room. When we stepped out into the cold cluttered garage that's never seen a car, she immediately lit the cigarette she had in her hand and opened the flimsy side door. "It was a lovely funeral, Al," she said, blowing smoke out into the air.

"It was indeed," I said, tired from the efforts of the day's talking. "They did a great job with the service—and that sister of Hank's made everyone feel at ease with the whole death thing."

"Yeah, she did. But I couldn't help but watch Margaret when everyone in the chapel applauded at the end of her eulogy," she said.

I grabbed her cigarette and took a puff. "I didn't see her. What was she doing?"

"Oh, she was just sitting there with her usual resting face. You know, that peevish look of hers."

"Right, of course," I barked out with laughter. "She wouldn't have found anything his sister said, let alone everyone clapping inside a church, comforting *or* respectful."

She grabbed the cigarette back from me. "Did Margaret get along with her?"

"Not really. She was standoffish with her too. She'd visit George in the hospital so Margaret could go home and rest—" I explained, thinking of how his sister's gesture was kind and thoughtful, "but Margaret insisted it should only be her staying with him." I took a deep breath before continuing. "His sister was dismissed as quickly as I was whenever I offered to help. I'm sure Margaret had it in her mind we would've ended it all applying the wrong ointment to his bed sores or tripping and pulling out one of his tubes." I paused and sat on a plastic step stool. "Whatever the reason, it was clear she didn't trust anyone to be in the room with him overnight. It was odd." I felt my heart tighten thinking about it. "Speaking of odd, Robert looks a bit different than I expected," I said, smiling as I looked at her.

There was a brief silence before Val spoke. "Really? How so?"

I stood up. "For starters," I said, "he's an inch shorter than you."

Val threw her head back, laughing at the high heel boots she had on. "Make that two inches," she said with a sweet seriousness in her eyes. "But I got to tell you, he's a gem. He's honest and good for me. No bullshit or baggage—unless you count his son, Keith."

"Good," I said, swinging the door absentmindedly to clear the smoked-filled air. "I'm happy for you—" I stopped with the door.

"What's wrong?" she said. "Is it that Robyn woman?"

"No," I snapped, my heart constricting again.

I opened the door further. "Look for yourself."

Val leaned over and poked her head out, quickly retracting it. "How *dare* he do this to Sam," she hissed.

My poor naïve daughter.

We hurried back to the kitchen, first to search for wine and then to search for Samantha. "She's probably upstairs crying," I said, holding up my glass for Val to fill.

"Okay, let me go. You'll only sugarcoat it for her," she said.

I shook my head side to side. "I won't," I promised, finding to my surprise I was feeling relieved. Samantha will now know he's a complete waste of time once we tell her.

Val threw me one of her looks. And in a flash, she was gone. I was right behind her until I felt this forceful tug on the back of my dress. I spun around.

"*Oh, there you are,*" Margaret said, excessively flapping her hand in front of her nose. "Smelling like cigarette smoke, of course."

My back usually tensed up whenever she'd look at me in her concentrated way to express displeasure in something, but this time, strangely enough, it didn't. I didn't feel the need to defend myself, nor feel bad about indulging once in a while in a guilty pleasure. For Hank, it had been his marijuana. And I never harassed him about it nor made him feel guilty whenever he'd want to sequester himself in the garage with his Ziploc bag full of weed. *Strip away the guilt and enjoy your life*, we'd say to each other—*virtue can be exhausting.* "I need to talk to Sam," I said patiently to her.

"Can't you speak to her later?" she said, her hand now on my arm. "We have a house full of guests."

I wiggled my elbow out of her grasp. "I'll be down as soon as I talk to her."

She looked around frantically. "Well, where's Hank then?" she grumbled. "Someone needs to help with things around here."

"Everyone looks fine and they all seem to be enjoying themselves, Margaret. Don't worry." And they were, as more people arrived, and more drinks were served. George would've been pleased.

"It's not a party for George, Allison—it's a funeral reception," she said.

I weighed my options before flashing her a quick smile in response to her icy stare. I'd made up my mind. "Back in a sec. Promise," I said before turning to the stairs, listening to her hiss about something as I raced up them.

Samantha was crying and Val was consoling her when I gently pushed the bedroom door open. The two of them were sitting on the end of the bed, amid the pile of Margaret's neatly folded sheets and knitted blankets. I hesitated a moment before I neared Samantha. "Aww... Sam. I'm so sorry you had to find out this way—"

"Find out what?" she uttered, freeing herself from Val's arms.

I kneeled in front of her, putting my hands on her knees. "Oh... sweetheart," I began, "Keith—"

"What about Keith?" she said.

Val looked at me with wide eyes before clearing her throat. "We were just talking about Grandpa."

"*Ooh*..." My eyes widened too. "I thought—"

"What were you going to say about Keith?" She looked back at Val. "Did you guys say something to him because I can't find him."

I wish I had the heart to tell her we just saw him getting into a white sports car with a pretty girl with purple hair behind the wheel, but I didn't. I couldn't.

Val stood up abruptly. "Keith's a cheat and in a lot of debt. Plus, he's been married and who knows what else. He's a loser," she blurted out.

Harsh.

Samantha stared at Val with a dropped jaw before whipping around to face me. "I know you don't like him Mom, but I love him. He might be older and a bit rough on the outside, but really... if you'd get to know him, you'd like him."

Oh, my God. Really?

Val put her hand on Samantha's shoulder. "I wouldn't be surprised if he's borrowing money from you too," she said.

Nodding vigorously, I opened my mouth to say something, and then closed it. I felt bad.

It was Val who broke the uncomfortable silence. She sat next to Samantha again and grabbed her in her arms. "You need to know this now so you don't end up getting hurt," she said.

Samantha pulled herself away. "What about his dad? It's weird you two are even together."

"I know, but he's nothing like Keith. And besides, he's the one who told me about him, not knowing you were dating his son. Believe me—if I wasn't your Godmother *and* pseudo aunt, I wouldn't be so protective."

Agreed.

When Val finished telling Samantha how Peter had blindsided her by an affair and how fucked up that left her after a twenty-year commitment in a kid-less marriage, I pulled myself up off the floor, hearing the crackle in my knees. "Keith isn't worth your tears—"

"Can you guys leave now," Samantha said dully.

Assured she got the message that Keith was up to no good, we both hugged her quietly before leaving her room.

•   •   •

"Don't leave before saying goodbye," I said to Val when we got downstairs.

I didn't hear her reply because I was too distracted. Distracted by the fact that Robyn was in *my* house. There she was, talking to Hank at the makeshift bar near the dining room table with a slim-fitting black dress that should've been on me.

She gave me a big smile, waving as if eager to say hello and offer her condolences. And so, as any polite hostess would do, I scurried over, hoping to meet halfway across the room. But by the time I squeezed my way through the small group of people and neared the bar, she was gone. When I turned around, she was sitting on the sofa, relaxed with some of the handsome men from Hank's office.

Moments later, Hank came up from behind. He pecked me on the cheek, smiling softly, clearly unaware of my insecurities about her. "Where've you been?" he said.

"Oh... I was busy upstairs," I answered, sparing him from my feelings and from the Samantha-Keith drama.

While he mixed a couple of vodka drinks for the next several minutes, I stood there sneaking looks at Robyn like a crazed jealous-hearted wife. When he finished adding the ice, I leaned toward him. "So, is she here for you or for Margaret?"

He knew exactly who I was talking about. "Ah, Allie, c'mon. You don't have to use that tone. I'm not interested." He rubbed the small of my back gently. "And besides, she's not my type."

"Yeah, right Hank," I said. "She's *everyone's* type."

He took a deep breath in. "She came to pay her respects. I told you... she used to be his investment broker," he said with some exasperation in his voice. "You have nothing to worry about."

I gave him a terse smile, feeling like I had to worry because he seemed to be standing a little taller and perkier as he joined his colleagues and Robyn at the sofa. I took a deep calming breath in, avoiding the urge to act out. And as I was pouring myself a stronger drink, trying not to think about the earring I'd found in Hank's car, one of George's friends with indiscreet hearing aids raised his glass, loudly announcing he wanted to give a toast. Soon the room was filled as others joined in to give their own heartfelt tributes. Even Samantha, who was now in the room drinking one of Val's cocktail concoctions, surprised everyone by reading a humorous poem she and Cameron had written about their grandfather. Everyone cheered when they finished, including Margaret.

The reception slowly ended after the last homage was paid to George. I started stacking dirty plates left on the dining room table when Margaret came over. Naturally, I thought she had come to supervise my clean-up efforts, but instead, she piled sausage rolls on a napkin and pulled me into the kitchen by my sleeve.

"I saw you watching that pretty redhead out there." She put an entire sausage roll in her mouth and seconds later, swallowed it. "Robyn once had her eyes on George, you know." She picked up another sausage roll and shoved it in her mouth. "She's about your age, maybe older," she mumbled between chews.

"*Really?*" I said, feeling better.

"Yep, I remember very clearly," she said. "She was in her twenties when she set George up in some investment... he was about Hank's age too." Apart from some laughter on the other side of the kitchen wall, silence filled the room. Margaret broke it when she said point-blank, "She still has it, you know." She must've read my face when she added, "Not the money, but the appeal."

I wasn't sure how to respond. Her words counted, even though it was a strange exchange between us. So I stood there watching her wipe away flaky crumbs around her mouth before she left me there, alone and thinking if Robyn had been capable of causing a shipwreck between George and Margaret, who was to say this ageless beauty wouldn't be capable of doing it again—and this time, according to Margaret, with someone closer to Robyn's age.

•　　•　　•

When we finished sorting out the last of the recycling bins in the garage, I felt armed with a reason to bring up Robyn's name to Hank.

"There's nothing really to tell," he said.

"Yeah, but your mother mentioned she had a thing for your dad when he was your age—so, I'm wondering what happened."

"Robyn was a very eager and competitive broker back then. That's all."

"Do you think she made a move on your dad? I mean... she *was* in her twenties, hot and probably wanting sex all the time," I said with conviction. "And to her, your dad must've seemed like the perfect older man—charming, successful... intelligent—"

"Oh, *c'mon*," he whispered, "my dad would've never crossed that line with her."

He's right. George was loyal to the bitter end.

"Yeah, well, maybe Robyn's hoping you'll cross the line with her," I muttered, *immediately* regretting my words.

He put his hand to his neck as if perturbed. "Stop. Just stop," he snapped, giving me a sidelong look.

Wasn't it every man's dream to be with a young, beautiful girl when they felt they'd passed their prime? I followed him back to the kitchen with a stinky garbage bin in my hand. I had to skirt the issue. *Conflict avoidance.* Yup, I'm good at that. I know it's an unhealthy way to deal with all the things going on in my head, but right now, Hank sounded and looked as though he'd had enough misery for the past few days. And my insecurities about Robyn were only going to push him away—and we've been there before.

14 – Blood, Sweat and Tears

Are you there, George? It's me, Allie.

It's been two weeks since your funeral. Everyone, including your three nephews, along with their wives and children, and then their children's children have returned to their busy lives. I think. Slowly, we're returning to normal at home too—except for our guest who seems to have settled quite comfortably into Samantha's room, and need I say, into the rest of the house.

No longer do I feel I have the 'rest of the house' as part of my personal space when Hank and the kids are out. No longer am I able to cherish the times of catching up on my favorite series or hanging out with my book characters.

Do we have a clean house? Yes.

Are we coming home to a hot meal on the table every evening? Yes.

Is laundry done, folded, and put away on the same day? Yes. Yes. And yes.

But with your wife here all day with a vacuum cleaner in one hand and a dust cloth in the other, escaping has become a necessity. Not to sound ungrateful for having a home that's running like a well-oiled machine by a house-proud mother-in-law, but I don't have much adaptive energy needed for this kind of disruption. Instead, I find myself sweating too much at the gym or drinking one too many at Val's. I'm

*even staying beyond school hours to keep busy. Good thing is my
classroom has never looked so cute and colorful!*

*Speaking of cute, I've been getting a lot of compliments on my hair!
It really seems to be my trademark these days.*

We miss you dearly,

Allie xoxo

"Almost done?" Margaret's voice sounded behind me when I'd finally
finished prepping a Valentine's Day craft on the dining room table.

I was halfway under the table picking up foil heart confetti that'd
fallen the floor. "Just a minute," I said over my shoulder. "I need to wipe
the table first." The last thing I needed was for her to spot dried-up glitter
glue and drops of blood from a painful paper cut.

She put down the placemats for dinner anyway. "Look at you, Allison.
It's no wonder you're so tired and looking worn-out all the time..." she
said. "All this cutting and gluing..."

I sighed when I saw the cardboard hearts I'd cut out earlier piled on
the end chair. Sadly, part of Margaret was right. At the end of the day,
shaping young minds is exciting, but it isn't worth the hours of prepping
crafts for them, and the bullshit of detailed reports and interviews with
parents who think their child is destined for greatness—unless I, or the
school itself, screws them up. However, it's the children's tears that come
with every runny nose, sore throat, wiggly tooth, broken crayon, and
family secret I'm *not* supposed to know that has kept me sane and
compassionate over the years. But now, the daily mission of figuring out
what's wrong so I can help them through their troubles is draining.

Still on my knees, I blew the last of the tiny pink sparkles off the chair
as Margaret stood there tapping her fingers on it. I pulled myself up,
noticing her foam tread slippers covered in them. She narrowed her eyes,
grunting something before pushing the chair back in under the table.

"There, all clean now," I said after vigorously wiping the table. "I'll go
get Hank for dinner." Without wasting another second absorbing her

tense energy, I went down to our half-finished basement in search of Hank.

Samantha, still in her pajamas, appeared at the laundry room door when I got to the bottom of the stairs. I assumed the stack towels she was holding were going back to the apartment with her. Although Hank and I were disappointed in her for quitting her program at school, we were relieved she'd made the decision to break up with Keith after learning, among other things, his short-lived marriage to a gorgeous Latin model. And since her rent had been paid until the end of spring, she was going back to find a mindless part-time job so she could figure out her next steps. I don't blame her. I would've done the same thing when I was her age. And besides, sleeping in a dark space next to the laundry room might actually lead to depression.

"Need help with your laundry?" I said, handing her the pink heart wreath I'd made for her.

She smiled sadly as she took it. "No, it's okay." Her swollen eyes drooped under the beam of one of the pot lights. "I'm almost done."

Nothing hurt more than seeing your child in pain. Sadly, this wasn't the first love experiment to have gone wrong for Samantha. Her weakness for that charming and ridiculously cute *bad boy* type with their mysterious dark side had only led to a series of heart breaks. I'm hoping she'll open herself up to a nice guy soon, like I did when I met Hank. There's such a thing as being nice *and* cute. "Okay, well, dinner is almost ready," I said, giving her a soothing hug.

"I'll be up in a minute," she responded, her arms limp by her sides. I gave her another big squeeze and then carried on to the far end of the basement.

When I poked my head inside Hank's recently constructed office, he was sitting in front of his computer. He was either here, the new "normal", tapping away on the keyboard while deep in conversation on the phone, or doing all that at the company's office downtown.

Startled, he looked up from his screen. "Dinner," I announced in a soft voice. I opened the door fully and walked over to him, admiring not only the moderately elegant and contemporary decorating I'd done, but the cheerful fabric wrapped DIY bulletin board I put together too.

After I pinned my homemade *You Color My World* Valentine's card on the board, I leaned over the side of his oversized office chair and kissed his cheek. He smiled at me and then at the card. "Aw, thank you. That's sweet," he said, giving my hand a gentle and reassuring squeeze. "I'll be up soon, babe."

"Okay, we'll wait for you." I kissed the top of his head this time before collecting three half-empty cups of cold tea. Sometimes a small part of me wondered if the romantic gestures between Hank and I were simply out of habit, or if they really meant something beyond trying to divorce-proof our marriage. Over the years, we've had our little signs of affection and gift giving on special days, like Valentine's for instance, but really, sometimes it all feels like an elaborate show from roommates who are being friendly to one another but not expecting to be best friends. I thought about this as I headed back upstairs.

•　　•　　•

We were in the middle of our chicken parmigiana dinner when Margaret announced out of nowhere, "It's time I sell the condo."

Hank stopped mid-chew. "*What?*"

Noooo. No. No. No. No. An overwhelming surge of darkness and anxiety rushed through me when she answered pertly, "Well, it's not exactly carved in stone yet, but it's something I've been thinking about."

Hank's eyes widened as he swallowed the food in his mouth. "But, why? You've been happy there, haven't you?"

"Well, not anymore," Margaret said, clearing her throat. "Most of the people I liked, moved out. And I don't even know anyone on my floor ... except for Edith of course—and God knows what I'll do if she moves too. The maintenance in that building is terrible—I sometimes vacuum the dirty hallway myself." She paused to take a bite of her chicken. "Thankfully Keith always sees that things get done when Edith and I need him—I don't know what I'd do without him," she said through chews.

My stomach churned for Samantha as she squirmed uncomfortably in her chair.

Hank cleared his throat and said before the words rolled off my tongue, "Out of respect for Sam, don't you think it'd be wise to find another handyman?"

"It's okay," Samantha cut in. "I'm *so* over him." She smiled at her grandmother before shoving a green bean in her mouth.

Stunned that Margaret seemed relieved to have Keith continue as her handyman, I whipped my head back to Hank. Hoping to see some disappointment in his face, he just sat there, wisely avoiding eye contact with me as he listened to his mother complain about her neighbors' poor English, the rising condo fees, the decreasing property values... *blah, blah, blah.* I knew there was more to the story than she was telling us.

I wondered if Keith had been bleeding Margaret dry because lately, she's been complaining about the cost of things at the grocery store, and once again, she's been going through our coat pockets taking the loose change in them and most recently, the five-dollar bill I'd put in mine. I haven't mentioned this odd and treacherous behavior to Hank because it seems he has money matters on his mind too. But perhaps it was time.

"So... would you be moving in here with us, Grandma?" Cameron interrupted, obviously undaunted by the possibility.

Noooo. No. No. No. No. Apart from my pounding heart and sweaty hands, a great silence filled the room. I pleaded inside my flustered head for Hank not to open his mouth. I was hoping he'd get my clairvoyant message that his mother moving in with us, beyond this *temporary* move, would be a bad idea. A very, very, *very* bad idea.

Margaret turned to Hank again, seemingly expecting a response to Cameron's question. But he didn't answer. He just sat there, staring at his breaded chicken smothered in bitter tomato sauce as though it were an oracle that held an answer.

15 - Money Matters

That evening, to Hank, I brought up Margaret's shattering announcement she made at dinner. "Why do you think she wants to sell the condo?" I asked, trying not to sound too distressed. "Do you think she needs the money?"

"I doubt it," he replied, pulling out his pajama bottoms from the dresser drawer. "She has access to their banking investments."

I allowed a moment to pass. "I have this gut feeling she's lending—or giving money to Keith." There. I said it. My mouth went dry.

"*Keith?*" He pulled his eyebrows together. "What are you talking about?"

"I don't trust him, Hank. Do you know he's—"

"Don't be ridiculous, Allie. I know he hurt Samantha, but I hardly think he'd be that desperate, or callous for that matter, to be borrowing money from my mother." He sighed in frustration. "And besides, she wouldn't without talking to me first."

I sat on our mid-century chair in the corner of the room. "How's she doing financially?" I asked, deciding it best to steer the conversation in another direction until I had concrete evidence of Keith swindling money out of Margaret. "I mean, was it all sorted before your dad got sick... the papers, the will—" I stopped because I was sounding a little like an absentee relative coming out of the woodwork to claim a piece of the financial pie.

"No, not really—but I need to have that talk with her. I doubt she paid much attention to it all," he said, breathing deeply. "She probably learned how to pay the odd bill here and there." He paused to pull his tightknit sweater over his head. "My dad probably guided her on everything. Beyond my duties as co-executor, he never shared his plans with me, so I don't know—he didn't have a company pension... his investments were for their retirement."

Retirement. The word echoed in my ears as I sprung up to close the curtains on all three windows this bedroom had. Call me strange, but not only did I like to sleep in total darkness, but I've had this fear for a long time now of waking up in the middle of the night to a gray scaly creature peering through the window in the process of my abduction.

Retirement. The word vibrated throughout my head this time as I reached under the bed for my yoga mat. *I get that George had retired from his years in banking... but what exactly would Margaret be retiring from?*

Hank threw his sweater on the top shelf of the closet. "The condo sale should help her with money in the future."

He'd been thinking about the next steps for her. Obviously. I unrolled the yoga mat and eased myself on it. Perhaps the *Riviera Retirement Residence* around the corner would be a good option. Their tagline, *A Place Where Retirement Serves You*, cost about seven thousand dollars a month. But if you could pay that kind of money, it'd be like one big coffee break with three gourmet meals a day, personal cleaning and laundry service, a packed social calendar, scheduled transportation trips to the mall, and even a concierge. Residents have access to a massage therapist and a hair and nail salon onsite too. And if that weren't enough, around-the-clock onsite home care is available, with someone delivering aspirins or sleeping pills to your room with a fresh glass of water if you wanted it.

Now that I think about it, the expense would be significant. Margaret's in her early seventies and in relatively good health. If she were to live a long and healthy life, we'd be talking close to a million and a half dollars for her to live out her golden years in such a place. Even with what savings and investments they had, Hank, I'm sure, would be concerned about the possibility of her outliving that money, especially since the final years would be the most expensive ones. Besides, he wouldn't want to see that kind of money going into the pockets of the rich over the next twenty years.

"I don't think I can send her back to her condo just yet." His face was a mixture of concern, exhaustion, and sadness as he sat on the edge of the bed. "She obviously doesn't enjoy living there anymore."

Annoyed and frustrated with the possibility of this unforeseeable imposition continuing, I clicked my tongue a little too loudly in exasperation before saying, "Yes, but—" I heard the floorboard outside our bedroom creak. It wouldn't have surprised me if Margaret was standing at the door with her ear pressed to it.

Hank gave me a quizzical look. "But what?" he said in a low, irritated voice.

"Nothing," I said quietly, stretching my legs out in front of me and relaxing into a full body extension like the yoga instructor demonstrated in class. This conversation is going to be hard, from all indications. I swung my upper body up again as I allowed a calm and balanced smile to spread across my lips before I reached down again, trying to touch my toes. "Let it all unfold," I breathed out, rising and clasping my hands straight overhead. *Let it unfold*, I'd say whenever Hank and I were on a prickly subject like Margaret. Let it unfold and let the fairies of the universe do their job. It's a much better choice than getting into an ugly argument before bed. Besides, anything I said would only come across as attacking him, which in turn, would only put him on the defense. But eventually, we have to make damn sure we're on the same page when it comes to her living arrangements.

Hank let out a long deep breath.

"What's wrong?" I asked, twisting my head toward him.

He slumped back on the bed running his fingers through his hair. "Speaking of retirement, you know we have little saved, right?"

I took a deep breath in, searching for the right response. "I know," I said slowly, as though the words were forced from me against my will. "I think about that too." My body suddenly tensed up and did whenever our discussions moved in this direction. As much as I wanted to let things unfold on the subject of aging and retirement, I hated thinking about it. The uncertainty of the *future* future filled me with an undefinable sense of dread.

"We're in our mid-forties and we don't have a nest egg," he said. "Plus, Cam's university years are fast approaching... you're going to need a new car soon... and it'd be nice if we could finish the basement *and* the backyard that looks like shit."

I closed my eyes. He was right. Until now, the thought of retirement had been a foreign concept to us—well, at least to me anyway.

When I opened my eyes seconds later, Hank was leaning over the bed, staring at me as I lay on the mat. "We need a plan. More income or less expenses... ." He paused. "Maybe it wouldn't be such a bad thing if she sells the condo. She could move in here and help pay—"

"You're joking, right?" I sat up straight, my stomach flipping.

"Not entirely," he said a little too quickly, "but it might make financial sense. Think about it, Allie. We could start saving money *and* get some projects done around here. We need to get a good return on this house when we sell."

"*Sell?*" I said in a panic, watching him get off the bed. "Who said anything about selling... I love this house—"

"I'm not talking about *now*," he reassured me. "But, sooner or later, it'll be too much house for us. And besides, we have to see our home beyond it being a nest... it's *gotta* be our nest egg."

The rights and wrongs about this particular topic were making me dizzy. I pulled my knees to my chest, breathing heavily.

In the next second, loud knocks cut through the thick, heavy energy in the room. "Dad, the shower's not working," Cameron complained through our door.

Hank exhaled loudly, shaking his head. "If it's not one thing, it's the other." He opened the bedroom door. "This is why we need a plan." He gave me a frustrated smile and then disappeared to the hallway bathroom with Cameron.

I groaned, feeling the blood thicken through my veins. Hank's idea of Margaret moving in with us to help solve our financial woes would most definitely lead me to running off to the interiors of Iceland or faking my own death.

16 - Move Over, J. K. Rowling

On Thursday, I arrived to school an hour early. Unlike most teachers, I wasn't going in early to prep. It was my escape from Margaret, dressed in her nightgown and a full set of Hollywood sponge rollers covering her head, stopping me at the front door with her damn lists. Lists that included various food items I needed to get or various repair jobs that needed to be done—like the shower in the upstairs bathroom.

With forty-five minutes until the first bell rang, I sat at my desk sorting through the daily boatload of emails on a colossal computer. There were always a few from teachers or parents and more than a dozen it seemed from our school's new headmaster, Thomas (who thinks he holds special powers), about weekly reminders and passive aggressive FYIs, like last month's expense report and next week's electrical repairs—along with many other facility defects needing attention. Surprisingly, and contrary to popular belief, this private school isn't overflowing with state-of-the-art equipment or Stradivarius violins for the kids.

Scrolling further, I deleted the unsolicited emails until the last one. I was about to hit the trash can icon when something caught my eye. Gingerly, I moved the cursor away. With curiosity, I opened it, intently chewing on a dry, ragged cuticle. My heart skipped a beat when I read the whimsical and colorful print jumping out on the computer screen.

Want to Become the Next Bestselling Children's Author?

YES! I've earned enough badges at this school. My heart skipped another beat when I read further.

Join Our Workshop and Learn How to Write and Sell Your Book!

My book? It was as if they, whoever *they* were, were talking to me. I re-read the words again and this time, envisioning *Allison Montgomery* written in cutesy bold font across the front cover of a wildly successful children's book. A burst of adrenaline flowed throughout my veins.

I took a deep breath, gazing out the window. Not only did the bright morning sun hitting the corner of my desk give me a renewed sense of optimism, but the thought of writing something other than an email or a 160-character text, did too. After all these years of shaping young minds with the stories I'd make up, here I was, full of them, and ready to share with the world.

Coco Chanel was right—a woman who cuts her hair is about to change her life!

I re-read the details again and before I knew it, I was pulling out my credit card to register for Saturday's workshop—without a second thought to having a scheduled dentist appointment. The magic of the universe was at work here, and I wasn't going to miss this nudge. Someday, I might stroll into a store and proudly see *my* book fill the shelves, and the money from it help to keep Margaret comfortable and happy at the *Riviera*.

After successfully registering for the workshop, I rescheduled my dentist appointment and texted Hank in excitement. And wouldn't you know it, the bell signaled the beginning of a new school day when I hit send. I greedily gulped down the rest of my coffee before throwing on my coat to greet the line of children waiting outside the door. I was ready to be with them today. After all, they were going to be my readers—my biggest fans, my greatest critics. *They* were going to be the reason and inspiration to write the best children's book ever. *Think big. I have my talents.*

It'd been a good day. I felt calmer with my students, including the classroom troublemakers and their unfiltered comments about my hair. Bouncing from one activity center to the next, I smiled and observed the children closely. I looked for potential characters traits, like a detective looking for investigation clues. In the teacher's staff room, the unconstrained and derogatory conversations with younger colleagues didn't seem to bother me like they usually did because I was too distracted with the thought of an exciting writing career that could also help fund our retirement. As we sat at the big round table eating lunch, part of me desperately wanted to tell them about my newfound dream as they mercilessly gossiped about the children's parents, and about the parents' children. But exciting as it was, I didn't. That *hmmm* or *blank stare* I might've received from a potential green-eyed monster in the room would've been taken personally. I didn't need anyone full of motivation and enthusiasm for their job killing my joy ride with eyeball rolls and negative comments.

Hank still hadn't returned my call or replied to my texts when I got home from school later that day. Some dreadful instinct told me he was avoiding me after I'd spoken up again about his relationship with his mother. In the past few days, he'd been favorably commenting on her meals, thanking her for the cleaning she did, asking her to mend his pants and sew buttons missing on his shirts and then dropping everything to watch back-to-back game shows with her in the evenings. Besides speaking up about his relationship with her, I *might've* blurted out she was a thief. Yes. A thief. Unfortunately, I didn't have the chance to expand on why I thought she was a thief, rummaging through coat pockets for spare change, because his phone rang. In a riptide of frustration, he'd stomped out of the room, carrying on with the caller as he grabbed his coat and walked out the front door.

Whatever I said this morning, I regretted. I blame it on my hormones. If it weren't for being that time of the month, when my coping mechanism and my ability to rationalize all that was going on around me wasn't so great, I wouldn't have called him a mamma's boy. *Would I?* And the little remark about being a mamma's boy was made *after* I told him if that he finds his mother moving in with us a good idea, then he'd better find a good divorce lawyer. Joking of course, but still.

I flopped on the sofa, taking a minute to regroup. I've missed the spacious, well decorated room and its soft carpet beneath my feet. I've also missed being a hermitic couch potato—more so, now that the house is really clean. With nothing else to do but open the blinds, I stared out the large picture window dreaming about my writing career. The scenery behind the glass and the perfect view of the big oak tree in the front yard filled me with hope.

I closed my eyes, enjoying the silence. Cameron was at Kyle's and Margaret was at her condo. Apart from Sunday morning church, Thursday night bingo has been the second highlight to her week. *Maybe that's what our pocket money was for.*

Because I had the house to myself, I happily settled on the sofa with a glass of wine and last night's pork roast, deferring the gym until later. But it wasn't long until my phone rang. I turned down the TV and answered. "Hey, Cam. How are ya?"

"Good," he said with enthusiasm. "I just dropped Dad off at the train station and now I'm at Kyle's. I'm gonna stay here and eat."

"Of course." I took my plate back to the kitchen. "I'm not cooking anyway since your dad has a dinner meeting."

"Okay, and by the way, Grandma said she's sleeping at her house tonight," he said.

The corners of my mouth turned up. "Oh?" I said, trying hard not to make a sound as I quickly busted a couple of dance moves.

"Yeah, she said Sam's bed is killing her back."

Well, sorry it hasn't been the Hilton, Margaret. "Oh, that's too bad," I said, displaying a good attitude for Cameron's sake.

"She said not to worry—it'd be just for one night," he said.

Just one night? My stomach plunged.

Seconds after Cameron and I said goodbye, my phone buzzed.

[Home around ten. Getting Uber from train station]

I felt a fluttering of wretchedness in my stomach. Before the world of texting, Hank and I once valued our time talking on the phone. But soon after texting became a thing, we could tell when each other's voices dropped from a distraction, whether it was me fiddling around in the kitchen or him responding to an email. Mostly because it's less disruptive when we're busy, texting each other to confirm dinner plans with friends or to find out when the other would be home meant we didn't have to get into the *How's your day going?* or *How you feeling?* conversation. We exchanged about twenty text messages a day, not including the ones we'd send when we were both home but on different floors.

I responded to his cold and distant seeming text with a warmer, wordier one. After all, I ruined his morning. And with all that's going on at work and at home, he didn't deserve that.

[Hey darling. Cam can pick you up. He's at Kyle's and coming home at the same time. I miss you and I love you! Sorry again about this morning. XO]

Two *long* minutes later, my phone vibrated in my hand.

[sharing Uber with someone]

There'd definitely been a *tone* to his simple one-sentence response. *And who was this someone?* I leaned against the kitchen counter, trying to keep my crazy thoughts from robbing me of the peace and serenity I could have tonight. *He's sharing an Uber with someone.* I twisted around and poured myself more wine. And when I did, I spotted my bright red sports bag sitting, as if waiting for me, on the kitchen chair. I could hear my heartbeat as I sighed long and deep, feeling slightly regretful and emotionally off. *Forgive Me, Red Sports Bag. I'm not being lazy—I'm no longer motivated to go.* It was a terrible feeling.

17 - MAMMA MIA!

When I woke up the next day, my mouth felt like it was overgrown with the key lime pie I'd finished while watching three episodes of *Renovate My Home*. Even though I'd had the house to myself last night, I went to bed early and fell into what I believe was a deep slumber after my head hit the pillow.

I could hear Hank in the shower, so I dragged myself out of bed and shuffled to the hallway bathroom. I paused at Samantha's door. It was closed, which meant Margaret had come home last night. Suddenly, as though the ground were shaking, I felt an unrelenting misery of a headache coming on and hurried to the bathroom.

I sat dazed on the toilet for a few minutes, sulking knowing Margaret was back. She's a regular fixture in the house now—we see her first thing in the morning, tearing apart the newspaper at the kitchen table, then again in the late afternoon, standing framed in the kitchen doorway giving a play-by-play account of her day, and then well into the evening, recounting to us, along with her opinions, the day's news—and not just around town, but around the world too.

After splashing cold water on my face and gargling a mouthful of Margaret's peppermint mouthwash, I passed Samantha's door again, thinking it strange—puzzling, actually. It was past seven and Margaret wasn't up. This would definitely be considered sleeping in for her.

Best to let sleeping dogs lie.

I made my way back to our room and then peeked my head inside the warm steam-filled bathroom. "Morning," I called out slowly to Hank, but no answer. I paused for a moment and then entered quietly. After pinching my cheeks and tousling my hair, I stripped out of my pajamas. I owed him a better start to his day than yesterday. And if I were being honest, I've been turning him down one too many times with my bloated stomach and nagging headache excuses lately. How many times can you say *no* to your husband before he reaches for someone else? And that *someone*—my stomach dropped—could've been the one who shared the Uber with him last night.

I sucked in my breath bravely, fighting the feelings I had about my nude body before pulling back the waffled weaved shower curtain. I pursed my lips. "How about a morning—"

"Mom!"

"Cameron!" I shrank back.

"Oh, my God!" he shouted, his mouth hanging open.

Shit.

Shit.

Shit.

I pulled the curtain shut and ran out of the bathroom. Mortified and stunned, I threw on my pajamas and sat on the bed, thinking of an immediate way to rectify the situation. Poor Cameron. To have your own mother see you naked in the shower was downright traumatic. And poor me. It'd been eleven years since I'd seen him in the buff and over that much time, many changes can occur. This *could* put him into therapy— him seeing his mother naked, offering sex.

It wasn't like we could avoid each other, so I waited for him to come out. There was no need for apologies. A simple acknowledgment would do. I tried to convince myself of that as I buried my head in my hands, rocking back and forth, feeling sick to my stomach.

"What are you doing?" Hank asked, standing there with his coffee when I lifted my head.

I blinked twice.

"Here," he said, handing me my phone. "You left it on the sofa last night."

I took it from his hand, barely acknowledging it. "Your son just saw me naked. And vice versa."

His face stiffened. "What?"

"I thought it was you in there," I said, blushing.

I could tell Hank wasn't himself. Normally, he would've found this amusing. He would've nodded with a gentle understanding. He would've playfully laughed and joked. He would've given me a big hug and a supportive kiss before saying *Aw, Allie. It's these little things you do that make me smile.* But he didn't. Instead, he gave off a humorless laugh before saying matter-of-factly, "He's never going to come out, you know."

"Why is he using our shower?" I stood up with wobbly knees. "I thought his was fixed."

"No, we're going to need to go beyond the walls. I think there's a leak," he said, sipping his coffee. "Go get your coffee. I'll smooth things over with him."

"Okay," was all I could say as he turned to face the TV.

"By the way," he said, searching for his morning news channel, "you have a visitor—"

Before Hank could finish his sentence, Cameron emerged from the bathroom. I quickly ducked out of the room feeling unusually vulnerable. But seconds later, I felt slightly better after hearing the two of them laughing when I got to the stairs.

I was about to descend to the kitchen but stopped. Besides something feeling off between Hank and I, there was something feeling a bit off with it being twenty after seven and Margaret not up yet. *Did I drink too much last night and commit a terrible crime?*

I pressed my ear against Samantha's door but heard nothing behind it. So, I opened it slightly and tiptoed into the half-darkened room toward the bed. When I got closer, a fleeting sense of relief washed over me. I had committed no crime because underneath the mound of sheets and heavy blankets, there Margaret was. Breathing, slow and deep. Her body, still and relaxed. And her face beneath the pillow was, I imagined, void of emotions and full of peace. Slowly, and very carefully, I inched my way back to the door. But without warning, she moved. I froze as part of her body twisted slightly up in the air and then down again to face the wall. She let out a deep yawn before sweetly mumbling into the pillows, "Honey, is that you?"

Surely, she was dreaming.

Then, in an unusually high, perky voice, "What time is it?"

Cameron, with Hank and Baily right behind, opened the door fully, "Morning!" he exclaimed as he pushed past me to get to this person in the bed.

Confused, I moved closer to the bed. There's no way this was Margaret that Cameron was hugging so tightly, and Baily was licking affectionately. I opened the blind for light and gasped.

"Morning, darling," my mother said, sitting straight up with a lively grin on her face.

"What are you doing here?" I beamed, leaping over Baily to hug her.

I turned to Hank, smiling. "Did you know she was here?"

He nodded, giving me a quick and indifferent grin.

I turned to Cameron. "Did you know she was coming—"

"Of course they did!" my mother said, beaming. "I finally got hold of Hank because you weren't answering your phone last night." She threw the covers off and raised her body out of Samantha's bed. "I left a message with Margaret yesterday saying I'd be stopping here before going to your aunt's," she said as she pulled the plush black sleeping mask off her head. "It was all so last minute, and I didn't want you making a fuss." She coughed a bit. "I was only stopping through to give my condolences to Margaret."

I turned slightly toward Hank. "That's *so* sweet of you, Mom," I said, perhaps with a little added emphasis for his benefit. I twisted back to her. "How did you get here from the airport then?"

"A good ole' taxi," she said.

"I didn't get *any* message from Margaret," I said, rolling my eyes for her to see. "You know I would've been there to get you if I did, right?"

She squeezed my hand. "Of course, darling. Not to worry. I'm here now, so that's what matters." I'm grateful she's able to accept Margaret for who she is. She didn't seem to mind that Margaret had conveniently forgotten to give me the message, making plans not to be here when she knew my mother would be.

Given that my mother was fully prepared to take the train to see her sister, I decided I would drive her. I've missed her, and even though she still offers her unsolicited opinions on things like my hair or clothes, spending time catching up is exactly what I needed. I was looking for someone who could take up the slack of a girlfriend even if for one day. Val's been busy with Robert lately to be that big, loud voice in my head offering advice or comfort when I needed it.

"I'll put some coffee on," I said and then we all left her to get dressed.

In the kitchen, after awkwardly saying goodbye to Cameron and wishing Hank a good day, I contemplated calling Margaret after notifying the school office I was... sick. Maybe I was looking for an apology from Margaret or at least an acknowledgement of her actions. But then again, I knew better. The last thing I wanted was for Margaret to turn it all around, blaming me for somehow not knowing my mother was coming.

• • •

"Hank seemed a bit cranky this morning," my mother commented as we sat at the kitchen table with our scrambled eggs.

"Yeah, he's probably upset with me for harassing him about his mother being here." I paused briefly. "I know he's grieving, so it's probably added stress for him. He doesn't want her being alone right now."

She gave me a sideways glance before turning her eyebrows down. "Is that all?"

"Isn't that enough?" My voice was small.

After giving me a penetrating look again, she lifted the corner of one of the placemats on the table. Underneath it was a neon blue *Post-it Note*— the same neon blue *Post-it Note* I'd left for Hank to read on the living room table last night. With my brain on wine, I'd made the lousy choice of confronting him with the "golden earring" on a small piece of paper.

I grabbed it from her hand, silently reading my messy handwriting.

Has Robyn been looking for this? Found it in your car.

What is it about red wine that makes me so stupid? I'd completely confused a bad idea for a good one. I was certain my heart was going to pound out of my chest.

My mother gave me an unbearable long-concerned look and said, "Well, it's a good thing I came into the living room first, Allie."

"What do you mean?" I swallowed hard.

"Darling," she began as she casually stood up from the table, stretched and then moved to the sink with her coffee cup. "It seems to me you're making up this silly story of Hank and this Robyn woman in your head."

I couldn't think of anything to say in response.

My mother came back to the table and put her hands on my shoulders. "Based on what you've told me about her so far, it's probably driving the way you've been communicating with him too."

"Yes, but that earring was in Hank's car. I know for certain it isn't Sam's, and Margaret doesn't wear earrings." Overcome with emotions, I took a deep breath before continuing. "And I found it the day after Hank's office Christmas party."

She gave my shoulders a supportive squeeze.

I twisted around to her. "I don't trust her."

"Uh-uh," she said almost in a whisper.

"I don't," I said again. "I see her *likes* and *comments* on Hank's posts. It's a bit stalky if you ask me."

"Stalky of you or stalky of her?" my mother asked.

I frowned as she cleared her throat. Now that I have *Facebook*, *yes*, *Facebook*, I can't stop myself from wasting time following Robyn and her updates—despite my best intentions of only using it to post *Teacher Time* articles to all my followers. All eight of them.

My mother took my hand in hers, clearing her throat again. "Allie, that earring was part of a set I bought you for Christmas—"

"*What?*" I squealed.

"Remember when I was visiting in December—"

"Uh, huh," I said quickly, nodding my head up and down.

"Well, after Christmas shopping with Hank and Cam, I was showing them the earrings on the way home from the mall... one must've dropped out of the box. I couldn't find it, so I had to give you that purple scarf, remember?" she said. "And I *was* going to buy you another pair, but when I saw it sitting on top of your note last night, I—" She grabbed the *Post-it Note* and wagged it in front of me. "I immediately hid it *and* the earring."

I breathed a huge sigh of relief as I slumped further in the kitchen chair. "So... he didn't see anything, right?"

She handed back the *Post-it Note*. "I hope not," she said sternly.

"Thanks for that," I said. "I feel better." But did I really because Hank hadn't said much to me this morning.

"Remember, Allie," she said, gently squeezing my hand this time, "insecurity is loud... and it can create a negative result."

I nodded, tearing the *Post-it Note* in little, tiny pieces.

"You two need to keep your communication lines open so you don't start drifting apart," she said, gathering plates from the table.

My eyes followed her to the sink. "I know, but it seems most of our communication revolves around Margaret these days," I said with a weak mouth and pouting lips. "It was better when our conversations used to be about George... or the kids or the house."

My mother nodded encouragingly.

To lift my mood, I stood up, stretching, and changed the subject—my new and exciting writing venture! And when I finished, she clasped her hands tightly and then pulled me in for a hug. "*Oh*, Allie, that's wonderful!" she cried, insisting we go to the overrated outlet mall and then out for a garlicky pasta lunch before the two-hour drive to my aunt's. How a mother's visit could clear up so many things in her daughter's head. *I hope Samantha and I get to enjoy this kind of bond.*

18 – Movin' in and Texting Out

Are you there, George? It's me, Allie.

I should be sleeping by now, but it's hard when your room smells of paint. Yes, paint. How long did it take for Margaret to decide after I left with my mother this morning that it'd be a good day to have Keith tear apart the bathroom wall to fix the leak and then finish painting our room?

Besides this, no one bothered letting me know she'd taken full control of the house again—arranging furniture in the living room, emptying the freezer, and refilling it with aluminum foil-wrapped and plastic bagged goods, and cluttering the counters with her useless appliances. Do we really need a bread maker the size of a smart car or a chicken rotisserie with spindly rotating bits?

If it weren't for chanting 'mind over matter' while waiting for my sleeping pill to kick in, I'd be in a padded cell with flickering lights and mean nurses, or worse, a prison cell for murder—sorry, George, those words might've gone too far, but isn't there some way you can be that little voice in her head—like a TV voiceover that provides a running commentary to help with her judgment of what might be considered good or bad, acceptable or unacceptable?

I miss you terribly!

Allie xoxo

The trouble with not being able to sleep at night is that it can make you feel like a zombie the next day. And the trouble with a drug-induced sleep is that it can also make you feel like a zombie the next day. *Which is better?*

Because I'd opted for a sleeping pill that didn't quite clear out of my system, I was probably the least responsive participant in the *How to Write a Children's Book* workshop. I need a different prescription because I'd barely managed to get my name right when we all introduced ourselves. And then I said I was in kindergarten. The instructor, though, spoke very gently to me after that—doubtless he assumed I was suffering from early onset dementia.

I recovered my wits somewhat but at lunch break, I snuck off for a twenty-minute nap. When I woke up an hour after, I felt confused and exposed. Confused because I thought I'd properly set the timer on my phone, and exposed, because of the location of my nap—inside my car parked in the middle of a busy downtown lot full of pedestrians and crazy drivers who didn't believe normal driving rules applied.

After wiping the drool from my mouth and the gunk out of my eyes, I hurried to grab a tall green tea and straighten my mussed hair in a coffee shop across the street. Ten minutes later, I was back inside the library, catching my breath. I hesitated to go back into the workshop and interrupt the speaker. I knew I was going to be seen an annoyance, an unfavorable latecomer who'd had the gall to walk in with a large hot drink, so I decided to wait for the next break.

When I sat on one of the hard-plastic seats outside the meeting room, my phone pinged through my purse. Eagerly, I pulled it out and read the text:

[Where are you?]

Stumped at first with the unfamiliar phone number, I chuckled inside when some of the digits finally registered. It was charming Mike—also attractive, extremely witty, and recently retired. He was here to learn the craft of children's writing after spending the last thirty years as an accountant. He'd told me his life story during the morning break, including details about his recent divorce from wife number three. When he'd given me his number and asked for mine, I was flattered, thinking I might be considered wife number four. It felt good. *Really* good. But silly me. What he really wanted was the useful writing links I'd discovered after signing up for this workshop.

I took a sip of my tea and replied with a slight smile.

[I'm sitting outside the door]

His reply came within seconds.

[Why?]

My fingers flew over the keyboard like a ninja. Charming Mike seemed like someone who loved to play.

[I fell asleep in the car. LOL! Too embarrassed to come in. I'll wait til 2:30]

His reply about a minute later.

[I can't see you outside the door]

Me, giggling to myself.

[You must be blind as a bat]

Him about a second later.

[What's wrong with you? You're acting strange]

And before I had the chance to reply, he sent another text.

[We need toilet paper]

Toilet paper? Well, the instructor did say he was going to show us some creative writing strategies. My fingers raced over the virtual keyboard again.

[Nothing's wrong... just wiped. TP? Sounds interesting. I'll get more from the bathroom and come back in]

Him.

[Are you drunk?]

Whoa, Nelly. I pressed my back up against the chair. Was there a joke in there somewhere?

Minutes later, he texted again.

[I'm calling Henry]

Henry? I jumped to my feet. How did he... wait... this wasn't Charming Mike who'd been texting me. Bloody hell, it was Margaret.

My chest tightened. I mean *really* tightened. *When the hell did she get a phone?!* I gasped for air, throwing my cell into my purse before pulling the heavy metal door open and walking back into the workshop. I didn't want to be sitting in the quiet and still hallway frantically obsessing about what this could all mean for me now that she has a *friggin'* cell phone—*and* has figured out how to text on it already.

The rest of the day, *thank God*, was delightfully insightful and informative as I learned about the writing industry. And after being around these aspiring authors during an early Japanese dinner, it gave me what I needed—excitement and a sense of hope, again.

When I got home, I threw my coat and tote bag on the hallway bench and headed directly for the stairs with a supersize pack of toilet paper under my arm. I was eager to find a quiet part of the house to start writing.

Unfortunately, my feet hadn't even touched the stairs before Margaret's chilling voice rang out like the voice of doom. "Well, *there* you are."

I turned to see her sitting in the wingback chair in the living room watching a basketball game on TV with Hank and Cameron.

She twisted her whole body around further. "We were beginning to worry about you."

I hardly think so. I texted Hank twenty minutes ago.

Forcing a smile, I kneeled to rub Baily's belly. "Yeah, well, I'm here now, but going up to change."

"How was the workshop?" Hank asked before quickly returning his attention to the game.

I stood up quickly. "Good!" I answered with a smile, pleased we were able to smooth things over last night. Though, it feels like we'd only put a couple coats of plaster on our *Margaret* issue—the stubborn issue in our marriage.

Cameron popped his head up slightly from the sofa, seemingly unperturbed by our incident in the bathroom yesterday morning. "Mom, it's your favorite team playing."

More like favorite logo and uniform color. "Oh yeah, right," I said, trying to sound mildly interested.

"I'll be down soon," I said happily. When I turned to face the stairs again, I caught sight of what was on the coffee table in front of Margaret— the empty box that presumably held her new cell phone with its tiny instruction booklet. I climbed the stairs wearily. Just knowing she's now part of the mobile world is unnerving. *Fuck, fuck, fuck.*

Shortly after settling myself on the bed, my head snapped up when I heard Margaret across the hall in Samantha's room. I leaped off the bed, hurrying to shut the door, but it was too late. She was already at it, holding a tampon box in her hand.

"I found these in your bathroom today," she said, shaking the box at me as it rattled. "Hope you're not using them."

I stared at her blankly. At times like this, I forcibly have to bite my lip to prevent myself from exploding.

"I really don't think it's wise for a woman your age to be using them..." she hesitated before continuing, "if you know what I mean."

"No, Margaret. I don't know what you mean," I countered, hoping to end the conversation as I hightailed it the bathroom. Though half amused, I swung around and faced her. "But, why don't you tell me."

"Because they can cause excitement." She eyed my waist before eyeing further down.

"You're kidding, right?" I shook my head before closing the bathroom door.

She muttered through it. "I'm sure your friend Val likes to put 'em up there."

Oh. My. Goodness. Where was this woman's filter?

I could hear her waiting outside the bathroom door, surprised she hadn't pushed it open, wedging her face in like Baily would sometimes do to watch me pee.

Minutes later, I heard her voice behind the door again. "Your phone's ringing."

Shit. I rushed to rinse my hands before she could answer it. But when I came out of the bathroom, she was standing there with a big smile slapped across her face. "Of course, Samantha. Here she is now." She examined my phone before proudly handing it to me. "You have the *same* one as I do."

I took a deep breath, exasperated that Margaret did indeed have the same device as *me* and that she was sitting on my bed now. I held the phone to my ear. "Hi, honey," I said as cheerfully as I could muster.

"Hey, Mom," Samantha replied, sounding much better than the last time we spoke.

Margaret flipped through one of my design magazines, pretending to be reading it. But I knew she was intently listening to Samantha and me talk about her new job at her favorite jean store.

Samantha stopped mid-sentence with a mix of frustration and weariness in her voice. "Oh, and guess what?"

I sat on the chair. "What?" I said cautiously.

"My car is in the shop again."

"*Again?*" I moaned.

Margaret's face was full of concern as she crossed her legs and folded her arms. "What's wrong?" she mouthed to me.

I shook my head, dismissing her while Samantha continued telling me about her car troubles. I knew what was coming next.

"I might need to borrow some money until I get paid."

Bingo.

I sighed deeply, getting up to close the curtains. "Maybe we can use our mechanic. He knows what he's doing," I said. "Obviously the one you have is costing an arm and a leg."

"It's fine," she said, sounding distracted by something or someone in the background. "They've already ordered the car parts—"

"I'll need to speak with your dad before we put any more money into it." What I really wanted to say was *before we put any more money into that piece of junk your grandmother helped you buy.*

I gave Margaret the same disgruntled look she gave me while I waited for a response from Samantha. "Are you still there?" I said after several moments of silence.

Margaret threw the magazine down and stood up. She motioned me to give her my phone, but I spun around. All I could hear were muffled background sounds. "Sam?" I said with a little less patience as I fiddled with the curtain tassel.

And then I heard, "*Is your mom still there?*"

My heart stopped. I would've recognized that voice anywhere.

"Yes. Sorry, Mom. I'm here—"

"Sam," I growled into the phone, "why is Keith there—"

"He explained everything. And he's not the bad guy you've made him out to be."

What had he fed her? Besides telling her she was the only one in his life. And this, after Val and I told her about the girl with the purple hair in the sports car picking him up on the day of her grandfather's funeral. *Lies. Lies. Lies.*

A sudden sense of Samantha feeling like a stranger overwhelmed me. My voice, cold. "Your dad and I have no money to loan you this time." I was angry she was back with this asshole—the same asshole who was here yesterday, fixing the shower and painting the bedroom. If only Hank knew what kind of person Keith was, I'm sure he wouldn't have let him in the house. Truth was, I didn't think we'd be seeing him again after Samantha ended their relationship. But then again, he's still Margaret's stupid handyman.

"What if she really needs the money?" Margaret asked after Samantha hung up on me for calling Keith an a-hole. "And what's all the fuss about Keith?"

"She doesn't need the money, trust me," I said, ignoring her second question.

Margaret eyed me suspiciously. "And how do you know this exactly?"

"Call it instinct," I said. "We're not sending her any more money right now."

"I think Henry needs to know about your unwillingness to help her," she protested, marching out of the room.

Not if I get to him first. I grabbed my phone off the dresser and lapsed into a dismayed silence as I texted Hank. While I waited for him to come upstairs, I changed into a t-shirt and leggings. There was no way I could start writing now—I was going to need a good workout at the gym.

After ten minutes of waiting, I noticed Hank's stupid phone charging on the bedside table. Aggravated, I went downstairs. And as suspected, Hank was talking to Samantha on Margaret's phone at the kitchen table. I could see the twinkle in his eyes as he spoke with her. It'd been hard for him to figure out where and how he fit into her life. I knew he missed their relationship before his role as a father had changed.

I waved my hands wildly to him. "Say, *no!*" I mouthed. "Say, *no...*"

Sure enough, he smiled, shaking his head at me.

I sighed heavily, watching how ridiculously happy he was to be that great ally of hers—guiding her in making smart decisions, supporting her in her bad ones, and letting her take the lead when it came to their relationship. I didn't want to burst his bubble. *How could I?* He was dealing with the loss of a parent and that bereaved struggle with intense emotions such as depression worried me. When Hank gets depressed, even mildly, it can be a dark ordeal.

I got his attention again, this time pointing to my gym bag.

"Just a minute, sweetheart," he said to Samantha.

He smiled broadly at me. "Okay, have a good workout."

I smiled in return which had nothing to do with happiness and left, slightly slamming the front door behind me.

In the car, my phone buzzed. Thinking it might be Samantha wanting to apologize for hanging up, I reached into my purse and read the message.

[Time for wine?]

A small grin blinked on and off my face as I backed out of the driveway. Instead of turning in the gym's direction, I drove around the corner to Val's. *She certainly had the best time sensor known to womankind.*

19 - "C" Ain't Just for "Cookie"

After finishing our second bottle of wine and a plate of cookies, I stupidly told Val about Margaret's tampon comment. We had a good laugh, but then she grabbed my phone off the kitchen counter, searching for the string of texts Margaret had sent me earlier. I could see the vein on Val's temple throbbing with a mix of mischief and anger. Did I mention she was also fighting with her boyfriend Robert? Suspicious of a heavy perfume scent on his shirt or something about an investment in Costa Rica—*or was it Ecuador?*

I tried seizing Val's hand from texting Margaret. Honestly. But she grabbed my hand away from hers and hit send. Without showing me Margaret's quick reply, Val, with a malevolent and precise smile spread across her face, responded. That's when I lunged at her. Unsuccessfully. After regaining my balance, I took a few steps toward her. "Give me my phone," I moaned, signaling impatiently with my hand. I knew Val too well and when her confidence level was at an all-time low, as it was tonight, her moral values vanished. She could be fragile and uncertain one moment, and then the next, be pulsing with boldness and audacity.

My mouth dropped in horror after reading Val's second message to Margaret.

[Maybe what you need is to stick a tampon up your c—]

I slammed my phone down on the counter. "Really?!" I squawked, my skin flushing. "Did you *really* need to drop the *c-bomb?*" Even I wouldn't use that word with my worst enemy. It's terribly offensive. I glared at her. "She's probably on her knees right now praying for you, Val."

"Sorry, I couldn't help it," she cowered before pouring more wine. She unwrapped her legs from the chair and stood up. "When it comes to Margaret, you have a tenuous grip on your boundaries. And she doesn't seem to have much respect for them either," she said.

"Well, I think you have a tenuous grip on reality... making all these ridiculous plans with Robert. And what's with you investing with him in some property down south—you barely know him." I softened my tone a little. "If he's anything like his lying, broke, womanizing son then he's playing you for a fool!"

Val's eyes widened as she looked past me. I followed her gaze and saw Robert standing in the kitchen doorway with an oversized bouquet of deep red roses.

Without saying another word, I spun around and grabbed my coat.

By the time I walked the seven-minute trip home, I was sure Val and Robert were in knee deep sexual reconciliation. *Assholes.* I was also sure when I made it to the front door, I had my keys and cell phone with me.

In my eagerness to get inside our warm house, I did what I had to do. Now, it could've been my brain was frustratingly cold or foolishly drunk, but either way, throwing snowballs at our bedroom window to wake up Hank was a dumb move. Most of the snowballs ricocheted off the bricks, missing the window altogether. But I was determined, so I stood closer to the window and aimed for the middle of it. And when I did, I slipped on a stupid patch of ice and hit my face on the edge of the front steps. I was crying when the bright porch light flicked on. Speechless, I lay there like a poor lost child, staring up at Hank as a tremendous stinging sensation radiated from the right side of my face.

Thirty minutes later, squealing stretchers, howling patients, and the smells of antiseptics in the hospital corridors filled me with more misery as we sat in the emergency room waiting for my name to be called for stitches. Hank took the hand that wasn't busy checking the gauze pad on my cheek and gently squeezed it. "Want another tea?" he asked, shifting his body in the hard bucket tandem seat.

"Nah," I breathed, relieved he wasn't upset about my reckless night at Val's or for robbing him of a goodnight's sleep. Resting on his shoulder, I twisted my sore head up at him. "Did you hear back from Cam?"

He glanced up at the TV monitor in the corner of the room, exhaling. "No... my phone's dead. But I'm sure he got the message." He stretched out his legs in front of him.

"What about your mother?" I took a deep breath. "Does she know we're here?"

"No... strangely enough, she went to bed without saying goodnight," he said.

"Mmmm," I murmured, knowing she was most likely livid with Val's vulgar text. "That *is* unusual... but I'm sure she was just tired."

He nodded when I looked at him for confirmation. "Hopefully we're home before she wakes up," he said. "She won't be too happy about all this."

I bit my lip and said nothing. *Are we twelve?* I squeezed his hand, stretching out my legs too. Slightly irritated, it still felt good surviving without our phones. Removed from the matrix, we distracted ourselves under the low lights from witnessing the surrounding emotions with junk food from the vending machines and simple conversation—conversation that didn't include Margaret or Keith. We cuddled like a happy little couple, completing magazine quizzes and teasing one another about aging body parts. Finally, cuddling in a little closer, we fantasized the notion of me becoming a notable children's author with lots of money before a tall, handsome nurse named Brendon called my name, breaking up what seemed to be a rare intimate time together.

Three hours and four stitches later, Hank and I were finally on our way to the car. We saw Helen, George's nurse, entering through the main doors. Presumably starting her shift. After exchanging a few words and catching her up on life without George, she straightened her coat and said,

"Tell Margaret hello for me. I didn't get a chance when I saw her at the bank the other day."

"Oh, I'm sure you were busy, but I'll tell her," I promised.

"Well, no. I just didn't want to interrupt her. She was busy with some good-looking fellow and one of the bank managers."

Good-looking fellow at the bank with Margaret? Only one person came to mind. I managed a smile as I turned to Hank. Not surprising, his eyes were wide. "Okay, Helen. I better get this one home," he said, gently bumping me before giving her a quick hug.

We walked in silence across the parking lot in the brisk early morning air. And it wasn't until Hank pulled out of the parking space that he turned to me. "What the hell was Helen talking about?"

I swallowed hard, trying hard to think of something to say other than *I told you so.*

"My mother at the bank..." he said, "going over papers with a bank manager... *and* with someone other than me?"

"I tried to tell you," I said. *Didn't I?* I cleared my throat, fully aware I haven't been the greatest communicator of late. The problem is, I've been so lost and distracted with my own stuff, it's been difficult to be effective and follow through with other people's shit. Even though Helen may have unknowingly provided a perfect segue into my suspicions of Keith, I regretted the timing. My stomach was aching, and my cheek was throbbing. I certainly didn't want to get into this with Hank now, especially with him driving, but I had to.

I leaned over, lightly squeezing his arm. "Keith is in a lot of debt and who knows what else..." I took a calming breath, saddened that our hospital date night was ending on such a low note. "And he's sweet-talking your mother into some loans. It's clear now."

Moments later, he let out a long, aggravated sigh. "And what about Sam? Has she been lending him money?"

"Well..." I smoothed the back of my hair down, playing for time as I waited for him to change lanes. "Probably," I muttered, knowing he'd soon connect the dots that Samantha's car repair bills had undoubtedly been inflated. My stomach spasmed thinking about her as we turned onto our street.

•   •   •

We nearly tripped over Margaret's luggage lined up at the door when we walked into the house. It was dark, except for the low light in the kitchen rendering a malevolent looking entity bouncing on the far wall. I slowly hung up my coat and put my boots away, blinking away the unnerving shadow.

Feeling a little unsettled, I cautiously followed Hank into the kitchen, but stopped dead in my tracks when I saw Margaret standing around the corner scowling at me. I glared back at her before she stepped forward and walked past me.

"Henry, I'd like it if you drove me home now," she said in a low gravelly voice, much like the creature reflected on the kitchen wall moments ago would've sounded.

"Okay," he said quickly, clearly not up for any conversation or argument with her.

After watching them leave in Hank's car, I slumped down into the sofa. I felt bad for him. He was most likely getting an earful from Margaret. I sighed deeply, draping myself over the sofa's soft arm, listening to the eerie silence of dawn. But it wasn't long before I got up again. My burning stomach needed food.

I noticed Margaret's phone on the counter when I was buttering my toast. It was just sitting there, calling out to me. Obviously, I picked it up and opened the messaging app. With greasy fingers, I curiously scrolled through Val's drunken text messages to Margaret last night. Seconds later, my mouth dropped as I stared at the screen silently cursing her. No wonder Margaret had left in such a hurry. Not only were Val's replies offensive and callous, but nowhere did they mention they were from her.

Naturally, Margaret would've thought they were from me—it was my phone.

I didn't bother with the toast crumbs on the counter and trudged back to the sofa, flopping on it. My body felt like lead as I lay there. The conflict. The drama. It was weighing heavily on me, causing an unpleasant state of uneasiness to roll in like a fog. I closed my eyes, permitting myself to detach from last night. And from the past few weeks, months... and years.

$$\bullet \qquad \bullet \qquad \bullet$$

"How's the cheek?"

When my eyes popped open, Hank was sitting on the edge of the coffee table looking drained.

I sat up, waiting for my vision to focus. "Sorry," I mumbled, feeling last night's repercussions of wine, sugary cookies, and a wipeout. "When did you get back?"

"Just now," he said. "You should probably go get your car from Val's."

I nodded, giving him a tired smile as I picked up three sofa cushions off the floor. "How did it go with your mother?"

"Well, she didn't say anything in the car but did when we got to her condo."

"What did she say?" I asked slowly.

As expected, Margaret told Hank about the uncouth texts she received. "Look, let her cool off," I said after telling him the texts were from Val. "Distance will do us all some good—and I know she won't want to hear from me for a while anyway." I sat next to him. "Did you mention anything about being at the bank with Keith?"

"Not yet. I will—later this week," he said. "I want to go over some papers with her... and find out her plans." He stood up. "In the meantime, Keith is not welcome here."

A-men.

"So, what about your mom—will she be okay on her own?" I asked, feeling as though I were on the brink of reclaiming my house.

"Maybe," he said, "but I'll get Cam to stay with her til I get back. He can—"

"*Back?*" I said, slightly panicky. "Back from where?"

"I have to travel for a few days," he said, sounding irritated. "I told you."

Right. He did, but in passing.

"Cam can use my car to get around," he continued before giving off a great big yawn.

I yawned too. "All right," I said, watching him climb the stairs.

For a moment, I put aside life's worries and focused on what was ahead—alone time. And plenty of it. A small smile formed across my lips as I sank back into the sofa again. My whole body buzzed at the thought of crafting out my children's book in a quiet, drama-free house for the next few days.

20 - He Loves Me, He Loves Me Not

Are you there, George? It's me, Allie.

As daunting as this may sound, I'm going on a healthy juice cleanse. Yep. I'm going to detox my insides until they sparkle. I need to— Saturday night's wine at Val's caused a series of unfortunate events ending with Margaret leaving at the crack of dawn on Sunday and me looking like the bride of Frankenstein with a two-inch slash across my face.

On a better note, the next few days are going to be distraction free around here. I'm going to get back to the gym and also write a children's book. I'm going to be quite famous, actually. Okay, maybe that's a pipedream but I need something that'll get me up in the mornings and make me want to sing. Find your passion, a reason to smile, or what's the point? Isn't that what you used to always say?

Keep you posted with all that's going on 'round here.

Allie xoxo

"Ready?" Hank asked, smiling as he watched me walk into the kitchen early Monday morning. He looked happy, standing there in his light gray jacket and dark denim jeans.

Perhaps he was relieved to be getting away from me.

"All set," I replied, smiling back.

He dumped his cereal bowl in the sink. It was nice to know we had our kitchen back and even better to know we didn't have Margaret hot on our heels putting the cereal bowl into the dishwasher.

As I ran the last of the carrots and a bruised apple in the juicer, Hank wrote out a note to Cameron and when he finished, he reached into his pocket for two twenty-dollar bills, placing them on top of it with his car keys. I looked at Hank. "Forty dollars for gas?" That, to my mind, simply wasn't going to be enough, because Margaret would have Cameron driving her all around town. Believe me.

"Right," he agreed. He opened his wallet and placed another forty dollars under the keys.

Feeling a flush of warm relief, I added hearts at the end of Hank's note and reminded Cameron to text me when he got to school. Even though he'd become a competent driver during his short time on the roads, I still had him text whenever he'd get to his destination or was going to a new one. However, this week, I was going to ease up a little. Texting every time he got to the grocery store with Margaret, or the bank, the drug store, the community center, the fabric store, you name it, would be onerous. And besides, he wasn't too thrilled about staying with his grandmother in the first place. Who could blame him? But once he settled in, he'd be happy to have the attention and the partial freedom of living away from home. It'll be good practice for me, too, because in a little less than two years, he'll be off to school. Coping with those sad feelings when seeing his bedroom empty, is going to be hard—granted it'll be clean, but still.

As predicted, traffic was heavy. I adjusted my mirror when we got on the highway, glancing quickly at Hank in the passenger's seat. For the past fifteen minutes, he'd been nervously sorting out work on his thin sleek laptop.

I tried to keep my thoughts to myself and my eyes on the road so he could concentrate but could hold back no more. "I'll miss you," I blurted out.

He gave me a quick but distracted smile before returning to his computer. I knew he had more important things on his mind than to worry about me for four days. Besides nailing his presentations, his mother was probably at the forefront of his concerns. In the span of twenty-four hours, she'd called or messaged at least fifteen times to complain, which amounted to about one-and-a-half complaints every two hours if we were to do the math.

Her guilt trips. In her world, using guilt as a way to get to Hank was her deadliest weapon. Yesterday, complaints had been flying left, right and center. She called to complain about the heating system in her condo, the wobbly refrigerator and all its strange noises, the lack of water pressure in her bathroom, and then the bent mailbox key. On top of all this, she'd forgotten her cellphone. Relentless? Yes, because she carried on via text after Cameron had returned from delivering it to her. She texted Hank to ask if she'd be charged long distance fees if she needed to call him while he was away—which I told him to say yes in all CAPS. And then she asked if he could come by later to see if her computer had a virus. Apparently, it was operating slowly, too slow to play Scrabble online she said. Did I mention she'd already complained about leaving her pills behind on the kitchen table and how much her legs and hips were aching without them? She'd ended her text by asking Hank if he was coming to drop off her pills and fix her computer if he could bring her teacup and dishes. She didn't want to risk them getting broken. Why wouldn't Hank be worried? Worried and drained with a mix of frustration, perhaps?

How George survived with her for as long as he did, bemused me. It couldn't have been easy for him. She'd depended on him even for the little things, and right to the bitter end. In fairness though, I was sure it hadn't been easy on her, either. However, she could've lightened up on him when he was weak. She'd get upset and lose it with George when her food tasted too unpleasant for him to eat, when his spirits were too low for her to lift, and when she'd find strands of his gray hair tangled in her toothbrush or mixed in with her dinner. Now, there might've been a marginal chance that this behavior of hers was normal. After all, she isn't a natural nurturer, but part of me wants to believe her behavior was an involuntary defense mechanism against the enormous loss she foresaw every time she looked at him.

Hank had finally finished what he was doing. He closed his computer, turning his head to me. "I'll miss you too."

It warmed my heart to hear those words, but it'd passed quickly when I suddenly saw myself from the outside. It was a bizarre feeling. Here I was, unsure of what part Hank was going to miss. Was he going to miss the *me* that was tired with work, frustrated with his mother and insecure with aging? Or was he going to miss the *me* before all the aforementioned angsts had set in?

I glanced at him when traffic picked up, grasping at reality. For the sake of him not having to feel like he'd have to worry while he was away, I leaned over. "I'll make sure to check in on your mother. I promise," I said, hoping I didn't sound too riled.

"It's fine, Allie. I told her I'd be busy for the next few days." He rested his head back into the seat, closing his eyes. "Cam will be there, and Edith will be around too."

Well, now I felt bad. Bad, because he probably felt he couldn't depend on me to be a supportive, loving and caring daughter-in-law to his grieving widowed mother when he was two thousand miles away. Although Cameron would be there, I think Hank would envision her waking up at midnight with the lights and TV still on or her shuffling around in her housecoat eating sweet, mushy corn out of a tin can. Images like these would weigh on him—especially after all the bloody phone calls and text messages yesterday. Meanwhile, here I was in the throes of peri-pause, left with the daily burdens, including dealing with a rambunctious seven-month-old dog all while trying to write a children's book.

Feeling a little defensive, I placed my hand on his knee when we stopped at the last set of lights before the airport entrance. "Okay, that's good... it's good to know she's capable of getting others to help too. She'll be fine," I said, immediately wincing for how quickly the words had come out of my mouth.

Hank kept silent, analyzing and processing like he always does. Although I'm not sure why—this wasn't the first time he'd heard statements like those coming from me. There'd been little variation to them over the years. I felt the familiar tension between my shoulder blades brought on with the mention of her name—ten ways to kill a marriage, and a mother-in-law is one of them.

"You're right. She'll be fine," he finally said, putting his laptop back in his briefcase.

I swallowed hard, hating myself. I shouldn't have mentioned his mother when we were about to say goodbye. There was no time to revive this grim mood between us. *Damn it, Margaret. Even when you're not here, you're still here.*

When we got to the drop-off area at the departure terminal, Hank reached over and gave me a quick kiss. "I'll let you know when I'm there," he said, getting out of the car.

"I love you," I said just as he was about to close the door.

He popped his head back in. "You, too," he said quickly.

A hurried goodbye was never a good thing, especially at a place already filled with nervous people rushing around for their flights. I watched him in the rearview mirror as he grabbed his luggage out of the back. When he closed the hatchback, I gave him a little wave.

Back on the highway, my gravity shifted again. Whenever either of us replied to an *I love you* with a dismissive and quick *You, too*, it usually meant we were upset. *You, too* in return to an *I love you* should be used with some caution between a husband and wife, because it can carry very little romantic meaning. Normally this wouldn't have been such a big deal, except he was going to be away for four days.

I struggled to stay positive as the sun warmed me through the car window. I continued driving, getting ready for the next exit. *But fuck it.* I needed a mental health day, so I picked up speed, skipping the exit and taking the next one that led home.

After leaving a message for Headmaster Thomas that I was still recovering from Friday's illness and would need at least three more days to recover, I clambered up the stairs to change into my gym clothes. Moaning when I caught a glimpse of myself in the mirror, I flopped on the bed. I lay there for a moment before realizing I didn't want to wallow in self-pity. *Nope, not today.* Besides getting to the gym and wanting to detox my body, I have a book to write. With a little gusto, I jumped up, grabbed my bag and headed out the door.

Gwyneth, with her clipboard, was patrolling the gym when I got there. To her credit, she did smile when I strolled toward the change rooms. Maybe because she saw some commitment from me instead of being another lazy donor. *That's right, darling. I'm here for a purpose, and not because I'm locked into this gym's pricey contract and feeling guilty about it.* After my workout, I drove across the street to the grocery store. Despite my casual goodbye with Hank at the airport, the day felt like progress. Even while I looked for a parking spot, I was mentally making a shopping list for the rest of my cleanse.

In less than ten minutes in the store, I had my basket filled with an assortment of greens and colorful fruit. I then perused the dairy section looking for on sale items, but suddenly stopped when I turned the corner toward the meat counter. Waves of anxiety reached their peak in seconds. I dropped my loaded basket on an empty bread rack and made a swift exit out the doors. I raced across the parking lot, checking over my shoulder. When I got inside the car, I slammed the door shut before letting out a rather loud scream.

Of all the people I'd have to run into today, it had to be her? With Edith? And smiling and looking like her old self? This was *my* territory. *My* neck of the woods. She didn't like paying the super expensive prices in an organic store like that. I took a deep calming breath, staring out the window. When I slowly released my breath, I noticed *McNab's Vacuum*, opposite ends of the plaza. It was decked out in red and blue sale banners across the front of it. *McNab's Vacuum*, a little shop Margaret saw when she'd come with me to my gym orientation a few weeks ago—the same stupid shop that sells handheld steam attachments for her vacuum cleaner.

Not surprisingly, my phone pinged with a text when I started the car.

[Are you following me?]

Before I had a chance to reply, Margaret texted again.

[Heard it was Val who sent the vulgar messages. Calling and apologizing would still be nice. Why aren't you at work?]

My stomach muscles tightened as I texted back.

[Not feeling well. Needed groceries]

Margaret, seconds later.

[If you have a virus, you shouldn't be out spreading it!]

This was going nowhere fast. I had to take control and end this because I was starting to feel like I *was* sick.

[I'll call you tonight]

As I drove home without my detox items, I thought of Val. It was times like this when I needed her the most. Unfortunately, neither of us had reached out to the other yet. And at this point, I wasn't even sure who was mad at who.

My phone pinged with texts right up to the time I'd parked in the driveway. I was hopeful one of those pings might've been from Hank... or Samantha. But when I looked at my phone, I breathed out slowly and steadily, visualizing only toxic air because every single text had been from Margaret.

21 - Toxic Detox

Once upon a time, there lived a wicked witch...

Nah. *Delete, delete, delete.*

In a land far far away, there was an evil monster...

Hmmm. *Delete, delete, delete.*

There once lived a horrible beast...

Yikes. *Delete, delete, delete.*

I shook my head, trying to clear out the dark thoughts in it. They weren't helpful when a blank document glared at me, waiting for a story. A friendly, happy children's story.

For the past two hours, Margaret had fired off a series of texts:

[Where are you?]

[Why are you not answering me?]

[Are you that sick?]

[I'm calling Henry]

Hence the mood.

I finally appeased her, sending a message that started with:

[Sorry for Val's unkind words] and ended with:

[Going back to bed]

I sighed and put my phone on silent mode.

Like one of Margaret's pots of stew, my stomach gurgled and bubbled as I tried to massage the discomfort of knowing it wasn't going to be soothed anytime soon. I had two more pre-made detox juices I bought at a nearby health food store to drink.

I took a sip of the thick green liquid, trying not to gag as I stretched my back on the kitchen chair. *Moldy grass clippings anyone?* If anything, I was hoping the broccoli and spinach concoction would magically help get the creative juices I knew were within, flowing out of me. Because I had nothing. Nothing. Not even a made-up story buried in my head. I was *stuck, stuck, stuck.*

I looked under my chair at Baily before slowly hauling myself up. "Come on," I said, feeling an intense urge to crack my back. "Maybe a walk will do us some good."

Outside, I couldn't help but notice all the for-sale signs hammered into people's lawns. I also couldn't help but notice Val from a distance walking out of a house with a sale sign in front. No wonder she was a successful real estate agent in the neighborhood. It was hot with amenities and empty nesters who were flocking to condo living.

Instead of yelling out Val's name like a hillbilly, I eagerly waved my arm hoping to get her attention. But she didn't look. My shoulders dropped further when she got into her car and drove away in the opposite direction. Disappointed? Yes. Especially since she hadn't returned my texts.

After a few more blocks, we walked back home. Apart from sad feelings surfacing when I thought about Hank being miles away, hurt feelings surfaced when I thought about Val. We hadn't spoken since Saturday. It was our first fight, a landmark in our relationship. And given we're equally stubborn and independent, the longer the distance between us, I think the harder it's going to be to make-up—especially at this point in our lives when we're both trying to keep our own shit together.

Once settled on the kitchen chair again, I noticed a missed call from Hank. *Damn it.* I texted him after my call went to voice mail.

[Sorry I missed you. Call back if you can xo]

Twenty minutes passed without a reply. I grabbed my computer and climbed the stairs with Baily behind. After propping my body up in bed with pillows, I opened my blank document, hoping I'd get some words down before my next liquid meal. I stretched out my legs and within minutes, I was fighting the urge to sleep. *Note to self—Don't get on the bed in the middle of the day with work to do and not expect your eyelids to want to close.*

I propped myself up more, watching Baily aggressively chew his way through a bone. With a wagging tail, he looked at me as if to say he was happy and content. I blew him a restless kiss and turned to my screen again, strangely thinking about our beloved cat, Ruby. These two creatures wouldn't have liked each other—given Ruby's *I'm human, aren't I* personality, she certainly wouldn't have melted with Baily's charming and playful energy. She would've ruled him.

For a minute or two, I thought about the disharmony that could've been between Baily and Ruby before something happened. My muse had returned from her long vacation. In the zone, my mind raced on. I had it. A story about a happy dog who was ruled by a mean old cat. I started typing. And typing. My cramped fingers struggled to keep up. I typed and re-typed, several times over. And in less than two hours, I had thirty-two well-constructed and wildly imaginative sentences fit for the pages of a children's picture book.

After reading the story over and over, I was confident I had a ready to publish children's story. *How hard was that?* At this rate, I could fill a bookstore's whole top shelf in no time. I smiled to myself, pleased of my accomplishment.

It was time to celebrate with my next juice—a lovely thick mixture of pineapple, oranges, and carrots. I cracked open the lid, instinctively smelling it first. I gasped but took a sip, nearly choking. When I looked over at Baily, my horribly empty stomach growled listening to him eating his kibble dinner. That couldn't be a good sign if I was drooling over dog food, could it?

It took time but after finishing the bottle in disgust, we went for a walk through the dimly lit neighborhood. Distracted by thoughts of my finished manuscript and the horrible taste in my mouth, I hardly noticed that Baily had led the way to Val's. *Who's walking who?* I hesitated to turn onto her street, but he pulled fiercely on his leash. When we got to the fourth house, I stopped suddenly. I tugged Baily back with all my might, keeping him close as I hid behind a giant elm tree. Like a crazed stalker, I peeked around the tree's thick trunk, watching Val get out of Robert's car. Hurt she hadn't returned my texts, my stomach sank further when I heard laughter through the still air as the two walked hand in hand into her house.

When we got back from our walk, I saw another missed call from Hank—a big reminder to bring my phone next time. *Damn it again.* I called, leaving another voicemail before sending a series of colored hearts and emoji kisses. But then upstairs, after a long hot shower, my face shriveled when I saw another call from Hank. *What the hell?* I could usually hear the stupid ringtone a mile away. I stood there a moment before drying the rest of my body. Not daring to dwell on the fact that Hank might be getting frustrated with this phone tag nonsense, I called again. Voicemail. So, I left the same message, but this time, assuring him I'd be doing nothing but waiting by the phone.

It was time for another root juice. I wrinkled my nose smelling it, and then, within seconds of bravely gulping it down, my stomach churned the water and juice, sloshing it all around. I always had a poor record with feeling awful whenever I missed a meal, but after missing three, I felt sick. Nauseous. Dizzy and sweaty—the sensation felt a little deathlike. *Houston, we have a problem,* I murmured as I crawled up the stairs, slowly, like an injured sloth.

Unhappy, I lay face down on the bed with the covers over my head. If I passed out, no one's here to help me. No one to call an ambulance or bring me water. I could only wait it out, accept defeat, and see if I would feel better in the morning.

Several hours later, I woke up stiff and achy. I stared into the darkness before grabbing my phone off the side table and then groaning deeply when my eyes adjusted to the bright screen, seeing missed texts and calls from Hank. I groaned again when I looked at the time. It was either too late at night or too early in the morning to call where he was. I just couldn't do the math. Sighing, I gently rolled back over. Maybe I really was sick after all. A simple juice cleanse wouldn't make me feel this bad, would it? I sat up quickly, a little too quickly but reached blindly for my computer off the floor anyway. Wasting no time, I googled if a juice cleanse could make you sick. Within seconds, I discovered it could. *Something to do with toxins and metals in your body?* Even though my initial research may have missed the part about the importance of pre-cleansing, I was done. It was over. I *hate* detoxes. I snapped shut the computer and then sank down on the bed with a piercing headache.

It was six thirty in the morning when I woke up, seriously imagining a truckload of water parked out front. After risking it all by drinking water from the bathroom faucet, I called Hank—quite sure it'd be earlier for him. Seconds later, he answered. Thinking there'd be a showdown, he surprised me with a concerned voice.

"Allie, I've been trying to reach you all day yesterday and last night," he said. "Are you really sick?"

Sick? Right. I forgot about telling Margaret that I was. I also forgot about silencing my phone so I wouldn't have to hear her messages arriving like a hail of stones yesterday. No wonder I'd been missing Hank's texts and calls. Besides feeling like I'd been losing my mind with the toxic detox, I thought I was losing my hearing. "No, but it felt like I was," I said, breathing heavily for demonstration, "but I'm better now." I closed my eyes, relieved my stomach and head were no longer aching.

Feeling a little emotional, I kept my eyes closed listening to Hank's soothing voice. It was like relaxing piano music as he told me about his presentations and seafood feast he had with his colleagues. I wished he was lying in bed, next to me. My heart missed him. I rested my head against the padded headboard, pulling the bed covers up, slightly laughing when I told him about the tortuous detox I had attempted. I wiggled my toes when he laughed too. It was a pleasant feeling. I told him about my completed book, my Val sightings, and how well-behaved Baily was and then we said our goodbyes. And this time, fully and passionately, Hank said *I Love You*.

With a big smile, I tried to make the bed but decided to let the sheets air out. *The world won't end if I don't make it,* I told myself. I was too hungry. Insatiably hungry. And I had no shame about quitting the cleanse, so I ate French toast and two boiled eggs for breakfast before taking advantage of my second sick day from work this week by going to the gym.

Feeling as though I had an intense hangover, and I'm not someone who functions well with one, I was done after twelve minutes of sweating out the rest of the toxins jogging on the treadmill. I grabbed my belongings out of the change room before waving a friendly goodbye to the front staff on duty. Where was *Gwyneth*?

In the gym's parking lot, I checked in on my mother and aunt with a phone call, frowning when I looked at the time after twenty minutes. The bloody malls weren't even open yet. If people aren't working, or volunteering, or at home taking care of their house or kids, what the hell do they do all day? Having a lot of free time ahead of me, like I did today and would tomorrow, wasn't giving me any sense of excitement or adventure. Sadly, part of me thrived on routine. I know what time breakfast is and when I need to make dinner. It was the transitional time of not knowing what to do next that was making me feel a little vulnerable and bored, bored enough to want some social connectedness other than to a dog. I sighed deeply, starting the car. I had no place I wanted or needed to go, so I drove home through the busy morning traffic.

Robert's car was in Val's driveway when I drove past her street. It made me sad again, especially after entering an empty house. Not long after staring at the ceiling from the living room sofa, I did the unthinkable. I resisted only momentarily before punching in Margaret's number.

22 - ABSENCE DOESN'T ALWAYS MAKE THE HEART GROW FONDER

I listened to Margaret's voicemail greeting, telling me what to do after the beep. I hate that beep—it gives me heart palpitations. I also hate leaving messages and I hate it when others do too. They're a relic of the past. I don't enjoy listening to someone ramble on to hear them say they were calling and that they'd try to call back later. If you're going to try later, then do it. I left a message anyway, because Margaret would see I'd called, and I wanted to tell her I'd call her back instead of her calling me.

"Oh, hi, it's me, Allie." *Cough. Cough.* "I'm calling to tell you everything's fine." *Big sniff.* "Almost better." I regretted starting this stupid message but cleared my throat forcefully and continued. "Okay... well... I'm going to lie down again, so I'll call you later." The moment had clearly passed of wanting to talk to her, so I hung up.

With my brain clicking into gear, I spent the rest of the morning researching literary agents to send my children's book to. Although part of me felt intimidated to be sending my writing to the heavy hitters in the book industry, the other part felt empowered. It's been a long time since I've tried something new, not counting a few labor-intensive meals I've learned the recipes for and mastered over the years.

Confident and eager, I found several literary agents in the country seeking picture book manuscripts as of... NOW! So I busied myself cutting and pasting the same message to nine agents and after sending the last one out on my list, I sat back, living the dream. I looked around the kitchen. With a clean house and laundry done, I was tempted to collapse in front of the TV, but I was pumped and ready to do something. I glanced over at Baily as I opened the sliding door to the backyard. Knowing full well he wouldn't understand what I was about to say, I said it anyway. "Okay, Baily. Go do your thing and then we'll go on the trails." He made some remark with his tail as he jumped up and ran out the door.

As soon as he was out, I anxiously checked my inbox for replies. Nothing. *Oh, the pressure.* The pressure of waiting to hear from an excited agent wanting to represent me was unbearable. Seconds later, I hit the refresh button. Still nothing. They must all be on lunch, I reassured myself. I needed a distraction as I waited for Baily's bark to come back inside, so I logged into *Facebook*. And while it was loading, I heard a rumbling car out front. I dreaded the thought of an unannounced visitor. Cautiously, I made my way to the living room window and hid behind the curtains. When I peeked out, the same white sports car I saw Keith get into on the day of George's funeral was idling in the driveway... *what the...* and then Margaret opening the passenger door... *hell?* Moments later, there was she, climbing out of the car, holding one of her Tupperware containers carefully in her hands. A face-to-face confrontation or negative energy creeping into my space was not what I needed. I panicked and ran up the stairs. Two steps at a time.

On the edge of my bed, I sat listening to the doorbell ring. And ring. Over and over. Finally, there was nothing. A long silence—my cue. I tiptoed to the window. But midway across the room, her shrieky voice filled the house.

"*Hullo!*"

I ran into the closet, closing the door behind me. For all she knew, I could be out getting fresh air or a prescription filled at the corner pharmacy.

Her voice grew louder, with a touch of irritation. *"Hullo?* Anyone here?"

When I heard footsteps up the stairs. My heart pounded right out of my chest.

"Allison?"

I was feeling a bit foolish, hiding behind racks of clothes from my mother-in-law. But I dared not move.

She was sounding wary. *"Anyone here?"*

There was a pause before I heard another voice. "Found it." Another pause and then the same voice saying, "Left it under the sink fixing the shower last week."

I remained behind the closet door, foaming at the mouth.

"Okay... well, I'll just have to call and tell her we stopped by," I heard Margaret say. "And I'm taking this soup back with me."

Without warning, my ringtone blasted through the closet. In a state of terror, I fumbled trying to turn it off, and of course dropped it.

It wasn't long until I heard Margaret outside the closet. And then, seconds later, she flicked on the light before pulling the door wide open— her phone still to her ear. She jumped back, seemingly disturbed. "What are you doing in here?" she said, noticing me struggling to put on my housecoat.

I bent over and grabbed my phone off the floor. "Never mind what I'm doing in here. What are you doing here with him?" I said, gesturing to Keith, who stood there, wide-eyed with an oversized wrench in his hand.

Margaret shook her head, looking puzzled. "Why weren't you answering me?" she said. "I called out several times, you know."

"I was getting dressed," I said firmly, tightening the housecoat that covered my gym clothes beneath. "And you should've let me know you were coming," I said, glaring at Keith.

"Well, Henry told me not to bother you, but I thought I'd bring the soup I made you."

Made me? Yeah, right.

"Call or text next time," was all that came out of my mouth.

She looked over at my unmade bed, shaking her head bitterly. She motioned to Keith. "Let's go," she said. "There doesn't seem to be much appreciation in this house right now."

I pulled her back.

She gave the hand I had on her coat a hostile look.

I was breathing heavily. "Just so you know, Hank is going to talk to you about how Keith here is taking you to the cleaners," I said. Normally I didn't like to subject myself to this kind of directness head on, but I stood there with cool and unflinching courage.

"I don't know what you're talking about." She folded her arms, looking daggers at me. "We're not going to the cleaners... we're going to the bank."

It was like speaking two different languages with her. Keith understood. "I'll be waiting in the car for you," he said all too quickly before disappearing out of the room.

A moment passed. "That was a little rude of you, Allison," she snarled. "He's gone out of his way today to help me do a few things. And then he's coming to fix my fridge."

"Oh, yeah?" I glanced through the window blind. "Because it looks like he's leaving."

"He's what?" She hurried to my side.

I sat on the bed. "Margaret," I began, exhaling deeply, "he's not the nice helpful guy you think he is."

"What are you talking about—?"

"He's a cheat," I said. And before she had a chance to say anything, I told her about his divorce and the many other girlfriends he probably has.

"That all sounds absurd. He loves Samantha... *and* he's taking her on a nice vacation to Costa Rica, just so you know."

"Oh, *really*?" I said, taken aback. "And where did he get the money for that—you?"

She shrugged, turning back to the window. "So you know, Keith's been fixing all kinds of things in my condo—and for free too."

Exasperated, I clicked my tongue loudly. "He's not doing anything for free Margaret if you're lending him money."

"Oh?" she said, whipping her head back to me. "So, are you a spy now?"

I shook my head. "No, Margaret. I'm not a spy." I reached over and grabbed a tissue from the nightstand, remembering I was supposed to be sick. "Val gets first-hand information from his father."

She threw her head back and laughed. The kind of laugh one gives when hearing a beauty pageant queen discussing world peace.

I blew my nose, ignoring her. "Why is he driving his sister's car?"

Margaret's face turned white. "Who told you it was his sister's?"

"Sam. Why?"

"It's his," she snapped. "And I would know."

So, she'd also helped him with a car.

"And why's he in so much debt?" I asked.

"Oh Allison, he's made a few wrong choices trying to survive out there on his own. He's had school loans to repay, and he's helping his sister with things. He's had a lot to juggle—"

"Really, Margaret?" I had to hold in my laughter. It was pointless dragging this out further. And I wouldn't be surprised if one of his girlfriends has been casted as his sister.

"So... are you going to drive me home now, or what?" she muttered walking to the bedroom door.

I immediately texted Cameron. Seconds later, I jumped off the bed. "Good news. Cam will be here in a half hour," I announced. "I'm going to have a bath," I lied, pulling out a pair of fresh underwear from the dresser, "so, I'll see you downstairs."

It wasn't long after Margaret left the room that Hank texted.

[You kicked Keith and dropped soup in the closet? Told her to walk home? Confused. I'll call soon]

I took a deep breath, responding as best I could.

[Kicked? No. Keith left when I told your mom about him. She brought him over. Dropped phone in closet, not soup. Asked Cam to come get her. She has a way with words]

When I got downstairs to confront Margaret about her grossly distorted message to Hank, she was busy on *my* laptop at the kitchen table. She twisted around when I was closer. "When did Henry say he was coming home again?"

"Thursday," I replied coldly.

"Hmm, I *thought* he said tomorrow."

"Then why did you..." I said, peering closer at the *Facebook* page she had open, "ask?"

She nudged me with her elbow, snorting. "Looks like he's having fun, doesn't it?"

Leave it to her to find a group photo of Hank and his happy celebrating colleagues with Robyn in the background. I yanked the laptop from her. "Why are you on her profile?"

"I saw a tagged photo of Hank and liked it," she said, shaking her head. "*Facebook* can be so addictive when you click on pictures and comments. It's like one big web out there."

I really wanted to hit her over the head with the computer, when I realized I'd forgotten about Baily—and leaving our little escape artist in the backyard, alone and unwatched for more than five minutes is a *big* no-no. Surprised Margaret hadn't noticed that Baily wasn't in the house, I placed the computer back in front of her, adjusting the screen. "Here," I said, stumbling over my words, "let's see what else Hank's up to." And then, without calling attention to myself, I moved over to the sliding door and peeked through the blinds.

No sight of him.

I suddenly panicked at the thought of Baily being terrorized by another dog or pinned under a car while Margaret sat there engrossed in *Facebook*—probably finding another picture to upset me with. I moved to the kitchen sink, desperately looking out the window while trying to look busy washing dishes.

Still no sight of him. "Shit," I said loudly.

"What's that?" Margaret asked without taking her eyes off the computer.

"Nothing," I mumbled before giving her a quick, but broad smile. Without wasting another second, I hurried out the front door. I frantically called out his name and then ran to the back gate. The opened gate, plastered with muddy paw prints.

Clad in my bright pink housecoat and Hank's big black boots, I ran to the end of the driveway, my voice cracking. "Baily, come!"

I ran down one side of the street, searching bushes and checking porches. "BAILY!"

Nothing.

I screamed his name several times more and as I was halfway up the other side of the street, I saw Cameron pulling into the driveway. Breathless, I stood there flagging my arms.

"WHAT'S WRONG?!" he shouted, getting out of the car.

When I got closer, I cried, "Baily's gone!"

Before Cameron had time to process my words, Margaret had opened the front door. "What are you doing out here?" she hissed. "Are you telling him about *Keith*?"

No, you idiot. "Baily ran away," I managed to say through a flood of tears.

"I'm calling Henry." And then she slammed the door.

•   •   •

Cold and tired, Cameron and I met on the front steps after searching for Baily in the neighborhood for the past hour. I gave him a tight and confident squeeze. "He'll be back. I promise," I said, tumbling into a shame spiral after looking into his sad and skeptical eyes.

23 - Lost and Found

George, are you there? It's me, Allie.

I don't plan to disturb you all the time. You're supposed to be resting, right? But in case you haven't been following the news down here, Baily's run away. If I told you I knew what to do, I'd be lying because we've searched all over for him. Just wondering if there was anything you could do from up above. We need your help!

Allie xoxo

The only thing we could do after calling animal control and posting on *Facebook* was to see if Baily would sniff his way home to his favorite beef treats we'd scattered on the front porch. I looked to Cameron while spooning out more of the soup Margaret *apparently* made for me. "We'll go out again after we eat."

He nodded sadly, but gamely.

Margaret huffed, eyeing her watch. "He's probably in *Timbuktu* by now."

"Oh, shush," I said, joining them at the table. "I'm sure he's not far and everyone around here knows Baily," I said, trying hard to convince myself more than anyone else at the table. "If they see him, they'll bring him back."

"Yeah, so then why hasn't anyone brought him home yet?" Cameron mumbled, clicking away on his phone, updating Samantha.

"Don't worry, Cam, they will," I said, trying not to feel the painful disconnect from Samantha lately as I thumbed haphazardly through the newspaper, occupying myself. It'd been three days, and she still hadn't called, only quick replies to my texts. Hank hadn't returned my call either but was texting for updates. The fact he hadn't mentioned anything about Robyn being at the same finance convention, broke my heart. But strangely, numbness was taking over because my attention was on Baily.

Minutes later, Cameron and I nearly fell off our chairs when Margaret abruptly broke the silence. "AMELIA!" she shouted across the kitchen.

I stared right at her. "It's *Alexa*," I said, frustrated she still hadn't grasped the wake word.

Margaret shook her head. "Oh, for God's sake—ALEXA!" she shouted this time, "WHERE'S BAILY?"

Within seconds, *Amazon's* personal assistant replied matter-of-factly, "BAILY IS IN NORTHEASTERN PARK COUNTY, COLORADO UNITED STATES."

Cameron and I exchanged looks, keeping silent.

"He's *where*?!" she shrieked.

"Margaret," I said, as clearly as I could, "*Baily* is a name of a town. It's in Colorado."

"Well," she said rather dismissively, "ALEXA, WHERE'S BAILY THE DOG?"

Seriously?

Alexa then replied, "BAILY THE DOG IS AN ACTOR, BEST KNOWN FOR A GIFT TO REMEMBER 2017, LIFETIME OF LOVE..."

Margaret rolled her eyes. "ALEXA, Find—"

"Alright. *Enough*," I said, rising from my chair. "*Alexa* won't know where Baily is."

She shrugged, leaning toward Cameron. "Well then, I guess *Alexa* ain't so smart after all, is she?" she whispered, her chin held high.

For the next ten minutes, none of us said much until Margaret broke the silence again. "We sure wouldn't be sitting around like this if Baily were here. Poor little thing." She shook her head, exchanging a glance with Cameron. "To leave him out there with the gate like that." She blinked twice and then cleared the table of soup bowls, mumbling to herself, "It should've been fixed a long time ago."

And there it was. I'd been wondering how long it'd take for her to make a snide remark about the broken gate. *Let it go, Allie.* Disheartened and antsy, I wiped the counter for the third time. I was already on the cusp of terrible guilt and certainly didn't need her to make me feel worse than I already did.

As I was deciding on whether to have more tea or crack open a bottle of wine before heading up the search party again, the doorbell rang. We looked at each other with some brightness in our faces, rushing to the door. I got there first and pulled it open, remaining cautiously optimistic.

"*Baily!*" Cameron and Margaret shouted from behind.

I stood there, trying to make sense of the sight in front of me. "How... Where... *Oh my God*, thank you!" I exclaimed.

Baily squirmed out of Val's arms, jumping into Cameron's.

She gave us a radiant smile. "I found him sniffing around my garage when I got home."

Hit with a wave of intense gratitude, I motioned for Val to come in. "Oh... thank you," I said again, glancing over my shoulder at Margaret and Cameron. "We've been so worried."

"We sure have." Margaret was beaming as she spun around. "I'll call Henry and tell him the good news," she said directly to me. Of course she'd want to do that. And she'd probably start off by saying *if it weren't for me*...and end with...*Baily wouldn't have been found.*

Val, with half a grin, pulled out two bottles of wine from her deep pockets like a cowboy whipping guns from his holsters, aiming them at Margaret who was halfway to the kitchen.

I leaned into Val, lowering my voice. "Do *not* give me any ideas."

•   •   •

"Here," Val said, handing me a full glass of wine. "All's well that ends well."

My eyes twinkled at the thought of having my best friend and dog back in one swift moment. "Indeed." In a celebratory mood, I clinked my glass to hers. She was here, Baily was home and Margaret was back at her condo with Cameron. It wasn't like me to give hugs, but I gave her another big squeeze. "I really missed you."

Val's blue eyes were warm. "I missed you, too," she said.

"Who knew it would take Baily to get us back in the same room," I giggled, motioning for her to follow me to the living room.

"How's Robert?" I asked once we got settled.

Val tucked one leg under her on the sofa. "As of today," she said, taking a big swig of her wine, "It's over."

"*Really?*" I said. In spirit, I was selfishly pleased.

She nodded vigorously. "I was at Robert's today, and when Keith got home, it all went sideways. He was yelling up the stairs after he slammed the front door. I jumped out of Robert's bed and hid in the bathroom, listening to them in the hallway. Keith seemed agitated. Something about an investment that went wrong or didn't happen." She paused. "And then I heard them talking about a huge property deal with condos and hotels before Robert called someone."

I nodded, thinking back to when Keith had been here earlier. Was that the investment that went wrong? *Maybe I botched up his plan to take Margaret to the bank.*

Val drew up her shoulders, staring into the distance. "I heard little after that. Robert went downstairs. But I did hear Keith say he was buying a one-way ticket to Costa Rica." She looked at me closely.

I considered this for a moment. "Costa Rica," I said, concentrating. "Where Robert has property, right?"

"*Exactly*," she growled. "It's some investment scam they're setting up. I'm sure of it and I don't think it's their first one either."

With Margaret's money, I assumed. A wave of nausea engulfed me.

She changed her position slightly on the sofa. "That's when I realized that all this time, Robert was trying to smooth his way in with me, hoping I'd invest in his big plans down south—and God knows what else."

I kept quiet, letting her continue as my mind went wild with thoughts of my dear daughter involved with Keith. "I thought I heard Keith leave, so I threw on my clothes and then tried to get out the front door before Robert came back up. That's when Keith stopped me in the hallway," Val said.

"He's such a creep," I said, mildly distracted before texting Samantha to call me. "I hope he *goes* to Costa Rica and never comes back."

Val grabbed her purse by the front door, still talking. "Keith freaked out when he realized who I was." She sat back on the sofa again with her big leather bag. "I think I've had enough of men like Robert, and besides, he didn't stop me when I walked out." She wiped the wine droplets on her chin before pulling out her phone. I momentarily shared her pain about bad relationships. Of truth, for a greater part of her romantic life since leaving Peter, most of her love affairs had gone south.

I shook my head in sympathy. "Better you know all this now than down in Costa Rica, handing over all your money to him."

She nodded. "*God*, I hate having to start over though... uncovering someone's secrets after the honeymoon phase of the relationship is over," she said. "It's exhausting—and at this age, the *baggage* is usually battered and seasoned."

I nodded in agreement, quickly taking on Val's negative energy. Feeling my anxiety creeping within, I took another big gulp of my wine, and then suddenly, without forethought, I was typing out a quick and somewhat cold text to Hank.

[Tell Robyn she looks great in the photos she posted on your business trip]

I looked back at Val, feeling guilty for not wanting to let her into my world right now. "Sorry, I was responding to Cameron," I said to her.

Obliviously, she held her phone to my face. "But guess what?"

"*What?*"

"Peter wants to talk to me—*see*," she said, showing me his message.

I read his text with wide eyes.

"Maybe he's come to his senses," she said, grinning as she replied back.

I nodded lightly, glancing at my phone to see if Hank had responded. Nothing, yet. *Shit. Maybe I shouldn't have sent that.* Silently cursing myself, I sent another one.

[Baily's back in case you haven't heard]

Of course, he's heard. Margaret called and left a message. Okay, you idiot, that text wasn't necessary.

I looked at Val, who was telling me how two people should try to live in harmony. "Uh-huh," I said, showing interest. But since she still seemed oblivious of my inner turmoil, I sent Hank another text.

[Do yoa mess m/e?]

I quickly re-sent another one.

[I meen miss mee/?]

Ugh! Where are your glasses?

I threw my phone on the table and turned to Val. "Sooo... when are you seeing him?" My heart pounding.

She tilted her head. "Seeing who?"

I sat up straighter on the sofa. "Peter."

"Oh, tonight," she said, smiling, "maybe."

169

I pursed my lips before smiling back. Despite Peter's cheating, he was good for Val. His cheating might've not happened if she hadn't been such a nightmare to live with before the *change*. Her conclusion, not mine. The number of bad hair days, her low sex drive and urinary tract infections she'd complained about, especially for someone like her who'd always enjoyed the perks of being a gorgeous, natural beauty all her life, had only heightened her mood swings. But now that she had settled into post-menopause, my guess was that Peter might've been welcoming back the Val he had married. And cherished. Her sex drive had returned, and slowly, so was her sense of well-being, it seemed.

When the wine was gone, we ordered pizza. And just as we opened two watermelon coolers Val found in the back of the fridge, Samantha called. Before I could answer, Val grabbed my cell, hitting the speaker. "Sam, sweetheart," she began, "Keith is—"

"I know," Samantha jumped in. "Grandma just called and finished giving me her opinion of him."

My mouth dropped. "She did?" *Huh.*

"Yes, Mom. She did... so, don't worry. I'm not going to Costa Rica if that's what you're thinking."

I breathed a huge sigh of relief. *Thank God* Margaret had come to her senses and talked some of that into her granddaughter. She must've been listening after all. Or she just wanted to take credit—credit for saving her granddaughter from running off with Keith. Frankly, it really didn't matter. *Whatever the motive, thank you Margaret.*

•   •   •

Hank was standing over me when I opened my eyes. Confused, I sat up, taking in his face and the messy living room before me. Ten minutes? Ten hours? I had no idea how long I'd been sleeping—the last thing I remember after walking Val to the front door, were my feet carrying me back to the sofa. I remember pulling the blanket from underneath me and sliding further down on the cushions, heartbroken because Hank hadn't responded to my string of drunken messages.

I turned to him, forcing a warm smile. "What time is it?" I didn't wait for a response. "I thought you were coming back tomorrow."

He looked pale in the morning light. "I bought the ticket before getting the news that Baily was back," he said wearily.

To Hank, the scene stepping into the living room must've looked disastrous—his wife passed out on the sofa with empty wine bottles, cooler cans, and a pizza box on the table.

"How come you didn't respond to my texts?" I said.

He puffed out his cheeks, shaking his head. "Allie, I'm too tired for this."

"For *this*?" I cried, following him up the stairs, dizzy-like. "Isn't *this* important to you?"

He seemed awfully calm when he answered. "Allie, if you haven't figured out by now that I would *never* jeopardize our marriage, then you really don't know me."

"What does that even mean?" My thoughts were muddled when we reached the bedroom.

"Look, let me get some sleep and we'll talk when I get up. It's been a few stressful days and I'm exhausted—and more from what's been happening around here." He lay on the bed, closing his eyes. "I'm not up for an argument right now. I don't feel well." He searched for my hand and squeezed it. "I love you. Nothing will ever change that."

I love you. I repeated those three words in my head. It was nice to feel his warm skin—albeit clammy.

There was this comfortable silence until I nudged him. "So out of curiosity, why was Robyn there?" I said.

He popped one eye open. "One of the guys invited her."

"Who?" I said softly, immediately feeling better.

"You don't know him, and believe me, you wouldn't want to," he said. "Apparently the two have more than a business deal going on." He let go of my hand. "Okay, I love you, but..." He took a deep breath. "Sleepy time..." he said, rolling onto his side.

Experiencing lightness, calmness even, I reached over, kissed his forehead and even though I wanted to keep talking about Robyn, I let him sleep. And as he did, I unpacked his bags, feeling all cheery, before taking a shower.

Twenty minutes later, as I was toweling off, I heard banging on the door. Impatient banging and then Hank shouting, "Allie, I need the toilet!"

"Okay, hold on," I said, struggling to unlock the door.

"Hurry!"

As soon I pulled it opened, he rushed past me. He made a fierce lunge at the toilet, violently vomiting into it, barely missing the floor.

I stood there watching, shocked. In all our time together, this was the first time I've seen him do this. Alarm grew as I watched him hover over the toilet, throwing up again.

I tried to keep the panic out of my voice. "Are you okay... what's wrong?"

He moaned as he hugged the toilet.

I hurried to rinse a washcloth in cool water before laying it across the nape of his neck. It was the least I could do.

He was slumped quietly now.

"Hank, are you okay?" I whispered, stroking his back. "Was it something you ate?"

He slowly got up to wipe his mouth with the washcloth and then threw it in the sink. "Maybe I have what you had," he said hoarsely, dragging his body to the bed. I followed with the trash can and then helped him into his pajamas. I watched him closely as I covered him with another blanket. "Feel better?"

"A bit," he said, kicking the blanket off his legs, "but tired."

I sat on the edge of the bed, watching him toss and turn for the next few minutes. His face was pale as beads of sweat rolled down his forehead. He rolled away from me, moaning as he grabbed his chest.

"What's wrong, Hank?" I stood up, seriously worried. "Are you going to throw up again?"

He said nothing and rolled over on to his other side, still moaning.

Suddenly I knew what was happening. It was ambulance worthy, so I scrambled to get my phone in disbelief.

It didn't take long before two burly medics with deep voices entered our house and within ten minutes were carrying Hank out on a stretcher and into the ambulance parked in the driveway. I'd hurried right behind them, noticing neighbors and motorists trying to get a good look at the situation. I tried not to be that hysterical and screaming family member acting out of panic and seeming like a threat to the medics as they pumped him full with oxygen. It'd all felt like a scene out of a TV drama, but I remained calm, reassuring and comforting Hank as we tore through streets with a blazing siren.

•   •   •

Hours later, I hit the dial icon on my phone. It'd been an agonizing time waiting for test results and now that we knew, it was time to let his mother know.

"Margaret, it's Hank," I said, breathing deeply.

"Well, it doesn't *sound* like him," she said coolly.

I shifted on the bed, letting out an audible sigh for her to hear. "I mean it's about Hank," I said, bracing for her reaction. "He's had a mild heart attack and we're at the hospital." I swallowed hard.

"*He what?!*" she screamed.

I knew she wouldn't comprehend everything, so I had her put Cameron on. And after reassuring him his father would be fine after a routine surgical procedure for a blocked artery, he said he'd come to the hospital with Margaret as soon as he called Samantha.

After hanging up with Cameron, I stared at Hank in the hospital bed. The sight of long clear tubes going in and out of his body as he lay there making little whistle snoring sounds overpowered me with intense emotions. I took his hand in mine. We have a long deep history, I reminded myself. And even though we're sometimes far more affectionate with Baily than we are with each other, we're still each other's *big love*—despite Margaret, the bumps, the twists and all the turns in the road, we've had the kind of love that moves in like a massive storm and then settles down comfortably and quietly for years.

24 - Change of Heart

Even though I'd only experienced two one-night hospital stays after each of my children's births, there was no way I would've wanted to stay more. It's like being thrust into a foreign country, unable to speak the language or understand the customs. And now, with Hank in the hospital, the never-ending beeps of monitors, the announcements of emergency coded messages, and the rounds of exhausted nurses coming in to check on him, only added to the imminent fear of surgery.

I dragged myself off the sleeper chair and opened the thick beige curtains, letting in the early morning light. The room was small, dominated by a bed, making it feel crowded. Luckily, our insurance plan covered a single room upgrade because room sharing at a hospital was like sharing a hotel room with a stranger. Honestly, there'd be no way another patient in here could put up with Margaret constantly poking her head in between the curtains, like she did with George's hospital mate when he was here.

"How do you feel?" I asked Hank, knowing he didn't get much sleep either.

"My brain feels fuzzy," he said, sounding strained.

"Yeah," I sighed, suddenly craving greasy eggs and bacon. "Mine too."

He pulled the sheets to his chest. "What time is it?"

"Seven o'clock," I said. "You still have four hours to go before surgery."

He moaned. "You should go home—take a nap... a shower..."

Certain my eyes had big dark circles under them, I shook my head, giving him a warm smile. "I'm not going anywhere," I said, searching for my toothbrush in the bag Samantha brought last night. Even though the bathroom in the room was for patients only, I was mindful of my hygiene and slipped into it anyway.

When I got out, Nurse Amy, who wore a deep scowl and looked like she'd rather being doing almost anything else, was checking Hank's vitals. Don't get me wrong, I have a lot of respect for nurses and the fact they want their patients to be submissive and compliant, but it was like a damn *Dr. Seuss* book around here. Like Amy, there were the rude ones, and then there were the lazy ones, the passionate ones, the wise ones, the nice ones, the chatty ones, the mean ones—the list goes on.

She asked Hank a series of questions before eyeballing the assortment of snack wrappers on the table. "You haven't eaten anything since midnight, correct?"

"Correct," Hank answered obediently.

"Good," she said before turning to me. "Only sips of water if needed."

"Right. Of course." I nodded vigorously as my shoulders tightened. "How's his heart rate? Do you think he's ready for surgery?" I struggled to contain my composure. "Will we need to sign a form of some sort?"

Not quite meeting my eye, she gave me a quick and precise response. "The doctor will answer all your inquiries."

Rude.

When she left the room, I managed a giggle as I rubbed lavender oil under my nose. "It'll also help diffuse the air in here."

He nodded his head, smiling faintly.

I took his hand in mine. "Feels strange, doesn't it?"

"What feels strange?" he murmured.

"Here we are," I gestured to him, "in a hospital room, waiting for a surgeon to cut you open—." I stopped. "Sorry, I think I'm more worried than you are."

He squeezed my hand. "Worrying is not going to change the outcome."

I shuddered. "But what if it's horribly painful?"

"That's what the happy, sleep juice is for. I won't feel a thing."

I picked up his wedding ring on the table. "Well," I said, twirling it around my fingers before putting it safely in my pocket, "I'd be scared... scared of strangers poking and prodding me—"

"They perform this type of surgery every day," he said, playing with the collection of charms around my wrist. "Nothing to worry about but the recovery."

I straightened my back. "You're right." *Be a buffer for him, Allie. Not an intensifier of his fears—if he had any.* I inhaled deeply and reached across the bed, giving him another soft kiss on the cheek. "Think I'll see if the cafeteria's open," I said, pretending the surgery was part of the day's routine.

"Good idea. Go and stretch your legs." He flashed me one of his winning smiles in his dreadful looking pale-yellow hospital gown. "Don't worry. I'll be here when you get back," he said with a wink.

•   •   •

I filled my cup with premium roasted coffee and grabbed a gluten-free egg wrap, noting that real progress has been made with healthier and more palatable options in hospital cafeterias. With my tray, I looked around, almost forgetting where I was and then chose a spot by the window that looked out to the empty courtyard. I sat down, but soon after a few gulps of my coffee and finishing only half of the wrap, I'd lost my appetite. The reality of sitting in the bright open space, like an exposed wire, threw me off. My motivation to eat had vanished.

I dabbed more lavender oil under my nose, deciding it was time for the horrifying task of leaving a voicemail for Headmaster Thomas. Despite having to perform on the spot and being judged for the tone and clarity of a detailed message, I didn't want to have to talk to him, explaining everything that'd happen right after taking the last three days off for being "sick".

Five, no, six rings and then, *please leave a message after the beep.* <beep> "Oh, hi. It's me, Allie." I straightened my back, my ears and face tingling. "Good and bad news." I took a deep calming breath. "Hank had a heart attack." *Should I say mild? No. A heart attack is a heart attack.* "The good news is he survived." *No need for details.* "The bad news is... he'll need some support and care after surgery." I took another deep breath in. "So, I'll most likely need a substitute teacher for part of next week." *Wait. This warrants a full week.* "I mean, for all of next week." I ended up fumbling the rest of the message before saying a quick goodbye and hanging up. I decided I'd text him later with a follow up email or phone call. *Be professional,* I thought. Sure, I'd been displaying a general lack of enthusiasm for my role at school lately, but that didn't mean I was trying to sink my own ship. I needed my job, especially since Hank would need to reduce his work hours.

Fifteen minutes later, I was back upstairs to find Margaret in the room. And in the corner, slumped down in the chair, was a seemingly tired Cameron. "Oh, hey," I smiled brightly when he looked up. "I didn't know you guys were coming so early."

"I'm not going to sit at home with my son in the hospital," Margaret said, angry for some reason.

Two's company. Three's a crowd. But four?

As much as I wanted to be at the hospital with Hank, being in the tiny room with his mother would be too much of an emotional minefield, so I decided to take his advice and go home and shower. After leaning over to give him a kiss on his forehead, I motioned Cameron to follow me.

"What's up with your grandma?" I said once out in the hallway. "Did she not get sleep?"

"Probably not. She was up late posting photos and stories of Dad on *Facebook.*"

"*What?*" I moaned, throwing my head back. "I wish she hadn't done that. Now everyone will be showing up here."

Cameron shrugged, keeping quiet.

I sighed, choosing to keep quiet too as I clutched him tightly. "Okay. I'll be back soon."

• • •

Samantha was locking the front door when I drove into the driveway.

"You're up early," I said when we met at her car.

"Yeah, I want to see Dad before his surgery."

I smiled. "He'll love that." And he would. I reached out and hugged her. "I'll be there soon. Just going to have a quick shower."

"Okay. Love you, Mom," she said before getting into her car and closing the door.

It warmed me to hear her say that. Unlike Cameron, who'd been a more emotionally attached child, it took her time to say those words openly and freely, even after telling her every day we loved her.

Exhausted, I collapsed on the sofa, ready to text Headmaster Thomas. With Baily by my side, I reached into my purse before realizing I'd left my phone charging next to Hank's bed in the hospital room. I groaned, throwing Baily a look. "Right now, I desperately need a shower." I let out a loud yawn, rushing up the stairs.

Baily jumped on the bed when we got to the room. Besides being left unattended in the backyard for too long, being on the bed was another *no-no* for him. He was whimpering as he sniffed out Hank's pillows. I didn't have the heart to order him off, so I lay beside him, sinking into our mattress while sniffing out Hank's sweet vulnerable pillows too.

One and a half hours later, I startled awake. "*You stupid idiot!*" I cursed aloud—the whole reason why I didn't want to come home and risk nodding off. I flew off the bed and scrambled down the stairs. Grabbing my purse in a mad dazed rush, I left Baily looking extremely bewildered as I shut the front door behind me.

Of course, after a frantic drive to the hospital, I looked like a complete mess when I got to Hank's empty room. I spotted my phone, noticing neatly underneath it, an envelope addressed to Hank. It was obvious Margaret wanted me to see it, so I read the *I Can't Imagine Life Without You* card inside.

My Dearest Son, I'm sorry you have been under such stress lately. You need a break and more support at home. Here's some money for you so you can work less and recover for the next month. And don't worry. I will make sure you are properly fed and getting the rest you need in a clean and tidy house. Love, Mom. Xoxo

Good grief. When will this mama bear ever stop feeling the need to take care of her cub? Her very grown cub.

When I was stuffing the card *and* cheque back into the envelope, there was a light knock on the door. But before I had a chance to answer, I heard Margaret in the hallway. "Sorry, but family only I'm afraid," she said with a sliver of hostility in her voice.

I stood still, suppressing the urge to jump out from behind the privacy curtain.

"*Oh, I came to wish Hank luck before surgery,*" I heard a familiar voice say. "And to bring a card from some of his colleagues—"

"It was kind of you to drop by. I'll make sure he gets your well wishes," Margaret replied.

"Thank you," the woman said. "And please give my warmest regards to his wife."

"Allison," Margaret said coolly. "My daughter-in-law's name is Allison."

Who was this woman Margaret was plowing down?

"Yes, sorry. Allison," she said with a bit of horror and awkwardness in her voice. "Forgive me. I'm terrible with names."

And then, "Henry loves his family very much. So, you really have no business being here right now," Margaret added smugly. "He already has a wife."

Robyn?

Think stalkers and mad exes next time you post an upcoming event, like a surgery on Facebook, Margaret. And did my mother-in-law just stand up for me?

My body got so hot I thought I was going to choke on my sweat. Unable to move, I remained behind the curtain listening to Margaret's heels clicking down the hallway, presumably showing Robyn to the elevator.

Strangely enough, I suddenly felt bad for Robyn. You can have compassion for your enemies, right? Doesn't mean you have to put them on your Christmas list. Whether she'd been too picky or needy, she hadn't been able to settle down with someone decent in her life. And according to Hank, there was no prospective person in sight—matters like this can make some people desperate.

Cameron spoke first when I got into the surgical waiting room. "What happened?" he said as soon as I reached the far corner. "We've been texting and calling you."

"I left my phone in Dad's room," I griped, waving it in the air. I inhaled deeply. "Baily was throwing up everywhere, and I didn't want to leave him." *Liar.* I sat opposite the three of them.

"Oh, *no*," Samantha cried. She paused for a moment. "I think he ate some garbage on our walk."

"He's fine now. Whatever was in his stomach, is out." *Liar. Liar.* "How was he before he went in?" I asked all three simultaneously.

Margaret piped up as she crossed her legs in front of her. "He seemed relaxed and in good spirits."

Surprised at her gentle tone, I sank back in the uncomfortable chair. "Good," I said, staring at her slightly. I was waiting for a jab from her, but there was nothing. No snide remark. No insult. And no mention of Robyn's visit. Instead, she smiled at me. And then, like the dedicated knitter she was, she pulled out a big wad of multicolored yarn and carried on with her latest knitting project.

I smiled too. And for the next two hours, I watched the wide oak door, and every turn of the knob with butterflies in my stomach, waiting for his pleased and relieved surgeon to come out with good news.

25 - How Long Can You Stay?

Are you there, George? It's me, Allie.

Day three now, and Hank's recovering well after surgery. He'll be here til next week, but he should be okay, thankfully. But that means Margaret and I will continue stepping on each other's toes in this cramped room.

By the way, I heard back from some editors! The bad news? None of them want to publish my book. It'll be their loss, so I'll try not to rub it in when I'm doing talk shows and hobnobbing with J. K. Rowling. You always told me to stay positive, right?

Allie xoxo

"You don't have to stay tonight," Hank mumbled from the bed. "Go have dinner with Sam. I'll be fine here."

I grabbed the awful-looking tray of half-eaten chicken and shriveled carrots in front of him and put it by the window. "Sure you'll be okay?"

He nodded.

"My body could do with a hot bath and mattress tonight," I grinned.

"Good... and besides, Cam should be here with my mom soon."

Right. She'd talked Hank into watching her favorite lineup of game shows and then the granddaddy of newsmagazines, *60 Minutes* with her. In this drab and sterile-looking room, it wasn't such a bad idea even though he was already on his way to *la la land* from the meds.

He opened one eye. "When will you be back tomorrow?"

"Whenever you want me to be," I whispered, playfully tugging on his arm.

He gave me a weak smile. "Noon is good," he mumbled. "I'm fine here." He lowered the head of his bed. "Got my drugs... TV... books..." He laughed slightly before closing his eyes again.

"Don't get too comfortable, Mister," I said. "I know you're enjoying the services and all, but we do need to get you out of here." I kissed his limp hand, straightening the pillows behind his neck.

•   •   •

On the main floor of the hospital, I ran into Helen when I stepped off the elevator. Wrapped in a thick gray coat over her uniform, she smiled a breezy hello. "We have stop meeting like this," she said.

We moved away from the doors. "Tell me about it," I laughed, which was not my natural one.

She tilted her head. "How's Hank doing?" she asked, rubbing my back ever so gently.

"Better than expected." I rummaged in my purse for my winter gloves. "But he'll be here until the end of this week."

She appeared to be struggling for words. "That's—that's good. He'll need the rest," she said before trotting down the corridor beside me and then suddenly stopping.

And then I stopped.

And then she leaned toward me, looking very serious. "Margaret told me what happened. Everything okay at home?"

I nodded, looking at her closely and ignoring my sudden uneasiness.

Helen offered a feeble smile, which of course is unusual for a big smiler like her. She motioned me to wait for her in front of the hospital's information desk. She stepped behind it, searching through drawers while a young and keen looking hospital volunteer sat on a tall stool watching her.

I distracted myself as I waited, instinctively pulling out my phone and sending Hank a series of yellow faced emojis winking and blowing kisses. Helen was still busy, so I sent another text telling him I'd be back to say goodnight after my dinner with Samantha.

Moments later, Helen seemed to have finally found what she was looking for and stepped in front of the desk again. "Margaret was mentioning the level of stress Hank seems to be under with work and at home."

"Oh?" I said, wondering what Margaret had said exactly. Not long ago, I was feeling happy, safe, and secure, but now?

She looked at me carefully with a polite smile. "I don't mean to pry, but is everything ok with you? Margaret's very concerned." She stretched out her hand, signaling me to take the pamphlet she had in it. "We have several programs here in case you're interested."

I looked at her expectedly with narrow eyes, unsure of what she was trying to say, when I saw Margaret and Cameron at a distance, entering through the main doors. I stuffed the pamphlet in my purse and managed a quick goodbye to Helen. "Let's hope this'll be the last time you see the Montgomery family here for a while," I said half-jokingly.

She nodded, smiling. *"Let me know if you're interested,"* I heard her say as I quickly turned the corner. *"There's a waiting list..."*

I had no idea what Margaret had told Helen. Not wanting to think about it further, I threw on my hat and decided to go to the gym before meeting Samantha. And when I got there fifteen minutes later, I noticed a hiring ad for a sales and reception position taped on the front desk. The gorgeous, athletic-looking brunette featured in the ad wore a confident smile beckoning whoever was reading it to join their team. *The fun and exciting team!*

I scanned to the remuneration section.

Weekend and evening hours, good pay and benefits, plus commissions.

I was forced to admit that the extra money would help if Hank had to slow down. Unless, of course, I was starting my next book—as soon as the first one took off. *Sigh.*

Gwyneth sauntered by as I was taking a picture of the ad. I suddenly felt awkward, wondering if she thought I was a kooky, middle-aged woman wishfully thinking about joining the fitness center's team. I turned to her and smiled, anyway.

She turned back unexpectedly. "Do you want to fill out an application and leave it with me?"

"Su—sure," I said, surprised I was considering this. "Do you think age is important?" I found myself asking.

"No, and honestly, most of the members are your age... so it'd be good." She paused. "Plus, you'd be less intimidating than someone like her," she said, gesturing toward the model in the hiring ad with her eyes.

You mean you, Gwyneth. And was it me, or was that a backhanded compliment she'd made?

Slowly, I looked at *Gwyneth* again. "Wait—is this *your* job being advertised?"

"Yep," she said proudly.

She must've had something better lined up. "Moving on to bigger and better things?" I said. That part may have come out sounding a little condescending, but for some reason, I couldn't help but feel uneasy around her. There was no common ground between us. She's young, beautiful and full of hope for the future. "So, what do you want to do?" I asked, this time with sincerity in my voice.

"I'm hoping to get a full-time teaching position soon," she said.

"You're a teacher? I didn't know that. Me too," I said, feeling more confident. "What grades do you teach?"

"Kindergarten!" she beamed.

"Kindergarten?" I repeated. "Me too."

"*Really?*" she beamed again, handing me the job application. And a pen. "You're *so* lucky to be teaching. I haven't been able to find anything permanent for a *long* time."

I looked up from the application. Eyes can truly show what you're thinking, so I relaxed my face and kept my lips straight. I couldn't imagine her having the patience and warmth to be around children all day. I chose my words carefully. "You will, don't worry. Just get yourself on substitute teaching lists and do some volunteering."

"Yeah... I'm filling in for someone now, and I love it. The kids all seem to love me, *even* the parents."

"Oh, terrific," I said, returning to the application in front of me. After a moment, my head popped up. "And if the school loves you, they'll want to find a way to keep you."

"Yeah, they've already hinted that I..."

I looked at her hard. "Hinted what?"

Her face turned white and rigid. "You're *Allison?*" she said, staring at my application. "*Allison* Montgomery?"

"Yeah," I said, not at all surprised she hadn't remembered my name.

She shifted her weight on her other foot, looking awfully guilt-ridden.

"Why?" I dropped the pen. And why did I have this funny feeling in the pit my stomach that *Gwyneth* was at my school *and* in my classroom, of all the classrooms in this city, teaching my kids?

She said nothing. And she didn't need to.

"Just so you know, I'll be back in the classroom next week." I paused. "But until then, enjoy," I added, trying not to direct my sudden fear and bitterness at her for possibly being fired and replaced as she continued telling me how much she'd been enjoying my class. "Make sure to leave the room nice and tidy," I said lightly after she finished. I stuffed the application in my coat pocket. *What the hell was I thinking applying for a part-time job selling expensive memberships to people like me?* After wishing *Gwyneth* the best of luck, I no longer felt like being at the gym.

In the parking lot, I called Hank, feeling deflated while waiting for the car to warm up.

Margaret answered his phone. "He's sleeping, so best not to disturb him."

Couldn't argue with that.

I put her on speaker while I drove. She chatted away, describing in detail the bouquet of flowers from Hank's team at work and then read out loud the entire get-well card, including the back, the brand and the price of it.

I interrupted her mid-sentence. "Is Cam still there with you?"

She must've not heard me, or chose not to, because she continued telling me, or lecturing me rather, how we needed to keep the house nice and quiet, and clean. She barely took in a breath and said, "He'll need to eat well, so I'm going to make all of his favorite dishes while I'm there... and drinking your wine and entertaining Val in the house will be out of the question... oh, and let's think about you sleeping in the basement so Henry can have his own space in the bedroom... away from all the noise and germs." And then somewhere mid-sentence, I told her my phone was about to die and hung up, exhausted and emotionally confused. Frustrated? Check. Guilty? Maybe. This woman was always running our lives and although I was still feeling good about her standing up for me with Robyn showing up at the hospital, I was already back to seeing her for the nuisance she was.

After finding a parking spot on a side street, I texted Samantha to let her know I'd be early.

She replied as I was putting on a fresh coat of lip balm.

[Ok we're already here]

We? Maybe Cameron decided to join us after all.

I scurried along the cold pavement until I got to the restaurant's window and saw my mother sitting inside with Samantha, waving me in. Thrilled with a big wide grin, I pulled the heavy door open to the delicious smell of searing steak.

My mom jumped up from the table and held her arms open as I rushed over. "Sorry, I should've told you," she said. "I came back from your aunt's a few days early and thought I'd stay and help—if I can."

I hugged her tightly and then stood back with a broad and enthusiastic smile. "How long can you stay?" I asked before I took my coat off and sat down. *Her staying with us couldn't have come at a better time.*

26 – A Spark Can Start a Great Fire

"Are we ordering wine?" asked my mother.

I peeked up over the tall menu in my hands. "I'm driving, so no. But you go ahead."

Our waiter, Jason, hovered near us and when we were ready, he gave a quick rundown of the night's specials. With limited eye contact I might add. After my mother quizzed him at length about the different cuts of steaks and which one was better (that's when he rolled his eyes), she ended up ordering shrimp linguini with a special cream sauce that wasn't even on the menu. And when she was about to question him about the restaurant's elaborate wine list, she suddenly stopped and gazed admirably at his long dark sideburns, telling him in her adoring and captivating way, how they helped to offset his long face and make him look like a handsome celebrity. Like Brad Pitt, she said. It sent a wide smile to Jason's lips, immediately turning him into a friendlier and more attentive waiter.

To this day, my mother always intrigued me.

With orders out of the way and drinks on the table, my mother went straight into all that'd happened in her condo village in Florida while she'd been visiting my aunt Viv, stopping whenever Jason checked on us. "Remember Bob?" she asked.

"Yes," I lied, because most of the men I've seen in that village looked the same with their silver hair and round faces covered in age spots and deep-set wrinkles, "what about him?"

"He died right in the middle of having..." Her eyes darted across the table.

Samantha nuzzled her nose into her hands. "*Grandma*, I'm twenty-one," she said. "You don't think I know about sex?"

Probably not. And she certainly doesn't need to know about your pregnancy scare either.

My mother winked at Samantha. "You're right—I have to keep reminding myself you're all grown up." She cleared her throat and continued. "Well, Bob, the stupid geezer, was having sex with Ruth on the third floor when his heart gave out—*and* right in her bed too."

I reached for another piece of warm bread, shaking my head with wide eyes. Bob, now that I remembered, was the community's social gadabout and Casanova with plenty of love and affection to go around to the ladies after being widowed for two years.

Samantha looked at both of us. "That's *so* sad."

I nodded, buttering the bread in my hand without taking my eyes off my mother. "What about Ruth's husband?" I asked, not at all surprised by the news. People at that age are probably hungry for companionship and feel freer to throw their hang-ups out the window.

"What about him?" My mother paused to take a mouthful of her wine. "He was moved to the dementia unit in the next building months ago."

I remembered Ruth's husband, Martin, too. A sweet, sweet man who liked to sit in the residence reception area and talk to anyone who'd listen. He refused to do anything or cooperate with the staff who'd come into his room, stating he was busy rewiring a freight train, the job he'd done over his fifty years of service with Union Pacific.

Like Martin, both my uncle and grandmother on my mother's side lost their intellectual lives to dementia. It frightens me to the core whenever I get really tired, and my brain becomes sketchy, like when I'd put the milk in the cupboard and the sugar in the fridge. And fear like this starts feeding my anxiety—enough so that I made a list of things I wouldn't want people to do if I become confused and disoriented. I wouldn't want family or caretakers to talk about me as if I weren't in the room. I wouldn't want to be treated like an imbecile nor dressed in a mismatched assortment of dreadful clothes with plastic barrettes in my hair. *Treat me like you'd want to be treated.* I went as far as framing those eight words so I could hang them above my bed if I ever lost it.

After hearing an hour's worth of gossip at the village, a real widower's sex paradise it seemed, my mother grabbed the dessert menu off the table. "You've been awfully quiet," she said, turning her attention to Samantha. "How's work and that little apartment of yours?"

"Good," she responded unenthusiastically. "Going with the flow."

My mom put the menu down and rested her elbows on the table. "What about the boyfriend you told me about?" she asked, leaning towards her.

Uh oh, a prickly subject.

Samantha shrugged her shoulders. Her voice was low. "It's over."

"Aw, that's too bad. You'll have to tell me more when you're ready." My mother gave me a quick look before turning back to Samantha. "You mentioned another school program. Did you get accepted?"

Samantha shook her head. "I'm still deciding whether to apply."

I reached across the table for the menu and then appeared busy with it, deciding between the chocolate cheesecake and fried ice cream. Even though Samantha and I have had a few nights to talk, she hasn't revealed her long-term plans, so naturally I was interested in hearing her tell my mother. And if she doesn't mention Keith or Costa Rica, I'd support her in anything.

"Any other plans then?" my mother asked, sounding genuinely puzzled with her short responses.

"No, not with school." I could feel Samantha's eyes on me. "But I'm thinking about moving home and finding a job so I can save money."

Smart, Sam. Smart.

Still appearing busy with the menu, I could see my mother nodding from the corner of my eye. "That's good, Sam. Nothing wrong with that," she said, looking at her steadily. "You'll figure it out in no time."

I kept quiet, listening to Samantha expand on her sentences while pretending to be searching for something in my purse.

"Yeah, I'm still interested in design and stuff like that." She exhaled, and when she did, I could hear her on the verge of tears. Her hands were squeezed together when I glanced up quickly. "Who knows, maybe I'll take a few courses here and there," she said.

Hank's heart attack had scared her. She rushed home, worried, and seeking, it seemed, family solace after being out in the jungle on her own, going through the ups and downs of life. And now that Margaret was back in her condo with Cameron, Samantha had her bedroom again. Her haven. For now.

Seemingly satisfied with Samantha's responses, my mother looked at me with a mirthful grin. "So, what about you, Allie?" she asked. "How's your writing coming along?"

I forced a smile. "Oh, I just finished sending my manuscript out to agents. Wish me luck," I said as I wrapped my two fingers together, waving them in the air.

"Why, Allie, *that's* terrific! How exciting to know we might have an author in the family soon," she said with big eyes.

"Hope so." I flashed another smile before drinking the last of my juice. I wish I could've beamed with inner confidence, but whoever discusses rejection emails. The thought of those impersonal one-line form letters trickling in, was discouraging. *Anyone who says rejection doesn't hurt is a liar.* I thought agents would've been jumping all over my Ruby and Baily story. Fighting for it, actually. Thought I would've had a contract signed and on my way to a fruitful writing career because according to *Google*, hundreds of children's books get published every year. Some of which are terrible. I should know. I've tried reading them to my kinders.

Shortly after dessert and in the restaurant's bathroom, which was clearly not a design afterthought with its metallic lime green finishes, I fished through my purse for dental floss. And when I did, I noticed the stupid pamphlet Helen had given me on behalf of Margaret in the side pocket of it. I pulled it out, gasping as the bold letters on the front panel jumped out at me.

ALCOHOL AND DEPRESSION

I opened the pamphlet slowly and inside on the left page was more bold text about the symptoms and causes and ways to help a loved one suffering. My eyes slowly moved to the right which revealed a list of programs and services at the hospital.

Sighing as quickly as I could, I stuffed the pamphlet back into my purse and marched out of the bathroom. *"Fuck you, Margaret,"* I muttered. *Note to self—Two steps forward, three steps back—it IS a thing.* She probably told Helen I was a blatant, shameless alcoholic who couldn't keep things together at home, including keeping Hank happy.

• • •

Cameron was sitting in the lobby when I arrived back to the hospital.

"Hey honey," I said when I got closer. "I thought you would've been home by now."

He shut his textbook with a snap and stood up. "Yeah, Grandma wanted to finish knitting Dad's socks."

"Aw, Cam. You poor kid." I reached into my purse.

"It's okay," he said when I tried handing him a twenty-dollar bill. "Grandma bought me something." He packed up his backpack. "Have you tried the poutine in the cafeteria yet? It's really good."

I shook my head. "No, I haven't," I said, distracted with the thought of Margaret upstairs with Hank. I gave him a quick smile. "Wait here, and I'll send her down."

Cameron nodded and sat back in the chair.

"By the way, thank you," I said.

"For what?" he asked.

"For staying with your grandma... and chauffeuring her around." I paused for a moment. "You're becoming an experienced and confident driver, thanks to her."

Cameron jumped up. "Wait, how long am I staying with her?"

I couldn't think of an immediate response because *a)* I'd given up his bed to my mother, and *b)* He'd been keeping Margaret distracted, enough so that she wasn't feeling the need to stay with us.

"Not long," I said, giving him a tight squeeze as I slipped the money into his hand. "I promise."

He shook his head with an expression that was half-frown, half-smile. "This is bribery, you know."

My son was of course, very smart. With a smile and a wave, I headed for the elevator.

"Cam's waiting for you downstairs," I said to Margaret when I got to the room. "I'm here now, so you can go."

Thankfully she didn't argue. In fact, she quietly packed up her stuff. When she finished, she gave a sleeping Hank, whose left foot revealed a speckled blue knitted sock, a kiss before giving me a stiff smile.

"Here." I handed her the *Alcohol and Depression* pamphlet as she pushed past me. "Helen thought I might need this."

She looked at it quickly before gazing at me.

My eyes narrowed. "Frankly I find this very insulting you would even think I had a problem, let alone speak to Helen about it."

She said nothing and motioned me to follow her out of the room.

"See, this is what's been causing Hank's blood clots and weakened heart muscles," she hissed in the hallway. "You're always stressed and worrying about things... then resorting to wine as a crutch."

I wasn't going to wrestle with her blame, and blithely accept that I caused her son's heart attack. "First of all, Margaret, heart disease runs in *your* side of the family. And second, I'm not an alcoholic, if that's what you're saying. Sure, I enjoy it, but one or two glasses every few days does not make me one."

"Hmmm..." she mumbled, staring down the empty corridor. "That's usually the first sign. Denial."

"That's *not* denial, Margaret," I said, fighting back the impulse to punch her. "That's being a sensible person with good taste. And besides, wine is a staple at every meal in some countries, just so you know." I shook my head and was about to add that red wine has a lot of proven health benefits, but I couldn't bear another moment standing in the hallway with her, so I turned around and strode back into the room.

Hank popped his eyes open when I neared his bed. "What was that all about?"

"Oh, nothing," I whispered, slowly taking his hand in mine. "We were just discussing recipes for a healthy heart."

"Oh..." he slurred, smiling. He turned his head the other way and drifted off to sleep again.

For Christ's sake! Imagine Margaret calling me an alcoholic. Though I will admit, every time I'm around her, I feel a desperate need for wine. Shocking, isn't it?

27 - As One Door Closes, Another Always Opens

"*Knock, knock,*" I sang joyfully over Val's shoulder.

She whipped her head around as we stood in line at our favorite café, giving a hesitant, assessing look before slowly responding. "Who's there?"

I grinned from ear to ear. "MARGARET!"

Val narrowed her eyes, but willingly played along. "Margaret *Who?*"

"Exactly," I replied, taking in the earthy warm scent wafting through the air. "*Margaret Who.*"

She furrowed her brow. "I don't get it. What's the punch line?" she said as we shuffled behind customers in the slow-moving line.

"Margaret *Who,*" I said, leaning in toward her. "That *is* the punch line. Cam and Sam have been taking turns staying with her. I've had three—*wait*—four glorious days without her in my home."

Val threw her head back and laughed, but suddenly stopped when the busy barista at the mahogany counter signaled us forward.

"I'll grab that table over there," I said quickly. Confident she would get my coffee concoction right, I raced over to the most sought-after table in front of the fireplace. I threw my purse down and exhaled a long, audible breath as I sank into the deep leather sofa.

It felt good to get out of the house, particularly with coffee machines whirring and flirtatious jazz music playing in the background. My body relaxed further into the sofa. Thanks to my mother, everything at home was relaxed too. She's an easy houseguest—respectful, self-sufficient, and extremely helpful. She has a peaceful, fun disposition as she happily goes about her day. Because of this, I could go about my day seamlessly too. I inhaled deeply with a smile. *I wish Margaret could take notes from her.*

Though part of me felt guilty about the number of days I'd missed at work, the other part of me felt indifferent—*really* indifferent, especially after my morning call with Headmaster Thomas. The conversation with him started off friendly enough, I suppose, but then my stomach shriveled up.

"So, how's Hank doing?" he asked after all the polite exchanges were out of the way.

"Good, good..." I said breezily. "It's a slow recovery, but he should be back on his feet in a few weeks or so."

"Oh," he said stiffly. "I'm sure you've been busy then?"

"Yes, helping him organize his medications, and of course, getting him to do his exercises." I took a deep breath. "And there's been a change in diet, so I've been experimenting with new recipes. You, know... making sure he's getting the best care at home."

"Uh-huh," he said. And then, "The *same* thing happened to *my* father." He paused a moment. "He fared well right after they sent him home from the hospital."

"Wow," I managed to say, clenching my jaw. "He *must've been* pretty strong."

And then I had to bite my lip when he switched gears to talk about the new policy at school. Something to do with the number of days teachers could take off with pay. As if my stomach wasn't already tense, he ended the conversation by saying how great the children were doing in the classroom with the supply teacher, Rebecca—a.k.a. *Gwyneth*. "The *very capable* substitute teacher," he made sure to add, contributing to my discomfort.

Jerk.

Val's arrival with our coffees brought me back to the present. She set them down and then tossed a napkin on the table before sitting across from me, glowing—a few good nights with Peter would do that, I assumed. From what she'd said, they were back together, but on her terms. They were going to live separately. Val wanted her rekindled love to grow slowly but surely, rather than quickly and spectacularly.

She unwrapped the bright yellow scarf from around her neck, "So how's your mom doing?"

"Good." I pursed my lips. "I'm going to miss having her here though."

She smiled. "When's she leaving?"

"Tomorrow," I said.

"Oh, then tell her I'll stop by tonight." She blew the hot steam off her coffee. "I have a bag of books for her."

"What kind of books?"

She gave me a smirk. "*My* kind of books."

"Your erotic romances that make those fantasy vampire trilogies seem like non-fiction?" I snorted. But then I straightened. "Since when did my mother start reading erotica?"

"Oh, I don't know," she said. "Maybe she's looking to rev up her sex life."

"Okay, stop there," I gasped, choking on my coffee. "I don't even want to think about what she's doing in Florida." I flapped my hand at her. "And whatever happens down there, better stay down there."

Val gave me this disgusted look. "Happens where?"

"*Florida*, Val," I shook my head. "Whatever happens down in Florida."

Val gladly changed the subject—her dinner with Peter the previous evening. As she was telling me about the new Italian restaurant they'd gone to, I thought about my mother and the secret life she might be living. Suddenly my thoughts turned to Margaret and how different she was from my mother. One boomed while the other scowled in their silent, but deadly battle. When Margaret found out my mother was in town visiting, she completely backed off—with the exception of calling Hank to remind him about his pills and then to ask if he'd eaten and what he'd eaten since she last called.

Val shifted her position on the sofa, still talking about Peter when her phone vibrated on the table. She ignored it at first but then answered. And after conducting what seemed like a one-sided fifteen-minute conversation with someone named Julia, she threw the phone on the table and frowned. And then cursed.

I gave her a serious look. "What's wrong?"

She reached for her phone. "The home stager we use is closing shop." She sighed heavily, tapping out a text to someone. "She's moving to the other side of the country," she said, without looking up. "And she was excellent too—had a good eye for decorating, especially for the shit-looking homes I've been listing. They're all in dire need of an overhaul."

"I could be your home stager," I said, completely out of nowhere.

Val's head popped up from her phone. At first, I thought she was going to laugh, but she didn't. She gave me a long, attentive look. "*You* could!" she grinned, reaching over to punch my arm. "You *have* the talent!"

"I wasn't serious," I mumbled.

She slapped the table. "Why the *hell* not? It's a *great* business!"

My heart beat out of my chest. *Me, a home stager?* A moment passed before I beamed back at her because the truth is, I do like moving furniture around at home, and I love home renovation shows. Whenever Hank and I used to go to Val's open houses, I'd often leave and wonder what the homeowners were thinking when I saw how they were showing the place.

"You could call yourself our stager *right* now." She paused for a split second before continuing. "Julia was staging *at least* eight homes a month."

My heart beat faster. "But wouldn't I need training—or some kind of license?"

She shook her head before sipping of her coffee. "It's an unregulated field. There's lots of programs, but that's for someone who doesn't know the business. I could train you," she said and then paused. "*Oh. My. God.*

You could get Sam to help you. She could study design. She'll add credibility."

I nodded vigorously. But then, "What about my job?" Dizziness was setting in. "I can't just quit. Hank will think I've lost it if I tell him I want to be a home stager."

She stopped smiling. "I'm not saying to give up everything this instant, but if we set the wheels in motion, we could make it happen."

Val walked me through the business of home staging, and although I drifted off a couple of times, assessing the possibility of it, I came back to her enough to understand most of what she was saying. I stared at her with a mix of awe and disbelief, gulping my coffee after giving her a half-crooked smile when she finished. "Okay, let's talk more," I said at last through a whirlwind of fear and excitement.

•   •   •

The savory smell of sautéed garlic awakened my senses when I walked through the front door. Pumped and energized, like how I felt weeks ago when I discovered I wanted to be a children's author. *I could still write and move furniture around in people's homes, couldn't I?*

I smiled as I kicked off my boots. An opportunity to ride Val's coattails in the real estate business could turn me into a staging diva, as long as we made sure goals and expectations were aligned. And then there was Samantha. We could become one of those mother-daughter teams, sharing clear-eyed determination about how to decorate and sell a home for top dollar.

"Sam's coming for dinner and staying the night," I heard my mother say cheerfully from the kitchen doorway.

Snapped back to reality, I gave her a bright smile. "Oh, great," I said, feeling remarkable good. "It'll be nice to have everyone here for your last night." I hung up my coat, deciding to keep Val's proposition quiet—at least until Hank was back to his old self.

Cameron and Hank were sitting at the kitchen table finishing my mother's crossword puzzle when I walked in. Cameron looked up. "Did you get my hot chocolate?"

I thrust out my lower lip. "Oh, sorry, Cam," I said. "I'll make you a better and healthier cup right now."

My mother jumped to the cupboard. "I'll make it, honey," she said, pulling out a sauce pan. "You go get out of your gym clothes."

See? This is what I'm talking about. Easy and stress-free around here.

I tried to ward off the guilty feeling surfacing deep within me because Margaret would be alone tonight. I took a deep breath, looking at Hank. "And your mother? Does she want to come over?"

He smiled and shook his head. "It's bingo night so probably not."

I smiled back, unsure of the most appropriate response. *I'm sure she'll be fine,* was what I finally mumbled when I left the kitchen. My cheerful mood shifted slightly. I knew that with my mother gone, there was a *big* possibility of Margaret resurfacing.

•　　　•　　　•

After a long-winded goodbye at the airport the next morning, I watched my mother saunter through the security gates. She turned around once more and with one arm loaded down with Val's books, she waved with the other. I blew her a kiss and waved back, smiling. *What happens in Florida, stays in Florida,* I repeated as I spun around and returned to the car.

My mind wandered back to Val's visit last night. In the kitchen, she'd hinted to Hank about the staging business, remarking about the latest house sale on the street, accrediting the stager she *was* working with. She leaned back in the chair, stretching her neck toward the living room. "Allie, I *love* the new arrangement in there," she said. "And the pillows *really* work." Clueless of her intention, Hank had asked her about the rising housing prices. It was a start. Who knows, Hank might be as enthusiastic about my home staging skills as much as Val seemed to be.

"How did it go?" Hank asked before I drove out of the airport parking garage.

"Good," I replied smoothly. "Did the kids get off okay?"

"Yep. Cam left for school with his bags," he said.

"Oh, right," I said, disappointed I didn't get to say goodbye before his ski trip with Kyle and his family.

"And Sam's just about to leave." I could hear him smiling through the phone. "*After* she makes me breakfast."

"Aw, that's nice. Hope the drive back goes well with that car of hers—."

"I'm going to miss her," I heard him say.

I sank back in the seat. "Me too."

"By the way, Val was looking for you," he pepped up. "She said something about you helping with decorating ideas. Not sure why she didn't text you... anyway, she grabbed your magazines."

I chuckled inside. Val was going strong. And then suddenly, fear rushed through me—the investment, the inventory, the storage space... and most importantly, Hank's reaction to it all. I sighed deeply and drove to the supermarket. After, I wanted to spend the day in a quiet house with Hank. I smiled, realizing we'd have the *entire weekend* to curl up with each other, catching up on life and our forgotten series.

An hour later, the bright sun warmed my face as I carted grocery bags to the front door. Even though my mother wouldn't be greeting me in the hallway and that I'd *just* dropped my keys between the porch steps, it was still a good day. The front door swung open when I bent over to dig out the fallen keys. "Oh thanks, honey," I said just as I got my fingers on them. But when I straightened and lifted my head, my happy expression turned to horror.

"I hope there's milk in one of those bags," Margaret said without batting an eye.

When I saw a pile of luggage at the bottom of the stairs, I stumbled and lost my balance. *Somebody pinch me, please.*

28 - I Had a Dream

At that very moment on the front steps when I saw Margaret standing at the door, I think I hated her—and I'd gladly eat a plate of Brussel sprouts and chug a beer, both of which I really dislike, to get off this island.

Margaret followed me into the kitchen after I grabbed the last of the grocery bags out of the car. She sat at the table, closely watching me unpack and put everything away. And while it would be of no great revelation to know she'd taken over the house again in the very short time she'd been here, I held my tongue, amazed at my own momentum, about her swift return and resumed control—for Hank's health and my love for him.

I held my tongue when I saw the living room furniture arranged to the way she'd had it two weeks ago. I held my tongue when I saw she'd emptied the refrigerator of leftover dishes and homemade sauces. I held my tongue at the sight of her antique silver tea set in front of the coffee maker, her crocheted doily in the middle of the kitchen table, and her stupid soup simmering in the big stainless-steel pot on the stove. And I really had to hold my tongue when I saw two full wine bottles in the recycling bin. I turned and stalked out of the kitchen without a word when I was done putting away the groceries.

"Don't you dare wake up Henry. He's resting and doesn't need you up there," her voice radiated through the hall.

Up there? "Up yours," I muttered, climbing the stairs.

I opened the bedroom door and tiptoed over to pull the TV remote from Hank's limp hand. It was routine now, curling up next to him to watch the news or play a game of backgammon on his iPad. Despite my resolution of not wanting to stress him as he recovered, I couldn't help but want to wake him so I could talk about the ongoing grudge match between his mother and me. I took a calming breath, and instead, sat on the chair. I was sure it hadn't been easy on him—being caught between two women he loved, trying to please both of us. No matter what he did, he was in a lose-lose situation.

Had this been before he was rushed to the hospital, maybe I would've told her off about coming back to our house and taking over again. Was it like George's battle with cancer, his death, and now Hank's heart attack, that I felt I couldn't do anything but to suck it up as I've done over the years?

I stretched out my legs on the ottoman, observing Hank sleep, head back, mouth open, as I listened to the steady hum of the heat blowing through the floor vents. But after five minutes, I was bored. I grabbed the iPad off the bed. Normally, I would've welcomed the chance to sit and do nothing, but I was feeling restless and anxious. And when I'm restless and anxious, I browse the Internet for live updates on the current buzz around the world.

Several windows were still open on the iPad. One being the home page for the *Riviera Retirement Residence* and another, real estate listings for similar three-bedroom condos like Margaret's. As I scrolled through, I looked at Hank with sympathy. I know I bring my fair share of the day-to-day minutia to him but having to worry over the future of his mother must be worse.

She must've brought up the sale of her condo again to Hank. Now that I think about it, I do recall hearing him questioning her about the age of her kitchen appliances and the number of parking spaces her unit came with. Could Hank be seriously thinking about her living under the roof of the retirement residence, or was it her seriously thinking about living under *our* roof for the rest of her golden years?

Without hesitation, I'd vote for the *Riviera* option. Hank could get his daily exercise by walking over to see her. But then again, Margaret could get hers by walking over to see us. Any day *and* any time. *Unless* Hank and the kids poked their heads in to keep her from doing so—maybe playing a game of dominoes or joining her for Sunday night dinners could help keep her at arm's length. Certainly, it wouldn't be me doing the visiting.

The vacuum cleaner turned on as I closed the iPad. *What the hell happened to our weekend?* I hauled myself off the chair and then clomped down the stairs and yanked the vacuum's plug out of the wall socket.

"*What?*" I heard Margaret utter in the dining room. Two seconds later, she appeared, with her hands on her hips. "What do you think you're doing?"

"Hank's still sleeping," I said, throwing the cord on the floor.

"Well, it's almost time for his lunch anyway," she finally said. "*And* by the way, I don't know who vacuumed in this house last, but the carpets are filthy."

Visions of wrapping the vacuum cleaner cord around her neck danced in my head. "My mother vacuumed on Wednesday," I mumbled, walking past her into the kitchen.

She followed right behind me, pratting about the importance of daily cleaning until I was ready to scream. Exhausted, and it wasn't even noon, I turned around, looking right into her eyes. "The carpets wouldn't get dirty in two days, Margaret."

She finally spoke again. "This house *needs* to be cleaned every day for Henry. Unless you want to see him in the hospital again," she fretted in a mighty sour way. I kept silent, making fresh coffee as she leaned against the kitchen doorframe. She shrugged. "I'll just have to vacuum later, I suppose."

A tiresome struggle is what this is. I don't think Margaret thought the carpets needed vacuuming. She just wanted to put a few lines in them—much like a wild animal trying to mark its territory.

Making her way to the kitchen table, she must've sensed my irritation because she flopped down in one of the chairs and then began flipping through the newspaper, pretending, I was sure, to be reading it as I carried on with making my coffee, keeping myself to myself.

Two-and-a-half minutes. That was the time it took for her to jump into a whole new ballgame, declaring out of nowhere, "Edith is a silly one."

Impossible.

I could see her shaking her head side to side. "Can you believe she almost sent someone two thousand dollars over the phone?" She got up from the table. "Want some soup?"

"Uh... no, thank you," I answered, completely baffled by her tactic of trying to suck me in by the facade of sweetness.

She looked over at me as she spooned soup into two bowls. "A con artist called her, pretending to be her long-lost grandson and said he urgently needed money... and can you imagine, she was about to get on the phone with her bank and wire him the funds..." Grimly, I remained silent and turned on the computer that sat on the table after watching her use another one of my decorative tea towels to wipe the drops of soup she'd spilled on the floor. "... luckily for her, I was there when she got the call. I grabbed the phone right out of her hand and gave him a piece of my mind," she proudly claimed, putting one bowl in front of me. "Good thing I've taken the time to educate myself on all the scams out there."

I nodded politely as she sat down. "I guess seniors are more vulnerable, more trusting, with more disposable income," I said, wishing I hadn't opened my mouth.

She gave me a harsh look followed by a slight smile.

We all knew who Margaret had been trusting—and she shouldn't have had anything to do with him in the first place. My fists clenched invariably. I consciously unclenched them, trying to relax.

I busied myself with the soup I didn't want, listening to her talk about Edith's naivety and then to the water churning through the pipes because the toilet upstairs was just flushed.

Margaret jumped up from the table and turned on the stove again. She took out another bowl from the cupboard before facing me. "Move over so Henry can sit there."

Paying no attention to the fact that *Cruella De Vil* was back, I slid my computer to the other side of the table and sat on the cold seat, excited to see a promising looking message from a literary agent in my inbox. I nervously clicked the unread email, waiting for it to load.

"Are you going to have more soup?" Margaret asked as she stood beside me with her hand on the bowl.

"Yes, take it. Thank you," I said.

"Yes, take it, I want more soup or no, take it, I don't want more soup?"

I shook my head, not at all surprised she needed clarification. "No more soup. You can take the bowl," I snapped a bit before flashing a quick smile and whipping my eyes back to the email in front of me.

> *Dear Allie,*
>
> *Thank you for considering The Writing Factory. Your book is fantastic! It has a lot of potential, and it would delight us to work with you. We would like to offer you an editing service to help polish it before we can offer you the best representation deal.*
>
> *Please follow the instructions we have included at the bottom of this email, and we can start working together right away!*
>
> *All the best,*
>
> *Kelly M. Smith*
>
> *The Writing Factory*

My lips formed a broad grin.

Your book is fantastic?

I jumped up from my chair and ran to the stairs. "Hank!" I yelled, barely breathing.

The best representation deal?

"Coming," I heard him say.

I leaned against the railing, and as I was about to run up the stairs, he appeared at the top.

"Good news!" I beamed.

"Oh, yeah?" He smiled when he reached me. "What is it?"

"I may be close to getting published," I cried, throwing my arms gently around him.

"*Really?*"

"*Yes*! And they said they'd be delighted to represent me."

"Oh, wow," he said. "That *is* great news." He gave me a long squeeze, kissing my forehead. "I'm *so* proud of you."

"Yeah, well you won't be for *too* long," Margaret snorted behind me.

I spun around and looked at her.

"Why would you say such a thing?" Hank growled.

"Because they're not offering you *anything*, Allison," she said with a smirk. "They're trying to get money from you. It's a scam aimed at desperate wannabe writers."

I turned to Hank, speechless, before facing her again. "What are you talking about?"

"I read the *whole* email, which obviously you didn't. And when you click on the link, you'll find out that the editing package costs over twelve hundred dollars, and the publishing program costs another fifteen hundred," she said. "I mean, *c'mon*... if the book was *that* good, they'd be offering to pay you."

I stared at her, dumbfounded.

She gave me a cruel smile before turning to Hank. "Henry, you read the email and see if you can explain it to her," she said, strutting back to the kitchen and mumbling under her breath, "Seniors aren't the only ones who are gullible."

29 – ESTRANGED

I threw myself on the bed after Hank confirmed, with an online search, that the *We Want to Represent You* email was, in fact, a scam. Was I really that dumb, no, naïve... gullible like Edith, that I immediately fell headlong into this, without as much as giving it a second thought?

He sat beside me. "Don't give up just because a few people said *no*," he said. "Not everyone's going to like your writing. Look at *J. K. Rowling*— she *still* gets one-star reviews."

I wanted to laugh, but I frowned instead, pouting almost. "Well, I know that kids..." I reached for words, "*my* kinders would like—*love* my story," I said firmly before pausing a moment. "Makes me feel like a failure."

He hastily chimed in. "Failure makes people grow," he said, clearing his throat. "Be persistent. It's key if you *really* want this. Send it out to more agents or write another story. Remember, it's better you try than to wonder what might've been."

"Yeah, I guess. It's just that I really thought it was a great story that would've been snapped up by all."

"It probably *is* a great story to someone out there," he said, gently poking me. "Keep pushing. You just never know... success might be right around the corner."

I sighed quietly. "I know. Just hope I'm not too old to be successful at it," I said, wondering if I could be successful with a home staging business. *What the hell did I know about it anyway?*

He stood up, arched his back and yawed. "*C'mon*, Allie. Age shouldn't determine if you're allowed or not allowed to start something new and be good at it," he said. "You just have to have enough passion for it."

I rolled on my back, looking straight up at the ceiling when Hank closed the bathroom door behind him. Was I really *that* passionate about writing, or did my subconscious trick me into believing I wanted... or needed, better yet, deserved to be successful at it after twenty years of teaching? Truth is, I don't think I'm that crazy about putting words on paper. I didn't enjoy the experience of writing the children's story. It was dreadful, like the stupid detox. I thought about this, drifting back to my high school days, as I stared at my hands, front and back. My school guidance counselor, I clearly remember, said I had enough talent for a career in creative design. She said I should find something I could do every day, all day to be happy. *Imagine that.*

I sat up when Hank came out of the bathroom. "Let's get out for a walk," I said, suddenly realizing that making the rooms of a home look attractive to a buyer, would really stoke the fire in me. It *was* my passion—not writing, forget that, but using art, color, accessories, and lighting that could transform ugly rooms into lovely rooms would. Plain and simple. It thrilled me to know I'd have an opportunity to turn this passion into a business. But would Hank be as thrilled?

We walked a slow pace around the block. And because the weather was unusually mild, Hank suggested we walk some more. I observed him closely for overexertion. "You sure?"

He took my hand, swinging it a bit. "I'm good. Don't worry."

We walked further up the street and then swung right. We continued another five minutes and when we stopped at the busy intersection, I turned my head toward the *Riviera* across the street. My mind floated in and out.

"Let's go check it out," I heard him say.

Involuntarily, I smiled. "Sure," I said, trying not to sound too eager.

Five minutes later, Hank and I were being shown around by what seemed like a caring and highly skilled staff member. It looked as nice as it did in the photos, feeling like a luxury hotel with outstanding services and a warm, friendly environment. She showed us the spacious restaurant, the rooftop patio, the exercise room, floor models of three different units, and then the games room. And when our quick tour ended, we grabbed brochures and promised we'd be back after carefully thinking about it.

Neither of us spoke until we exited the well-kept grounds full of perfectly shaped evergreens and garden beds. "So, what did you think?" I said, decidedly overwhelmed.

"Oh, it's beautiful, but expensive."

"I know. It's alarming how expensive these places are," I said, noticing he wore a grim defeated look.

We continued walking in silence and then I reached for his hand, squeezing it when we walked along a well-worn gravel path, a shortcut to our street. "Oh, there's another one of Val's listings," I said, pointing to a wooden sign full of eye-catching imagery and information.

He sighed heavily. "I should've gotten into real estate," he said. "House sales are at an all-time high. Easy money and little stress, looks like."

The perfect segue. I swallowed hard. "Did Val tell you about her home stager leaving?"

"Uh, no, she didn't," he replied. "Why would she?"

We slowed while I explained the opportunity. He listened carefully, asking questions, and then after I finished, he shook his head nervously— a bad sign. "It sounds risky to me. We have to be careful since I won't be able to work at the pace I was before. And what about your dream of writing?"

I stopped in my tracks, feeling an emotional downward spiral coming. But I took a deep breath, forging ahead. "I'm not sure I have enough passion for it, Hank. Honestly. I merely stumbled upon it—I was passionate about the vision and hope of becoming a successful author making lots of money." For effect, I sighed deeply. "It was wishful thinking without the spark, I guess."

He walked behind me, silently processing.

I twisted around, panicky of what he'd say next. "Hank, I really think I can do this. I'd be making twice as much as I make now."

"So, you want to quit your job?"

"Not right away," I said. "But maybe I could start learning with Val on the weekends."

I continued describing the potential of the business. I told him the number of agents in Val's office, the number of listings the office had, and the profit we could make with each staging. And by the time we got home, he looked tired—but *not* uninterested. "I don't know," he said tenderly, taking off his coat. "There's a lot happening right now, so I'm not sure it'd be the best time to start a business." He threw his hat on the top shelf. "We'd have to take out a second mortgage," he said.

I stared at his sweaty forehead. "Yeah, but home staging is pretty much guaranteed. Look, you're tired. We can talk later."

"Okay," he said. "Let me think about it more."

I reached up and touched his shoulders. "And remember what you said... age shouldn't determine if you're allowed or not allowed to start something new and be successful at it," I said, giving him a wink.

Then came Baily, charging down the stairs with a mouthful of... *something*.

"My mom must've fallen asleep," he said, turning to the stairs. "I'll go check on her."

I kneeled on the floor. "Okay, I'll be up soon," I said, pulling cotton balls out of Baily's mouth. "Oh, and we should also continue our conversation about the *Riviera... and* your mother," I said, mumbling the rest of what I wanted to say to no one in particular as I headed into the kitchen, "because there's *no way in hell* she's living here with us—"

"Don't worry," Margaret said, angrily pushing past me from out behind the kitchen wall. "I'm leaving." She was about to storm up the stairs, but stopped, shouting up them, "Henry, can you bring my bags down—oh, never mind." She glared back at me. "The least you can do is help me get them and drive me home."

"Fine," I retorted. The sight of her standing in front of me, waiting for me to retrieve her bags, made the corners of my mouth twitch.

•　　•　　•

Margaret was sitting in the car, huffing and grumbling when I squeezed her last bag in beside the ridiculous tea set she'd carefully packed in its original box from the sixties. Her head spun around when I slammed the hatchback door, and then her eyes bore through me as I got into the car.

Whatever all her looks and noises were about, I gave her no reaction. I took a deep breath and released it, reversing out of the driveway.

We drove in silence until we stopped at the intersection where the bright red and ochre brick *Riviera* stood. I pictured Margaret standing at the regal-looking window on the seventh floor, smiling and waving at everyone—and me, standing behind her, smiling with arms ready. *Just. One. Push.* I'm half joking, of course. But I'm also half not joking.

"I'm not going to live there if that's what you're thinking," she muttered from the back seat. "Those places are where people go to die."

My hands gripped the steering wheel. "It's not a nursing home, Margaret. It's a retirement residence where you can thrive and be... well... happy." I shook my head at the thought. "No one is telling you to live there. But it might be a nice option if you're considering selling your condo."

"There's no way I'm letting you guys ship me off to a place where they'll treat me like an invalid."

I wouldn't have any problem living in a place where I'd be fully taken care of. Hell, I could live there now, on a part-time basis. I smiled tightly, gently stretching my stiff neck and tight shoulders. "Don't worry, Margaret. Living in a place like that would be like living in a hotel with all the amenities. They want their occupants to be as independent as possible." When I looked in the mirror, she was staring out the opposite window, shaking her head with sad eyes. "It would ultimately be your decision," I added in a low voice.

She raised an eyebrow. "*Really?* Because it seems clear to me you and Henry think otherwise."

"We want what's best for you. If you're selling your condo, you'll need a plan, right?" I said, suddenly vaguely conscience she might be terrified of feeling abandoned—much like how some kids feel about their first time at daycare. That is, until you get a phone call twenty minutes later by one staffer telling you how happy they are, dancing with other children and splashing in the water center. I looked in the mirror again, trying to catch her reaction but there was none, so we drove in silence until the next intersection.

"What did you tell Henry when you went upstairs to get my bags?" she said coldly.

"Nothing. He was on his phone."

"Don't you think he's going to worry when he sees I'm not there."

Uh, no. "He'll think we went out," I replied. "I'll call him when we get to your place."

"Oh, never mind. I'll call him myself." She held her phone up for me to see in the mirror.

"Wait. No. Let *me* call him," I snapped back. "He's going to get stressed listening—"

"Henry?" she said after clearing her throat.

Dammit, Margaret. The only thing I could do was listen, listen to her babble away unless I pulled her out of the car and wrestled her to the ground.

"Sorry I didn't say goodbye, but Edith needed my help," she said to Hank.

Edith? How did she get into this?

"Yes... yes." She heaved a loud deep sigh. "She's driving me home right now." There was a brief pause. "Yes, yes," she said, responding to whatever Hank was telling her. "I will. And don't you forget your pills in the kitchen. I organized them in your dad's old pill container." And when she finally finished telling him about the meatball dish she'd left in the fridge, she hung up.

"Hope you're happy," she said, adjusting her seatbelt. "I had to lie so he wouldn't worry about me being thrown out by his wife."

Thrown out by his wife? Reminding myself that peace is in my hands as she punched my buttons, I made myself smile, concentrating on maneuvering the car through the construction zone ahead.

When we reached her condo building, I insisted on helping her with all her things, but she insisted on being dropped off at the front door and doing it herself. "Tell Henry I'll call him later," I heard her say through the hatchback before slamming it shut.

•   •   •

Twenty-five minutes later, I was home re-sorting the cupboards and rearranging the living room furniture. When I finished, I flopped haphazardly on the sofa. As I was waiting for Hank to come down, my phone pinged with a text.

[Do not use my turquoise teacup please]

Delete. The weekend was going to be spent resting and relaxing with Hank, not thinking about Margaret and her damn teacup. My mind sauntered around locking her out of our home completely.

I dozed off but was awakened fifteen minutes later by another text from Margaret. This one informing me she'd left Hank's shirts in the dryer. With a profound sense of detachment, I went through the motions of pulling myself up and then lugging myself to the basement in a complete fog. My trance-like state was broken back in the kitchen when my phone flashed with a series of texts from Val. Julie the stager was selling her inventory.

"*Thirty thousand dollars?*" I cried through the phone. "For what?"

My stomach dropped as Val ran off the price list of items. "It's a good deal," she said. "Everything she's listing is high-end... the sofas, the wall hangings, tables, beds—"

"I thought we were going to wait until the end of June?" I said, feeling queasy and unsure suddenly.

"Now's the time, Allie. Spring is around the corner, so you need to be up and running well before that. It's going to be busy. But don't worry— a lot can be done evenings and weekends." I could hear Val clicking away at her keyboard. "It's a *really* good deal. Just talk to Hank and let me know. I told her to give you at least a week before trying to sell it to someone else."

Thirty thousand dollars? Who has that kind of money lying around, waiting to be invested? We certainly don't.

Seconds after saying goodbye, my phone pinged again. I felt like a sealed vessel about to explode as I read the text.

[Hi mom, we r going to stay until Monday afternoon. Can you call school? Pls. xoxo miss you]

Oh, to be young without the responsibilities. When I was his age, I took a lot for granted. There's something about youth that makes you feel like you'll be that way forever, but you have no idea how life changes and how good you had it until you've already grown up. *How ironic.*

[Ok. Have fun. Miss you too! xoxo]

I smiled deeply when I heard Hank trotting down the stairs. I was ready to begin my weekend with him, hopefully this time without an unwanted houseguest or a roaring Hoover in the background.

30 – Out of Sight, Out of Mind

Monday morning. The kids were excited to see me, and as much as I'd missed their cute, adorable faces, everything felt strange—like a post-trip doldrum when you've been away all lively and full of energy on a fun-filled vacation and then you come back to the realities waiting at home. But this time, the realities were waiting at work.

I gathered the children around for circle time, preparing myself for the usual round of questions and unwelcome comments. *Your hair looks funny. What happened to your face?* they'd asked as they pointed to my recently waxed eyebrows. *Is your husband dead? Your teeth are yellow. How come? Can you put crayons in the microwave?*

However, this morning had a particular focus.

Where's Miss Rebecca?

When's Miss Rebecca coming back?

We think she's pretty.

"Don't you think I'm pretty?" I asked, feeling a bit rejected.

They shook their heads, *No, you're too old,* they'd said collectively. I sighed, feeling the heat in my face. And then they went on. And on, until snack time. *Rebecca, Rebecca, Rebecca.*

And then as if speaking to me, and only me, Headmaster Thomas had walked into the lunchroom and reviewed, again, the procedures for taking extended periods of time off. He gave us a wide smile and then ended his *lecture* with a not-so-gentle reminder that classroom evaluations were next week. As the younger, more eager staff sat around after he'd left, talking about their stupid reality shows, my mouth went dry. No longer feeling the need to pretend to fit in with the people here or with the school's expectations, I felt faint, unsure if I was on the outside of Hillmount, looking in, or, in the inside of these four walls, looking out. I knew I was getting the cue to leave. *But now would not be a good time.*

·　　·　　·

My kinders leave at two thirty-five. I'm allowed to leave at four o'clock. But today, I was ready to leave at three o'clock. After spending almost five and a half hours with twenty-three six-year-olds who were prone to tantrums, I was exhausted. And, after hearing the name *Rebecca* roll off the tongues of children and staff all day, I had to admit I was beginning to harbor a bit of resentment toward her. I did get it, though. I hadn't been giving my students my all lately, and they deserved better.

After the last carpet was rolled and put away for the custodian's Monday night mopping, I tinkered around the classroom for another ten minutes before looking at the clock again. It was only twenty after three. *Fuck it.* I was too tired to stay. So I put on my coat and gathered the rest of my things before closing the classroom door behind me.

And wouldn't you know, as I turned the corner, there was Headmaster Thomas, in the hallway, talking to the parent of one of my students. I froze, but it was too late. He'd already seen me. I had no choice but to continue walking down the hallway toward them, clad in my winter coat and boots, with my purse in one hand and car keys jingling in the other.

Headmaster Thomas glanced at the clock on the wall above Matthew's mother's head. He smiled stiffly when I got closer and then continued standing there, giving no suggestion of what was really on his mind as Matthew's mother and I started talking about Matthew and how cute he was, but how much of a troublemaker he could be. And then, "Oh, that

Matthew fell in *love* with Rebecca, let me tell you," she said, shifting her attention back to Headmaster Thomas. "What a teacher she is."

I blinked at both of them. "So... so I hear." *Great. Now the parents were in love with her.* I could stand this no longer, so I gave the excuse of running late for an appointment. I waved goodbye and headed out the side door to the parking lot. This was after Headmaster Thomas's eyes rolled up at the clock again, I think.

•　　•　　•

"How was your first day back?" Hank asked, loading his morning cereal bowl and coffee mug into the dishwasher.

I leaned against the counter, staring at a metal spatula on top of the stove. I didn't only have to deal with Margaret, but now, I'd have to handle a classroom full of kindergarteners who simply didn't want me anymore. "It was okay," I replied. "The kids were happy, but then after that wore off, they wanted to talk about Rebecca and how she could make perfect snowflakes and sing silly songs."

He scratched his head, looking frumpy and disheveled in his blue woven kimono robe. "Hang in there," he said, giving off a loud sneeze. "Spring break is coming up in a few weeks."

I nodded gratefully, sitting on one of the kitchen stools. "Is Cam home?" I asked, fiddling with the salt shaker in front of me. But before he could answer, I gave him a warm smile. "Sorry, I haven't even asked about you, *and* the cold you seem to have now."

He shuffled along the counter, giving me a run-down on his day, including his food intake and energy level.

"I'm glad you're feeling a bit better," I said, watching him swallow the last of his pills. "So, where's Cam?"

He coughed slightly. "Upstairs."

"Oh," I sighed. "I thought he would've come down to say hi. Guess he didn't miss me that much."

Hank gave a nervous laugh. "I'm sure he did. It's just that he can't..."

I jumped off the stool. "Can't what?"

Hank looked at the floor, taking a deep breath before lifting his eyes. "He thinks he may've broken his—."

"*What!*" I cried, rushing out of the kitchen before Hank could finish.

Upstairs, I pushed Cameron's door wide open and there he was, sitting on the edge of the bed, in what seemed like agony. I kept it to simple yes and no questions about his final ski run on one of the trickier hills in Mountain Springs before seeing it was after four on his wall clock. Too late to take him to our family doctor, I insisted on driving him to the hospital for an x-ray.

Three hours later, Cameron was sent home with a prescription for his throbbing pain and crutches for his sprained ankle. Disappointed he didn't get a leg cast for his friends to sign, he was more disappointed that his injured ankle was his driving one. No cast and now he couldn't drive?

"Not you guys again," I heard a woman's voice behind us as we were heading to the main exit.

I spun around, and sure enough, it was Helen.

We were able to keep the congenial conversation to a minimum. "That's four family members at the hospital in the last three months," she said.

"I know," I said, shaking my head as I looked at Cameron's swollen ankle.

She chuckled before hugging us goodbye. Moments later, she disappeared around the corner toward the elevators as Cameron hobbled beside me.

•　　•　　•

Cameron's phone lit up with a text as we were waiting outside of *Tony's Pepperoni*. He shot me a half-crooked smile after reading it. "Something about a teacup she wants me to bring over tonight... and some book *or* books?" he mumbled as he re-read the text again, sneezing. "Am I staying with her tonight?" he said with a small frown on his face.

"No... and tell her she's going to have to wait. You won't be driving for the next four weeks and your dad... well, just tell her she has to wait."

"Can't you go over?" he sputtered.

"*No*," I said, slowly opening the car door. "I'm not driving there and back so she can have her precious little teacup. Tell her she'll have to wait or get a taxi to come get it."

"*Wow*, Mom," he said, cracking a smile. "That's a bit harsh."

"Ha," I said, reaching for my wallet. "But, still. Tell her *no*."

"I'll call her," I heard him say as I shut the door.

Back at the car with our hot pizza, my phone buzzed in my purse.

I untwisted my seatbelt. "Can you grab that in case it's your dad?"

I could see Cameron shaking his head after he checked. "Sorry, Mom," he said. "It's a text from Grandma."

"Great. Now she's texting me." I gave him a sidelong glance. "What does she want *this* time?"

"She said I shouldn't have been allowed to miss school today to ski. And that's why I have a sprained ankle... and a cold."

I should've known she was going to blame me. I was inclined to believe she was also going to blame me that Cameron's sprained ankle represented another driver who wouldn't be able to take her around town.

When I grabbed my phone out of Cameron's hand, it buzzed again. Without thinking, I automatically read her loud and angry text.

[HANK SHOULDN'T BE EATING PIZZA FOR DINNER!!!]

Irritated, I backed out of the parking space with a tight smile. I genuinely, desperately, needed this woman out of my life.

•   •   •

By Thursday, after all the kids had left for the day, I collapsed in my desk chair. The past three days had been hectic. Not only was I busy with school, but I was busy at home with Hank and Cameron recovering from their aches, pains, and winter colds. Then there was Val, waiting patiently for my answer regarding Julia's *thirty-thousand-dollar* inventory. All this was making me feel a little achy myself.

Speaking of aches, Margaret had been quiet since the pizza scolding. However, Hank had been giving me updates, albeit unwanted ones, like how she'd taken the initiative to call a plumber to fix her leaky toilet. And then he'd laughed and said she'd had the same guy fix her refrigerator and T.V. too.

"Strange though, I haven't heard from her since," Hank said later that evening. "I've called Edith, but she hasn't been answering either."

"Maybe your mother's been out and about with her," I said.

He wiped his puffy nose. "I thought Edith had to stay off her foot for the next two weeks."

"Oh, right," I said, completely forgetting her big toe was apparently swollen from gout. "I bet she's been helping Edith get to the doctor's or get groceries... I'm *sure* she's fine."

"Yeah, maybe," he said. "But I'm concerned. We talk or text every day, no matter what."

True.

He looked at me, startled. *"What?"* he said, because I was sure I had some kind of expression on my face.

I pulled on my yoga pants. "Nothing," I said, shaking my head side to side.

"What, Allie? I know you want to say something."

"It's just that you worry so much about her. I'm *sure* she's fine."

"It's been almost three days, and she hasn't called once. Don't you think that's a bit strange?"

I thought about this for a moment. "Good point." I sat next to him. "It *has* been three days." *Huh.* This definitely raised a few red flags—especially since she knew her son and grandson were fending for themselves with colds and damaged body parts, alone, for eight hours a day.

Hank gave me a concerned glance after his call went to her voicemail again. Soon after, the familiar look of worry spread across his entire face.

I stood up, exhaling impatiently. "Okay, I'll go."

"Thank you, Al," he said through coughs. "And we'll talk more about the inventory investment you brought up last night. Promise."

My head snapped back. *"Really?"* I exclaimed, forgetting *all* about Margaret.

"Yes, but don't get *too* excited." He gave me a tight squeeze. "I'm waiting to hear from the bank. We'd need a loan but without having to put our house on the line. And there'll be some heavy fees involved, so you know."

I nodded with a pounding heart. Thrilled he was putting the wheels in motion, I kept a straight face. "I'll call as soon as I get there," I said, dashing out of the bedroom, almost skipping down the stairs and out the front door.

31 - The Fall of Cruella De Vil

When I stepped off the elevator in Margaret's building, an array of spices and sounds seeping through the doors filled my senses. I turned left and walked down the warmly lit orange hallway that'd always made me feel I were inside a squash. At her door, I glanced over my shoulder at Edith's, tempted to rap on it first. But I wished myself luck and then lightly tapped on Margaret's.

After no response, I knocked again. This time harder.

Nothing.

"She probably won't answer," I heard a voice behind me.

I turned to see Edith peeking her head out into the hallway.

"Oh, hi there," I said as she opened her door further, revealing baby blue sweatpants and the red turtleneck sweater Margaret had knitted for her birthday last year.

"She hasn't been answering her door since Tuesday," she said, wiggling her pants further up her waist. "She said she was spending the next few days in bed because of her arthritis."

For Margaret, staying in bed all day would seem like a hell of a lot of work. "Oh," I said, curiously looking at Edith's foot to see if she really had a big red toe. But all I could see were thick white socks inside her navy-blue slippers.

A real hugger like Helen, she opened her door fully and moved out into the hallway, stretching out her arms to clasp me. I returned her hug and then stepped back, turning my attention to Margaret's locked door. Her avoiding Edith was out of the ordinary—she'd been a good friend to Margaret, and the two of them depended on each other whenever they were struggling with an illness or injury.

From the time I'd known Hank's parents, I'd never had to use the spare key to open the door. It felt a little strange doing so, especially on my own, with a neighbor standing behind me. "I better let myself in then," I said, inserting the key into the lock and slowly opening it. *Good Lord*, I didn't want to meet any casualties. Our family had been through enough in the last couple of months to add *tending to sick Margaret* to the list. *Who would do the tending?* I shuddered at the possibilities.

Edith followed me into the condo. It was dark, except for the kitchen. With her close behind, we stepped over Margaret's shoes and winter boots scattered on the long Persian rug in the front hallway. I flicked on the switch that controlled the hall and living room lights. "*Margaret?*" I called out, glancing around quickly. "It's me, *Allie*."

"Look at this mess," Edith gasped.

I took a few steps toward the kitchen. Not only was a mildewy scent of stagnant water coming from it, there was a mass of dishes with partially consumed food piled in the sink.

"*Margaret?*" I called again, kicking off my boots.

Edith was still behind me, tsking away with her tongue. "*Look at this place*," she kept repeating.

My eyes focused on the living room. Tissue boxes, magazines, and sections of newspaper filled the sofa, with an abandoned vacuum cleaner lying on the floor next to it. Everything seemed out of place, completely out of character for someone like Margaret who'd let a messy house ruin her mood. I took a deep breath in, listening to the voice entrenched inside that something wasn't right.

Edith continued shaking her head and then followed me toward the bedroom.

The door was closed. *"Margaret,"* I said nervously, unsure of what I'd find behind it.

I struggled with the knob with shaky hands before pushing the door open a crack. It didn't go any further until I forced it against whatever was stuffed behind it. Opened fully, there she was, in bed, under the covers with George's red checkered robe on top. Piled high beside her were his clothes, a jumble of photographs and more plates of half-eaten food, which I suspect was the cause of the pungent smell filling the room and the rest of the condo.

"Margaret?" I said a little louder.

She didn't respond.

My legs became liquid as I called her name softly this time. *"Margaret?"*

Seconds passed before she merely lifted her head. An immense inward feeling of relief went through me as she moved her legs ever so slightly.

I stood there for a moment, speechless because *never, never, ever* have I seen her like this with her deep horizontal forehead lines. She didn't look like herself in the dim light of an antique bedside lamp. As I edged closer to her, she looked pale, fragile and weak.

"What are *you* two doing here?" she muttered weakly.

"Didn't you hear me knock?" I said as my heart pounded unusually hard.

"We called your name out a dozen times too," Edith added as she dashed around the bed to turn off the TV which was showing an excited contestant jumping up and down after winning a Jeep Convertible on *The Price is Right.*

"Hey, I was watching that," Margaret growled.

"Are you sick?" I asked, because her eyes were heavy, and she was moving her head slowly. "Or did you take something?"

She raised her head again. *"No,* I'm not sick, and *no,* I didn't take any drugs, if that's what you're thinking, *Dr. Smartie."* She pulled herself up in the bed, shaking out the covers on top with her swollen fingers and knuckles. When she did, I caught a glimpse of the raggedy pink nightgown and slippers she had on. *Slippers in bed?* Something *was* clearly wrong.

"Let's get you up and walking around," Edith said behind me.

"*No,*" Margaret replied. "I'm perfectly fine here, *thank you* very much."

"Tea—we can have tea," I suggested, looking at her helplessly. And then suddenly, she whipped off the covers, knocking pillows and photographs on the floor.

Edith returned to her condo and within minutes, brought back a plate of banana bread after helping Margaret out of bed and making tea.

Margaret, looking rather disheveled, sat at the dining room table while Edith told us about the latest adventure she had on the phone with a computer tech guy who had helped her through a malfunction. As she continued talking about how confusing computers could be, I looked over at Margaret. Something still wasn't right with her, but I didn't tell Hank that when I called him. Instead, I went along with Margaret's fabricated story—something about Edith's inflamed toe and sore back.

After an hour of sitting around the table, Edith stood up. "Okay, well... I'll let the two of you get caught up now." She patted Margaret's shoulder lovingly. "My show's about to start." She gave me another big hug after I walked her to the door to say goodbye. She leaned in and whispered, "I think she was just lonely, but look at her now."

I glanced over my shoulder and saw Margaret straightening the placemat in front of her as she took small sips of water. "Hmmm, maybe. I'll stick around and make sure she's okay," I said. "Thanks, Edith."

I took a deep breath in after closing the door, bracing myself. Margaret had actually been pleasant, perhaps because Edith was here. As mentioned, my mother-in-law could be sweet and kind one minute, bitter and mean the next. However, sweet and kind Margaret had manifested for over an hour now, which made me even more curious as to why. *Naturally.*

A little unsettled with *this* Margaret, I busied myself in the kitchen.

"Leave the dishes," I heard her say. "I'll do them later."

"Okay," I said meekly, pouring more tea before returning to the dining room.

"Go sit down, and I'll make us a fresh pot," she said, getting up from the table.

What was happening? Surprised and bewildered, I did as I was told, pushing a few books and magazines out of my way before sitting on the stiff and unyielding camel colored sofa.

I stretched my neck toward the kitchen, feeling bold and in the moment. "Why haven't you returned our calls?"

Sure enough, she didn't respond.

I spent the next few minutes sitting in silence before she came out of the kitchen. She placed a fresh cup of tea on the coffee table and then sat in George's chair. She looked over with intense eyes.

I'd never seen her in this light before, and it was scaring me. More awkward silence followed so I took a sip of the hot tea, burning my tongue. She wasn't answering any of the questions I had about her whereabouts for the past three days, and she certainly wasn't giving me the impression she was going to answer any other questions I had.

Margaret sank into the chair as she reclined it. "I miss him," she said with trembling lips.

Apart from being unsure of who this woman was sitting across from me, I wasn't sure if she meant she missed Hank or had missed George. I kept silent. *Likely my assumption would be wrong.*

"Getting old isn't for sissies, Allison." Not looking for a reply, she continued. "Now that Edith is moving," she paused, "I won't know anyone in this building anymore—"

"Edith is moving?" I gave her a concerned look. "When?"

Margaret shook her head with sad eyes. "I don't know. But soon."

"I'm sorry to hear this. I know she's been more than just a neighbor to you too."

She shrugged. "It's bittersweet," she said before breathing deeply through her nostrils. "I'm bitter she's leaving me all alone, and she's all sweet and happy because she'll be moving in with her son and his family. And her grandchildren *love* being with her and so does her daughter-in-law."

Was that an overtly hint or a subtle one? I tried my best to smile, shaking my head and pretending I didn't understand her. I certainly didn't want her getting any ideas of moving in with us, so I hastily changed the subject.

"What about your bingo nights? I thought you *loved* playing."

"I don't like it anymore," she said, looking directly into my eyes. "Most of the people are under forty, or English isn't their first language, so they're always asking for the numbers to be repeated. It's *too* slow." She stared off into the distance this time.

Her thoughts seemed disconnected and before I could open my mouth, she spoke again, regarding another concern. "And you guys only come to visit out of obligation."

I adjusted my shoulders. "What do you mean we only come out of obligation?"

"You only visit or call because you feel you *have* to—not because you *want* to," she said. "And I only hear from all of you when *I* call you."

I didn't respond as I shifted uncomfortably on the sofa.

She stretched out her legs further in front of her. "Wait. Henry does call me every day." She paused as if mulling it over. "But then again, that's probably out of guilt."

I figure it was safer to remain silent because she seemed more interested in what she was saying than in my reaction or response. As her thoughts went back to George, her sadness and vulnerability shocked me when she admitted she was lonely, and now that he was no longer here, she'd been missing that sense of purpose she'd had when trying to keep him alive and comfortable as he suffered through his pain—*and the uneasiness that came with contemplating his own death*, she'd said, closing her eyes.

I did not realize this.

I broke the silence, several moments after she finished talking. "George was in good hands with you," I said, hoping my carefully chosen words would provide comfort. *Yes,* comfort. I was trying to comfort Margaret. Just knowing that, felt odd but nice. I tried not to smile. "And he survived for as long as he did because of you." I grabbed my tea and gulped the rest of it, choking a bit as I felt my heart slightly slowing and opening. "You still have all of us to worry about," I added, trying hard to lighten her sunken spirits.

She nodded and closed her eyes before moving the lever to the upright position. "You, know, Allison, I've had my fair share of people to worry about," she said, giving me a tight-lipped smile. And then for the next hour, she told me about her family—the family, she said, which comprised of her and her brother. "Or so it was supposed to be," she cried. She reached over for a tissue on the small, unsteady table and then told me about her brother, the brother who'd died at the tender age of four from a mysterious illness. And that brother, who I remember Hank telling me about, died when she was ten. *Yes, Allie. Margaret was once ten. She was young and vibrant and after looking at Hank's photos of her, way cooler than I thought.* She continued. "It left a gaping hole in my parents' hearts. And do you know what my mother did?" she asked quickly. "My mother drank to cope, and why? Because my father had a nervous breakdown, you know. And back in those days, when a person went a little cuckoo, do you know where they'd go?" she said. I watched as she got up, unsure if I was supposed to answer her little fill-in-the-blank quiz. "They'd go to a mental hospital," she said in a loud voice that made me jump a little. "I never knew him after that. He was never the same when he got out of that looney bin." She glared at me. "You know, a lot of senior residences have the same effect, except you never get out." *Is this why she had firmly resisted going to live there? Was she afraid of not being the same?* I doubted even Hank knew about this.

She sighed deeply as more tears welled in her eyes.

I'll admit, I was getting a bit teary eyed too. Her shoulders slumped when she sat on the sofa, looking defeated. And that's when it hit me. Here I was, looking at a woman struggling with a deep pain. The loss of her father and brother had had a profound effect on Margaret at a young age, and it seemed she'd never come to terms with it. She was drowning in a sea of grief, and even more so after having lost George. No wonder she eyed me every time she saw a wine glass in my hand. Like her mother, I was coping in her eyes too—with what exactly, she probably wondered.

But how did this explain her behavior toward me?

She must've read my mind. "On the day Henry was born, I vowed never to let him out of my sight. Especially when I found out I couldn't have more children," she said.

I sucked my teeth. "Why didn't you tell me any of this before?" *Because we could've skipped a whole lot of misery and frustration between us.*

"Well, I'm telling you now," she said in a low, moaning voice. She grabbed her rose pink teacup abruptly off the table. "George always seemed happier whenever you were around," she added before disappearing to the kitchen.

I watched her as she rinsed dishes, unsure of how to respond to the sudden change in topics. Maybe she felt like she'd lost all the men in her life. *Shall we include Keith on this list?* Not only did she miss George, but she missed that sense of purpose she'd had with him. Her greatest fear, I think, was losing that with Hank. Or losing Hank altogether.

She came out of the kitchen with a glass of water. "I know I've treated you badly over the years, but that's not to say you haven't been a little unwelcoming at times yourself."

I didn't answer. How could I? We were both guilty of harboring negative feelings toward each other. I busied myself wiping crumbs off the table and into a napkin. I didn't know what to make of this, except perhaps she'd been expressing her internal agony through her behavior. Or perhaps she felt she'd earned the right to say and do whatever she was thinking or wanting around me.

She leaned against the wall and heaved a heavy sigh. "The bottom line is, I only ever wanted what was best for my son. And I knew it'd be my job to love and protect him from the day he was born."

I held my breath, waiting for the right words to come out. "Yes, Margaret. But you need to understand he's also my husband," I said before clearing my throat. "And it's been my job to love him too."

"*Mmhmm*," she said, barely audible. Her red swollen eyes glazed over in a thousand-mile stare. "Maybe a part of me was jealous, since Henry has always been so devoted to you," she said.

I considered this for a moment. "So, do you think you've been spending all these years trying to show him I wasn't the one?"

Dead silence.

We stood there, neither of us saying another word. Something was happening. I was aware I was in unfamiliar territory with her, and it seemed she was aware of being in new territory with me too. We were processing, processing seeing each other for the very first time, I think. It was a bizarre feeling. The commotion went on within me, so much that I moved forward, readying my arms to hug her. But before I could stretch them out, she reached behind me. I heard her draw a breath. "I'm getting tired, so if you don't mind seeing yourself out, I'm going back to bed," she said after switching the kitchen light off.

"Of course," I said, recoiling. Standing there like a dummy, I watched her drag her feet back to her room. For a moment, I took in the condo where the sound of George's warm laughter had rung out so loudly. I couldn't help but laugh too. I pondered on Margaret's words, her fears, her crushed hopes. *Her frailty.*

• • •

I felt completely drained. And oddly, completely alert as if electrical currents were charging through me. The past few hours at Margaret's overwhelmed me with emotions I'd never expected to feel for her. I tried to view the past from her perspective. When I'd come into Hank's life, there she was, this seasoned and dedicated mother who'd raised a healthy, strong son, and there I was, working in a sports bar, marrying him and then doing everything wrong. No wonder she couldn't help but criticize. She simply longed to be in her son's life throughout, and even more so, now that George was gone. That still didn't give her the right to treat me poorly, however it did explain a lot.

It had me thinking, though. Would I be the same kind of mother-in-law? *Uh. Probably not.* When I got pregnant, both times, my first few reactions were *What the hell...?* and *Shit!* Don't get me wrong, I *love* Samantha and Cameron dearly. I've loved being a mother, but ever since becoming one, my life has revolved around them. I'll be happy, relieved and content, enjoying the fond memories of raising them when they go off and start their own families. I will not be sad because I'll be too busy enjoying my newfound freedom.

"Oh, by way, I called your mother and invited her for dinner tomorrow night," I told Hank as we climbed into bed that night.

"Oh wow, okay." He smiled awkwardly. "Let's see if Sam can come too."

And then, for the first time in a very long time, the worried expression on his face softened as I lay in bed next to him with the evening's images at Margaret's whirling before me.

32 - New Tricks for an Old Dog

Are you there, George? It's me, Allie.

Margaret has stopped, or has almost stopped, behaving like... well... like a mean old mother-in-law in the past twenty-four hours. She's only called Hank once, and that was to return his early morning call. And her one text to me, which began with 'Hi, Allie' and ended with 'Talk to you later, M' was to confirm the time I'd be picking her up for dinner.

Margaret told me about some parts of her childhood. I'm sure you were aware of those, which perhaps is why you married her. You were able to see beyond her big-mouthed acts to see the real her, right?

I'm beginning to understand she might be human like the rest of us, with fears and insecurities. Whether she's up to something, who knows, but I'll keep you posted.

Love Allie xoxo

Friday night. We all sat down to a tasty Asian dinner from our favorite restaurant. Takeout at the end of the week was typical for us but eating together at the table was not. Hank would eat in his office while finishing the last of his work, Cameron would be watching T.V., and if Samantha were home, she'd be asking to take her plate to her room. And me? I'd usually be at the kitchen table getting caught up on the latest worldly gossip with a grocery store tabloid. But tonight, for some reason, I didn't care who *Brad Pitt* was secretly dating or what the latest *Royal* drama was.

Margaret said little while each of us took turns talking about our week. Was she her usual negative self? Not really. Sure, there were a few comments, but mostly, she was positive. She stepped out of her comfort zone and tried the miso soup and sushi rolls without a word after. I'd give her a *C* minus at best—she was definitely trying. Bear in mind, this grade comes from someone who'd routinely score her an *F* every day.

As I was forking more noodles onto my plate, my phone rang out on the coffee table with *Uptown Girl*. There was a moment of silence as everyone looked my way. But knowing it was Val, I simply shrugged and returned to shoving noodles in my mouth.

Shortly afterwards, in the middle of Samantha's bizarre customer story at work, Hank dropped his spoon on the floor. Margaret quickly reached down to get it, and as a non-believer in the ten-second rule, she went straight to the kitchen to get another one. When she returned, my phone sang out *Uptown Girl* again. She threw the clean spoon on the table before rushing to get it.

"No, no, no Margaret, it's fine," I told her. "Just leave it."

Proof of her selective hearing syndrome, she grabbed it and then placed it squarely in my right hand.

Hank motioned me to take the call, so I dashed off to the kitchen, holding my breath.

"Didn't you get my text?" Val asked as soon as I said hello.

"No, what text?"

"The text to call me right away," she said. "I've been hanging around, waiting to hear from you."

I clamped my eyes shut. "Sorry. I didn't see it."

She sounded weary. "Have you decided on the inventory yet?" she said. "Julia has others interested too."

"Hank's eighty percent on board," I said, sounding eager but terrified of plunging into a hefty investment.

"Okay, but make him hundred percent on board," she said calmly.

"I will." I paused, my balance a little thrown off. "Don't worry," I assured her. I took a slow, deep breath. My mind raced with speeding thoughts because of the stupid article that flashed across my screen when googling hot staging ideas last night. The *Ten Ugly Truths of Becoming a Home Stager* caused the harsh voice inside to come out full force. Once again.

"I didn't think we'd need you so soon, but we're swamped. And we need to stage these homes so we can get agents through."

"*Really?*" I gulped.

"Yes," she said encouragingly. "And I don't want to risk losing you to a hungry stager ready to jump in."

Was I *really* ready to transform dreadful looking rooms into stunning ones with color coordinated furniture and matching accessories? However, wasn't that what motivational speakers hammered on routinely? *Start before you're ready.* Don't wait until you feel knowledgeable, confident and market savvy to get moving on a dream or business idea. *Like my feeble attempt at writing a children's book?*

I took another deep breath, trying to sync my throbbing heart with my breath. "Val, this is *really* happening, isn't it?" For a split second, I marveled at the idea of being my own boss, getting myself immersed in the tactics of accomplishing something by working my ass off. "I'll tell Hank it's now or never," I said, gripping my phone so hard, it hurt.

"What do you want me to do with these?" Margaret asked just as I hung up.

When I turned around, she was standing there with two half-eaten containers of food. Surprised she was asking rather than telling, I took them from her, put the lids on and then stuck them in the fridge. By the time I closed the fridge door, she was back again with three glasses. "So much water wasted in this house," she muttered, pouring them into the various plants she'd lined up along the kitchen windowsill. When she was done, she smiled before returning to the dining room. It was intensely satisfying. *Was I starting to believe in this new Margaret?* Maybe her world had suddenly come into focus. Somewhere in my body, arteries vibrated through my skin.

Five seconds later, Hank appeared in the kitchen with his empty plate.

My grin was wide and obvious. "That was Val needing an answer on the inventory."

He sighed heavily, setting his plate on the counter.

I stopped smiling. "What is it?"

He lowered his head in disappointment. "I didn't want to have to tell you this, but I got some rather discouraging news from the bank before dinner."

"*Oh?*" I said in a panic. "*That* doesn't sound good."

"*Well,*" he began reluctantly. "Banks aren't willing to give out money like they used to unless it's tied to a house...so I don't think I want to gamble on the inventory." He paused for a moment. "And plus, we'd need to store it, maintain it and move it. I don't want to get into debt if I can't work at the rate I was."

I nodded, forcing a smile. *Disappointment has to be one of the most uncomfortable feelings in life.* Here I was, ready to take a leap of faith into unchartered waters, building my wings on the way down. And now this sudden loss between reality and my expectations of owning a piece of the home staging industry had me close to tears. It was an unpleasant feeling.

Hank rubbed my shoulders. "We can talk more when my mom leaves."

"Talk about what?" Margaret asked when she entered the kitchen again.

Hank and I exchanged looks.

"Oh nothing, Margaret. We're trying to decide whether to build a wooden deck in the spring or not," I improvised, pointing to the backyard through the window.

Her face fell. "I'm not dumb," she said. "You two are up to something, and if it's that *Riviera* place, forget it. I'd rather stay in my condo."

"That's not it, Mom," Hank assured her, seeming a little agitated.

"Then what is it?" she asked, turning to me. "You *know* I don't like to be lied to."

It took me a long time to answer. "It's nothing. We're just considering a small business," I finally said.

"Decorating homes, right?"

Hank rubbed his forehead and then ran a hand through his hair. "How did you know?"

"My eyes may be failing me, but my ears aren't." She gave us a knowing stare. "I hope you're not getting a loan from a bank—they charge *too* much."

Hank and I exchanged looks again. *I guess she would know after the fiasco with Keith.*

"I don't want to see you borrowing money," she added meaningfully. "I'll give it to you—"

"We're not taking your money, Mom. You'll need it to live."

"*Live?*" She looked ready to laugh as she shook her head. "If you want me to live *and* be happy," she said, looking at Hank after glancing at me, finishing her hypothetical statement proudly, "then I can sell my condo and move in here."

Ever hit the peak of a rollercoaster, especially when you're not a huge fan of them, and it's just about to drop four hundred feet? Well, that's what it felt like, like a tidal wave of fear and wooziness after hearing those words I'd been dreading for so long roll off her tongue. *Move in and then what? Allison can suffer health problems?* Recent studies have shown that living with a destructive force such as a mother-in-law is bad for your health, causing high blood pressure and diabetes. *Two hens cannot share a house.* This will kill me. I will die.

"And there'll be money so Allison can get started with the business sooner, rather than later," she said to Hank. She whipped around to me, adding, "You'll make a good decorator."

Did I just hear she believes in me? I was stumped on what to say next, too much was happening, so I stood before Hank, motionless, watching his enthusiastic nodding strengthen her resolve as my heart beat out of my chest.

Margaret fixed her eyes on both of us. "It seems to make perfect sense, *right?* I can give you the money for the business *and* pay for the stinky old basement to be fixed up for me."

Obviously, she'd been thinking about this.

Hank continued nodding as if this were the *one and only* answer to all his worries. He looked relieved. I felt out of equilibrium. But I asked myself, *how badly did I want to do something that would fulfill me?*

"The basement would *have* to come with a separate entrance," I said, hearing the words leave my mouth and dangle in the air.

Margaret rolled her eyes. "If that'll make you happy, then *fine.*"

I broke out in a cold sweat. "And I don't want you coming up here, whenever you please, to clean... unless I *really* need the help," I commanded, ensuring at least my sanity.

Her brown eyes darted around the kitchen. "Fine by me," she agreed with a crooked smile.

The floor shook beneath me as I cleared my throat. "And you don't need to be up here making dinner every night, because I can cook, you know."

With her mouth wide open, she was starting to look a little unsettled. She folded her arms across her chest. "*Fine,*" she muttered.

I breathed deeply, willing myself into a *Zen-like* state of mind. "Okay, maybe Sunday night dinners," I finally said.

•   •   •

I cried my way through evaluating Margaret's proposition that night with Hank and concluded that her money would no doubt move us forward. Hank could cut back at work, and I'd be able to transition from a *worn-out teacher* to an *enthusiastic stager* quicker. Who knew it was going to be Margaret, *the mastermind*, behind all this? With strings attached, of course. But maybe one day she'd be ready for the *Riviera*—once the sensation of living underground with a lack of sunlight had made her go a little stir crazy. But for now, I'd need to wrap my head around her being under the same roof as us, full time. Perhaps she'd channel her energy away from me and more toward making the basement her new home.

·   ·   ·

The instant my kinders had all left on Monday, I went and knocked on Headmaster Thomas's office door. He looked up from his desk and through the narrow window pane, motioned me to come in.

I got right to the point. "I have some good news and bad news."

"*Oh?*" he said, leaning back in his green leather chair in the corner of his pompous looking office. "Is it about your evaluation tomorrow?"

I shook my head. "*No*, of course not," I said through clenched teeth.

He cocked his head to one side, leaning forward while looking puzzled. "Okay, well, start with the bad news."

I stood taller. The moment I'd been waiting for was finally here. *Resignation fantasy*. I cleared my throat, ready to give a PowerPoint presentation detailing his ineffectiveness at this school and his inability to manage and treat his teachers with respect. I wanted to see his smug smile shrink into a sheepish grin, but I stayed professional. "I want to inform you that I'll be leaving my teaching position at Hillmount to seek out other opportunities—"

"When?" he said, looking up over the rim of his glasses, completely deadpan as he drummed his fingers on his desk.

My shoulders dropped. No *please don't leave, but the kids will miss you, I hope you'll reconsider?* came out of his mouth. I took in a sharp breath, pulling myself together. "Well, consider this a two-week notice," I finally answered, keeping details to a minimum. He, of all people, certainly would not be privy to the reason of my departure. "And the *good news* is... I know *exactly* who can replace me."

He nodded his head vigorously when I told him who. It was a win-win for him—my resignation *and* a superstar replacement who'd show enthusiasm, loyalty, and gratitude for a full-time teaching job. Easy to manage in his mind, I'm sure.

Dick.

After leaving his office, I was full of hope and wanted to celebrate. So, I decided to visit Margaret. *Yes, Margaret.* I felt like it, without quite knowing why.

She smiled when she pulled opened the door. She smiled wider when I held up a brown paper bag. With a twinkle in her eyes, she took it from me. "*Muffins?*"

"Your favorite," I grinned.

Humming quietly and then loudly, she bounced to the kitchen for napkins and then sat next to me on the sofa. "Did you read the newspaper today?" she asked, smoothing down her hair.

"No, *why?*"

"Keith and his father are soon going to jail with their investment scams," she said. "Apparently they were part of some big operation in Costa Rica."

"*Really?*" I squealed, my mouth dropping and my whole body relaxing.

Margaret's head bobbed up and down as she opened the bag, inspecting inside.

I lightly slapped her leg. "I'm so thrilled to know this," I said, suddenly distracted by her long, disappointed face. My back straightened. "What's wrong?"

"I don't like carrots muffins." She wrinkled her forehead and vigorously shook her head. "They give me all kinds of gas."

When the hell did she stop liking carrot muffins? She makes carrot cake all the time. Isn't that the same thing?

She put the bag down in front of her and then reached over, gently squeezing my knee. "But thank you anyway," she said with a warm, genuine smile. *But thank you anyway?*

Did you hear that, George? Maybe Margaret is learning. Or maybe I'm learning I need to accept her for who she is. We're family after all, and we should love each other. But doesn't mean we have to like each other... all the time.

I smiled back, feeling lighter. Almost freer as we sat holding hands. "*So...* tell me more about Keith and his father..."

33 - Dear Rebecca

If I'd been told when I became a member at New Body Fitness that I'd eventually be handing over my class of kinders to you, I would have laughed off the idea quite frankly. Yet just that is happening! I have no doubt the children are in good hands with you. You'll make a wonderful teacher—they love you!

Now, on to more important things. You're less than a year away from marrying your sweetheart, Andy. He sounds like a great guy! But based on what you've told me, his mother sounds a lot like my mother-in-law, so here's some advice per your request.

For starters, a few code words your mother-in-law might be trying to say.

Phrases	*Code for...*
Can I help with anything?	*I don't think you know what you're doing.*
Why don't I bring dinner tonight?	*My son's probably starving with your cooking.*
You don't mind, do you?	*You have no choice here because I've already decided on something.*
Why don't you and Andy give yourselves a break and go out tonight? I can babysit.	*Your house could do with a thorough cleaning. It's disgusting.*

She may ask if you're hungry, and if you say no, she may still give you a bowl of soup anyway. Remember, she really isn't listening to you and may not really care what you think... just so you know.

Your future mother-in-law might not apologize or confess to being wrong. She thinks she's always right, even though most of the time, she isn't.

Try to see the humor in situations, especially when she communicates to you in very subtle ways that you're not good enough for Andy. The good thing is, you'll be one step ahead now that you have, and what she might approve of, a real job. This might earn you extra points and respect. Oh, and speaking of humor, laugh at all her jokes. Hopefully she will likewise laugh at yours when a lame one breaks out. Throw your head back and laugh like she's just told the funniest thing. It sounds foolish, but it does help with easing up the tension you both might feel toward each other (the potential downside to this is she might consider you a bit dumb, but we all know you aren't).

Most of the time, she'll come to your home unannounced and want you to welcome her with open arms. Don't be fooled into thinking she's coming only because she wants to see you. It's for the inspection of your house and your kids, so this is where you need to define and enforce your boundaries. Present a united front and make sure you and Andy approach her together and let her know your concerns. So, from the very beginning, make it clear about where, and when, you don't want her interfering. Will she be angry at this move? Definitely. But eventually, she will learn to back off.

Andy might side with her, so beware. He may be torn between respect for his mother and his commitment to you. While it might sound bewildering right now, you should know it's a pretty common feeling with men who love their mothers. He loves you, always remember that—unless there's another woman involved.

You don't want to put him in the middle, so keep things smooth between all of you as much as possible. If her complaints continue, smile politely and ignore them. It's hard to argue with a smile. It'll rattle her for sure.

Some mother-in-laws love an audience. And like mine, yours might not be a nice person, but she might do nice things and people will fall for all that charm. You don't need to change their minds. Let them enjoy. Most will not understand what problems you have with her, so it is not worth complaining to them. Besides, it is usually not a good idea to air out dirty laundry. Refusing to stoop to her level of criticism puts you on a higher plane. Be the mature one.

Now, there might be days when she appears normal. You might be tempted to think things are getting better, and so you drop your guard. But then out of nowhere, she may turn on you again. Be cautious of this particular pattern, that's all. Never let your guard down, and always be pleasant when possible, avoiding tension and conflict to the best of your ability.

Remember, Rebecca, keep reminding yourself it's unlikely she will ever change. You might have to write her off as being a positive person in your life—unless you uncover the real reason behind her behavior. And if you do, you may understand her a bit more and discover she might be human after all. It took me two decades of groaning to finally uncover the reason behind her behavior and every other thing she did that made me unhappy—and in these last two weeks, I've lost six pounds, interestingly enough!

And as much as you can, try to maintain peace in the home without showing signs of fear. Nonetheless, don't expect the two of you will be best friends. The beauty of this type of relationship is how much you can learn from each other and also how much you can learn about yourself. You might discover this kind of relationship might help you grow, much more than you would have, in say, a relatively normal relationship. Being with her just might help you develop patience, grace, and respect. If you can meander through this relationship, might I say no other one should scare you. Ever.

Hope I haven't frightened you!

I wish you all the best!

Your Wise Old Sage,

Allie

P.S. And this is important. Failing to give your mother-in-law grandchildren will not go over well throughout your marriage. If that's your choice, stick by it and don't be intimidated. You can talk to my friend Val, if you need to.

P.P.S. I never did tell you this, but I think you look a lot like a younger version of Gwyneth Paltrow (Google her name if you don't know who I'm talking about).

About the Author

Carolyn Clarke is founder and curator of Henlit Central, a blog focused on 'life and lit' for women over 40. *And Then There's Margaret* is her first novel. She has been an ESL teacher for over sixteen years and has co-authored several articles and resources with Cambridge University Press, Macmillan Education and on her award-winning blog ESL Made Easy. She lives in Toronto, Canada with Tony, her two daughters, and bulldog, Sophie.

Note from the Author

Word-of-mouth is crucial for any author to succeed. If you enjoyed *And Then There's Margaret*, please leave a review online—anywhere you are able. Even if it's just a sentence or two. It would make all the difference and would be very much appreciated.

Thanks!
Carolyn Clarke

We hope you enjoyed reading this title from:

BLACK ROSE
writing™

www.blackrosewriting.com

Subscribe to our mailing list – *The Rosevine* – and receive **FREE** books, daily deals, and stay current with news about upcoming releases and our hottest authors.
Scan the QR code below to sign up.

Already a subscriber? Please accept a sincere thank you for being a fan of Black Rose Writing authors.

View other Black Rose Writing titles at
www.blackrosewriting.com/books and use promo code
PRINT to receive a **20% discount** when purchasing.

Made in the USA
Las Vegas, NV
15 August 2023

76132126R00152